Student

***

Nell Kalter

Copyright © 2011 by Nell Kalter

Printed in the United States by Create Space.

Kalter, Nell
Student : a novel / Nell Kalter
ISBN: 1466242582
ISBN-13: 978-1466242586

1. College—Fiction. 2. Sororities—Fiction. 3. Film School—Fiction. 4. Coming of Age—Fiction.

Printed in the United States of America

www.studentnovel.com

For my father, Michael Jay Kalter, the *real* prose pro.
Here's the book you always said I had inside me...

Part One
January–April, Senior Year
The University of Delaware

Rachel pulls off my pants and lifts off my sweater. My head gets stuck in the roll-neck, and I am, for what seems like hours, drowning in a sea of itchy grey wool. I had already peeled off my shoes, the new black boots that were a gift from Clay. I had wanted those boots for a long time, ever since the Sorority Rush Expo held the previous autumn, when I had seen the masses of already-initiated sorority girls, most of whom I pretended to hate, wearing them. Did I look as glamorous as they did in dark, tight jeans and tees with patterned sorority letters sewn on to them? No, and the reason was, *had* to be, shoe lack. So now, armed with those four-inch heels that were entirely inappropriate for traipsing around even a well-paved campus, I was complete. But I didn't know that. At the moment I didn't know much of anything, except I did remember that I was wearing my pretty green satin thong, the one with lace around the sides. I had put up my own hair in the bathroom several crawling minutes ago, steadying myself against the sink. Lori had banged on the door to see if I was alive and to swear that she'd been at the Balloon searching for me all night. Me at the Balloon. Dare to dream a dream. Now the machine is being played, and it sounds so far away, so either the volume has been pushed down low, or I am falling out of myself, down, down. Lindsay, my fourteen-year-old camper from last summer at Chen-A-Wanda, chirps, "Happy birthday! I'm calling for all of us! Rebecca wishes you a happy birthday, and Brooke and Jill. Don't get too drunk!" *So sweet*, I mumble into Cookie Monster's fraying chest, his insides tumbling onto me in the same way that my tears used to tumble onto him. He was about to be placed in the geriatric ward for stuffed toys. And didn't Jill tell her parents on visiting day not to give me a tip me when I was her counselor? Okay, so

I didn't like her either—she complained when it rained or if an activity required that she walk up a hill—but I was the counselor, the cool one, the one with the hair in the sleek ponytail and the feet in high-heeled black boots, and I was going down by the millisecond, and my eyes were feeling so very heavy, but I thought I might have the strength to hang on.

Six in the morning, and I'd almost given up the hope that I'd ever feel anything but completely nauseous again, but I decided to just deal and bring my blanket and pillow with me into the bathroom so I could stop making the frequent trips down the hall. I lay down on the dirty mat, covered with toilet paper scraps and many shades of pubic hair in various stages of growth, and leaned my face against the coolness of the toilet seat. I suddenly remembered being fourteen years old, right before that summer, and feeling so sick one morning that it was like my insides were coming forward to strangle my outside. And how after my body had done a supreme battle with itself, how I closed my eyes and woke up a few hours later with my face pressed against the toilet seat, the coolness keeping me sane, the cleanliness of that bathroom keeping me focused, and my father sleeping straight through my war.

I couldn't move, I couldn't eat, I certainly couldn't lie on my belly, and the only thing that was on TV? *My Girl*. The *sequel*. I was in the throes of hell; I thought I was probably being roasted mind first. I didn't get much sleep, but in the few short hours that my body blessedly kept running, it snowed about twenty-five inches. And all I could think of when I opened my shades to get some light in my dungeon was that I used to make angels, and it was a good thing I wasn't hungry, because I didn't have any food, and now I'd never be able to get any unless I tobogganed to the store. And if the snow kept up, maybe my class would be canceled on Monday, and I could wait to do my Film paper on the stylistic conventions evident in Woody Allen's early work.

Four hours later, and I had shifted twice, and my visitors had become frequent. I had been offered tea, I had been served cloudy tap water, and I had hidden my eyes and turned away from toast that was sweetly and lightly buttered. I had been regaled with stories of my silly behavior from the night before. I'd had to plug up my ears and squeeze shut my eyes when it is relayed *what* exactly I ingested. And I had silently and verbally cursed Bill Riley for buying me that cup of milky poison that I sucked greedily through a straw, wishing, not for the first time, that I could suck on him, and tell his girlfriend, who happened to be forever joined with me in the bond of our sorority, to get lost.

I had stopped spewing bile, and I had eaten a bagel, thoughtfully provided to me by one of the sweet conspirators who did me in the night before. My house was loud; everyone was up and looking for ways to pass the time. Two p.m., and it looked like there was no chance of anyone going anywhere. Once the TV came back on in a burst of static, reports jammed the airwaves that anyone caught driving would be in big trouble with the governor. Bad, bad drivers. I decided to venture from my sweaty bed and join the land of the lascivious livers, armed with my video camera for protection. I felt the coldness of the floor through my bunchy white socks that Rachel always yelled at me for wearing. I also saw that they are inside out, knowing Kathleen would freak if she saw that, because that is the one thing that drove her completely crazy. What killed me was hair on the shower walls—almost anything else, and I could take it. It would have really helped in this house where twelve of us lived if we all couldn't stand the same things, but there really were no collective horrors. I couldn't have cared less if dishes piled up in the sink or if someone used my toothpaste and didn't squeeze from the bottom. But hair...I walked into the room that Kim, Rachel, and Justine shared, marveling once again how well they use the space. When Elizabeth and Gina lived in this room last year, it seemed so cluttered, so dark, so tense. This year it was bright and flowery, and the door leading to the fire escape was always open so we could smoke in there. At the moment, though, I couldn't even imagine breathing anything foreign into my body, and since I doubt my body would accept it anyway, for once I felt, despite my sickness, in perfect accord. Like I just read *Siddhartha* or something.

Snow looks so bright when seen through a video camera. When my mother and my stepfather came up the day of my birthday to take me and Rachel and Kim out to lunch, they presented me with the coolest gift, the camera and a tripod. I hadn't yet ventured outside in this blizzard, but I had videoed through cloudy windows that we never cleaned, and all I could see was miles of snow. It made our street look so serene. If I filmed from Jessica's room, which looked out the back of the house, I could see the top of a strange car that belonged to the strange guy that Lori brought home randomly from the bar the night of my birthday. When he parked it outside, the weather had been clear. An hour later or so—the details are fuzzy because I was passed out cold—the weather had changed, and a clearly vengeful God had dumped a ton of snow. And now this person that Lori didn't really know, but now knew that she didn't really like, was snowed in with us and had been for three days. When I'd make my way down to the kitchen for tea, I'd find him watching television, which finally came back on a day ago. One time I saw him looking through the sorority photo albums that usually just collected dust on the shelf above the coat rack next to the front door. I'd kind of mumble a hello at him, and one time I asked him to get me a Splenda off a top shelf because I still didn't have the strength to move a chair and climb it; and as he reached up to the top of the pantry, I wondered how long a mild alcohol poisoning could possibly last and if it was worth it for me to learn this guy's first name.

School was canceled again, and if I had to stay in that house for one more minute, I was going to shoot myself and the person closest to me, which I guess would be Lee, because she was right next door. But I didn't hate Lee that day. I did for about a week, but it was for a reason so inconsequential that I couldn't even remember it, and she never knew it, and she probably hated me as well, so it's okay. We were getting along now, and it was for real. I was getting along with everybody, so that made life coast freely because I didn't have to waste precious moments pretending. I wondered sometimes how people thought about me, especially my friends. I knew that they liked me, but I also think they thought I was a little boring, what with my constantly planned plans and my good girl grades and the consistency of Clay.

Clay. My boyfriend for three and a half years, my cord to stability, my beloved, my mushball, my long-distance love. We started going out the summer before my freshman year at camp, where we were both counselors. I thought he was a very sweet guy that I was not in the least bit attracted to, but the guy that I had been seeing for about a week (which is a long relationship in camp time, where a minute seems to last a decade) was smooching with someone else across the bar, some girl with big boobs and frizzy hair, a cool girl who I liked, but not at that moment. I certainly didn't like the guy I had been seeing, Ryan. But most of all I didn't like myself, because what was wrong with me? I was thin and everybody said I was pretty, and I was wearing my black halter that always seemed to work with reeling them in; I knew I was severely lacking in some way, that I must be, and that these teenage years would slide right by me as I watched them go, and I would be alone. I felt gooey and slippery, and ready for a new challenge. And that night I got Clay.

It started as a transitional thing, an ego boost, a route that led away from boredom and routine that can be so stifling in camp, anywhere really, but sometimes I would sit back and long for the stability. With Clay I got it, and it came hurling in bursts. I felt quickly accepted, by him and by myself because he accepted me, and I felt thin and pretty again. Amazing how much weight I could lose in one night, or maybe the mirrors were just different in my bunk than in the bar, or maybe it was post-hookup glow that sheds pounds like our mouths shed rapturous spit that we both lapped up knowingly and uncaring. Stuck in the moment, grasping hold of a new identity, I plunged in face first, and for once I didn't hold my nose. I knew I'd be safe.

And I was and for a long time I lived in a fairy tale, and besides the fact that he went to school in Michigan and I went to school in Delaware, I felt fulfilled. And then I just didn't.

I think I just became sick of it all. Sick of the phone calls, sick of the family schmoozing, sick of the shitty sex that he found so exciting, sick of the airplane rides, sick of the flannels he wore, sick of the television always tuned to ESPN that I heard through the phone and saw when I was visiting. Sick of the stupid jokes, of his arrogance, sick of being thought of as not fully formed, sick of not being fully formed. Tired of my urinary tract infections, bored with his plans for himself, and way too attracted to his friends, I knew it was time to get out. And it had nothing to do with Luke.

Now Luke…that was an entirely different story. I was fifteen when we became friends, sixteen when we had sex for the first time in his best friend Vicky's bed, and seventeen when I fell in love with him on the deepest level I had thought possible. I had quilted journals, four of them, devoted entirely to the daily confusion that Luke's presence created in my life when I was a high school girl—when the look he gave me on one particular day or the look he chose to withhold from me on another day could impact every aspect of my life, including my breathing. He made life tumultuous for me back then, which is to say that he made it interesting and exhilarating, but I think it was only exhilarating in retrospect; at the moment it was occurring, it was crushing, demoralizing. Memory-inducing. Things had ended with us long ago, badly. He fell in love with one of my oldest friends, and it happened in front of me, at my house, at my party, the one in late spring that I had orchestrated for the sole purpose of having him sleep over. But he and Ellen had bonded over his newfound hobby of tripping out on acid, a hobby I didn't encourage. I thought the trees on our frequent hikes looked beautiful without altered senses, but she happily was willing to join him in fantasyland, a mythic place where just the two of them existed. He had still wanted to be close to me, but I just couldn't be exposed to their bliss, and I couldn't stand the knots in my stomach that came from compromising myself as I pretended to be "just fine" as the avid audience around me saw my rejection, daily, in close up. So I extracted myself from that pain, fleeing to summer camp to become a counselor, shrouding myself in s'mores, bunk politics, and, eventually, Clay. But I couldn't help it. I still thought about Luke. Even at twenty-one I thought about him. I thought about a lot, but usually when I thought about Luke, I thought of one moment in particular, when the world opened up and I could taste the lemony tang of promise that awaited me because I was me and at that precise moment in time, that meant everything and anything, and I knew in my heart, my soul, my toes, that I had it. The moment: lying on my double bed, River Phoenix staring down at me from my walls, wearing flowered pajamas that I got from my mother for Chanukah, I nestled the telephone into my neck and told Luke all about the symbolism in *JFK*. We talked for a long time that night—we always did—but this time I felt a rapture deep inside me, and it was because he challenged me, and because when I was with him, I challenged myself. He lived so in the moment. Everything was about passion, and his lips were so red, and I wanted to remain on my bed, in that moment, forever. And it didn't even matter that he wasn't really there with me, because had he been under my comforter with me, I wouldn't be there and I wouldn't be alone and I wouldn't be myself. And it was at that moment, when I was a senior in high school, that I loved myself fully for the first time and accepted who I would become.

I think I lost a lot of that with Clay, the self-assuredness I was about to stumble onto with my arms open really, really wide. It was easy to. And Luke and I hadn't spoken for a long time. It was easy not to. He stayed buried with the real me, coming to the surface in nighttime theater that began and ended with several standing ovations and an armful of pink roses, while I never left the nestled safety of my bed, maybe moving only to play an old R.E.M. song once again on my CD player.

Almost a month had passed since the big snowfall, and life progressed as it seemed to in those days, seamlessly. The weeks flowed into one another, and next thing I'd know it was Tuesday again, and I'm not sure that any collective amount of hours in my life ever passed by as quickly as the hours did in the first months of my second semester of senior year of college. I lived by a pretty set routine and I loved it. None of my classes started before eleven. I'd walk the same route each day, since almost all of my classes were in the same brick building, Memorial Hall. Every single day I would marvel at the absolute beauty of the campus, how much it looked like my idealized vision of a college. It was as though a production designer had literally constructed my fantasy with a large budget: paved cobblestone walkways, landscaped daffodils

15

and hedges, bricks for as far as the eye could see, fraternity boys in faded backwards baseball caps playing hacky sack, people whizzing by on bicycles, and the sun beginning to shine again. I took solace in my capacity for appreciation, and I tried to memorize the details. On my walks alone, I began to realize that my time there was coming to a close, that in a few months I'd be gone, that the steady campus life would continue for others but not for me, and each morning started to feel lined with a sense of poignancy. I wondered if there was any way to slow down time, actually slow it down, and I began to feel a sense of quiet desperation that confused me, so I kept it to myself.

And then it was almost spring, and the thought of ending it all with Clay increased and then decreased hourly. The sun began to beat down, and an image began forming in my head that couldn't be described but hinted to me that I had been missing out on something. Confronting what was troubling me on the deepest level was emotionally exhausting, so I tried to attribute my confusion to something else, and settled on stress. Spring was rough for me. I spent all of the time that I usually spent on shaving my legs and doing leg lifts so I'd look good in skirts running home between classes to check the mailbox, praying constantly. I did every potentially lucky and superstitious thing I had ever heard about. I chanted and om-ed, yoga-style. I stared at the sky and avoided cracks in the sidewalk. My knuckles were pink and raw from knock-knock-knocking on wood. I refused to move my eyes away from the magical minute of 11:11, and felt a deep power swell inside of me when I could make it all the way to 11:12 without blinking. I needed, I wanted, I longed for acceptance…into New York University's Tisch School of the Arts.

I had spent most of first semester studying for the GREs. Three times a week I met with my Princeton Review instructor and the other kid in our class and revisited the land of exponents, antonyms, and a section involving logic that I ended up doing really well in. Really well. My teacher was a girl about my age named Jules, who had just graduated from Delaware with the same major as me: English/Film. She was thinking about heading off to NYU for her master's, as I wanted to, but I spent much time that I should have spent comprehending my reading persuading her to head out west to the California schools so she wouldn't take my slot at Tisch. Calculating, yes, absolutely, but she was blonde and cute and would probably do really well in LA, so I never felt too bad.

I took my GREs on December 9 at the crack of dawn in the midst of a blizzard. I sat next to this girl who used to be friends with the loser girls that I lived with sophomore year, someone I disliked, who I knew probably disliked me, and on that fateful snowy morning, I shared my breakfast of M&Ms with her, hoping I'd get energy and she'd get fat.

So testing finished and transcripts ordered and sent and recommendations pleaded for, my applications were being reviewed by five schools: USC, UCLA, American, Miami, and New York University. I remembered how I used to walk by the downtown Manhattan campus of NYU when I lived in the city with my father, and how all of the students entering and exiting the heavy glass doors had worn black clothes and looked so chic and cool and so, well, *stimulated.* That building seemed to glow as though it was lit from within by movie Gods and Goddesses. I knew that one day I wanted to be there, to study from the greats, those who had been mentioned in the footnotes of my Film textbooks. NYU was beyond difficult to get into, and I was beyond aware that I was not the only one vying for a coveted slot. All the schools that offered what I wanted to study were tough, and I had applied for the same program in all them: Cinema Studies, or Critical Studies, as USC coined it. I knew that my chances of getting into any of the schools were slim; not only were the programs crazily competitive, but my grades in my first two years of college were hopelessly mediocre. I had preferred to spend more time in fraternity house basements or obsessing over my long-distance love or delivering cigarettes and diet Snapple to older sorority sisters who had demanded tasks like that from pledges, and I had done those things instead of hitting the books. So now my grades, though excellent in the last year and a half, still fell cumulatively just below a 3.0; my GRE scores were average, and my writing was scrutinized and probably thought to be fluffy, though entertaining. Knowing that I probably needed divine intervention to help me out, and conveniently forgetting that if I had to identify myself as something it would probably be as an atheist, I decided to hold a prayer session.

It was April when I decided that spirituality might help me in my quest for a graduate degree, and by then I had heard from four of the schools. I was two for two: two wins, two losses. Two schools I gave thanks to, while two schools I plotted a fierce retribution against, one that I'd be sure to carry out when I had the time and energy to seek it.

American and Miami welcomed me, but the California schools bid me *adieu* before even bidding me *bonjour*. And NYU apparently didn't yet feel like writing me back. I was certain that my twenty-page application, each page of which I had kissed chastely before mailing, had been shredded into little, itty bits, and had been used as packaging to mail presents to those fuckers who had been accepted into my program. I watched the stars for a clue, but they just sat there staring right back at me, so I gathered Kim and Rachel, and invited Jessica, but she was on the phone, and the three of us went outside to the porch and sat down cross-legged next to the porch swing. I lit the vanilla scented candles and we joined hands. It was the middle of the day, about three o'clock, and anyone who walked by turned to look at us curiously. We ignored them and closed our eyes. I spoke first: "Please, let me get into Tisch. I want it so much, I will work so hard, and I will make everyone including myself proud." Rachel spoke next: "Please let her get into NYU. She is a wonderful person and she totally deserves it. She will work so hard. She stayed in to study so many nights when we all went out. She's sacrificed a lot for graduate school." Then Kim spoke: "I can't imagine anybody wanting to get into NYU more. Please give her the chance to do what she wants to do so badly." We held hands for another moment in silence, and I thought to myself "Tisch, Tisch, Tisch" and also "They really took this seriously, they are such good friends" and, randomly, "I really need to break up with Clay." Then I tried to blow out the candles, but one stayed lit for a while.

The days began to pass so quickly, and I decided during this time that if I didn't get into NYU, despite the positive aura I had painstakingly surrounded myself with, that I would either go to Miami or throw myself off of a bridge. When I went to visit Miami, I squelched the plans for my post-NYU-rejection demise. The school was beautiful, the classes seemed cool, the professors were accomplished, and Dr. Harris thought that I should go there. Dr. Harris…

Jonathon Harris, Director of the Journalism program at my school, and film professor extraordinaire. I had taken two classes with him last semester, Hollywood and the 1950s, and 100 Years of Cinema. This semester I was also in two of his classes, Film Theory and Criticism, and Feature and Magazine Writing. Three days a week, I had two classes with this man, and I fell in a new sort of love with him. It wasn't a sexual attraction. But I was so intellectually stimulated by him, my brilliant professor, who spoke of Jacques Lacan and Laura Mulvey, of Kerouac and Scorsese, who refused to wear suits, not even plaid ones with elbow patches, and who smoked Winstons on his breaks between classes. Somewhat perversely, he reminded me so much of my father, as a professor and as a person. I just knew he held the secret combination in his messy attaché case that would open up the world that had remained double bolted since my father had died, the world of knowing…just knowing. Not what would happen next and not how it all happened. Not even why it all happened. Just that it was all happening now, and life was no longer about the routine, but about the moments when your laughter radiated and your voice shimmered and your smile would stretch so wide that your cheeks would hurt. Back to those distant, faded, yellow days.

I studied my ass off for Dr. Harris's exams, all of which were long and detailed and way too intricate to answer in the fifty minutes allotted to us, so I always stayed after until he kicked me out of the classroom so he could go smoke another Winston. He asked us in our exams to write clearly and concisely about the relationship of the films we had seen in class to the readings we had read outside of class. His questions were always thorough and insightful, and I longed to answer them in a way that would make him proud and would create a band of light around me that would match the one around him, though mine would surely be dimmer. I read and read, then watched and watched, and finally sat in my seat with my hair away from my face, my hands sweating and clenched, and I wrote. And wrote. Then everybody else from the class left, and I wrote some more. I handed in my exam to him with a breathless smile and an exhausted shake of my head and wished him a good day, and I left the classroom full and proud and knowing that first my feet would take me to bed to catch up on sleep, but then they would take me someplace real, someplace special, someplace where Dr. Harris was the majority, and intellectual intercourse would be as common as saying "Bless you" when somebody, anybody, sneezed.

And every day I would walk into class, and Dr. Harris would look expectant and say, "Jaye? Any news?" And I would just shake my head and tell him I hadn't heard yet. Was NYU on vacation? And my friends would tease me about how I was in love with my professor and I would laugh and protest, but then one day I passed his pretty wife who was Director of the Honors program at my school and who came from Arkansas like him and who kept her own last name when they married, and I quietly hissed at her when we passed each other, my lips snarling like they hadn't since high school, since Luke, and I began to wonder.

I was still talking to Clay every night; our conversations were always the same, and I was just so bored. I loved him, of course I did, but I started feeling like I was on a different path. I wanted freedom. I wanted to graduate and go forward. I wanted to read and write and watch movies that never played in Delaware. I wanted to leave Long Island for the summer and go to the city. And last summer I had heard about a course at this place called the New York Film Academy that taught moviemaking in six weeks and was located just two blocks up from my old apartment, and I decided that this coming summer I was going to start the rest of my life. I called the school, had an interview over the phone that amounted to the Director stoically telling me that I would have to be prepared to "eat, sleep, breathe, drink, *live* this program." I assured him in my best big-girl voice that I was prepared for the time and energy I needed to commit to this class, and not only was I ready for it, but I was looking forward to it. He seemed satisfied, especially when I told him I'd mail in my deposit soon. When we hung up, I realized I didn't find out if I had the weekends off or not.

And then one weekend night, most of us stayed in and watched movies, and Rachel tweezed my eyebrows while Kim went down the phone list of all of our sorority sisters and talked about who she did and didn't like, so it was just a relaxing kind of night. Jessica had gone out, though. A little after 2:00 a.m., she came flying through the front door and raced up the stairs with a look of pure confidence on her flushed and sweaty face. We all immediately thought she had hooked up. But she hadn't…yet. She had just left the Balloon, where she saw this band for the first time. They were so amazing, and the lead singer was so beautiful, and he sang "Smoke Two Joints," the Sublime song that she loved, right to her, and they had invited her upstairs to eat pizza after their set, and she was so excited just recounting the experience to us. The band was called The Assassins, and they would be playing next weekend at the Balloon, and we all had to go and collectively dribble and drool over the newest men in her life, but the lead singer was hers. When I crawled into bed that night, I finally admitted to myself that I was truly and completely exhausted from being catty, that I didn't want to be that girl anymore; it was time to outgrow those mean girl tendencies. I felt stickily suffocated. I needed to feel something new. Slamming my eyelids shut and locking them for the night, I drifted into myself and away while planning what outfit I would wear to see this motley band of boys next week, wondering vaguely if they could inspire within me some newfound jitters.

It had been a shocking revelation to me that I loved bars. There were three main bars at college, and that semester we visited them all. I liked Kate's, the bar with the big booths, the awesome appetizers, the top floor where we always ended up, and the huge mounted televisions that played hockey and baseball games. My favorite bar was the Balloon, with its sawdust all over the floor, a crowded bathroom I would never use, and live music playing three nights a week. The Down Under was the bar you could get into with shitty ID. That's the one I had gone to as a freshman. They had a good happy hour and a mirror in the bathroom that was known throughout the state as the best skinny mirror in all of existence. *Everyone* looked amazing in that mirror. I often contemplated ripping it from the wall and walking around campus with it strapped to myself so that reflection of me would be constant. I used to use my sister's expired license to get in there, and every time the bouncer looked at it, with its picture of my sister and her blondish hair and her hazel eyes and let brown-haired, brown-eyed me in, I was just bewildered. But most of all, I loved that all the bars were crammed with people I knew. I hadn't loved the social life at school during the first few years; that used to scare me because I had bought into the expression that the best time of life is college, but I was not having the best time. Standing around in crowded fraternity house basements, dodging cigarettes that seemed to want to burn sizzling holes through my Lycra shirts just never felt like where I should be. By the time I became a junior, fraternity parties seemed so childish, so people moved on to apartment or house parties. Those were so much better, smaller and more intimate; but at the end of the night, most people would make their way to one of the bars on Main Street to be there in time for last call and to scope out who they would take home that night. If the chosen bar was anything but the Down Under, I couldn't get in, so it wasn't really until I was a twenty-one-year-old legal senior who couldn't be handcuffed and frisked for entering a bar that I started to love going out at school. I still didn't drink often. Every time I ingested any alcohol into my body, I woke up the next morning throwing up runny green stuff that smelled like Coors Lite. Ignoring the fact that I had just missed failing every science class I had ever taken and that I didn't understand shit about the medical profession, I diagnosed myself and decided that I must surely be lacking that necessary enzyme that breaks up alcohol, and that was why I got sick when I drank. Never mind I had no idea what an enzyme was. It made sense to me, and also worked as an excuse to others about why I wouldn't drink, which sadly came up more when I was a senior in college than when I was a size-two-jeans-wearer in high school.

I went to almost all of my classes almost all of the time, and when I didn't go, it was usually because I had wardrobe anxiety and couldn't find something to wear or I felt too fat to wear what I was already wearing. But I always went to my classes with Dr. Harris, and my love for him grew along with my love of film studies. Or maybe it was the other way around. We did the most interesting reading in his class, and one day we learned about this woman named Laura Mulvey, who was this famous film theorist who talked about how men look at women in film and how sadistic that look is. And we read a lot on the subject of "the gaze" in cinema and in real life and how women are not only watched by men, but they constantly stare at themselves as well. And at first I thought, no way, but then I read this article by some lesbian theorists who wrote that women are always conscious of what they are doing—whether they are walking across the room or weeping at the death of their father, they are always watching themselves walk or weep. When that section of the article was read aloud in class, I felt stunned and I put a big circle around it in my notes and then quickly turned the page of my notebook because I didn't want anyone else to see that something so coldly academic could get to me like that. Or maybe I was just afraid to admit to myself that I had always lived my life as a spectator, especially when I wasn't so sure that I was ready to suck down some ice cold water, tie my hair back, build up my endurance, and become part of the game. And later on that night, as I was studying my notes from class, I thought about the day of my father's funeral. I couldn't remember where it was held; I'm not sure who I sat next to, and I think that all of "Thunder Road" was played, but I can't be certain. But I clearly remember that my hair had just the right amount of curl and it felt soft and looked shiny, and a lock of it kept falling across my left eye during the Shiva call.

The weather was getting to be so beautiful outside, and the seats of my car were so steamy and hot, and I started walking more and more. My weight always fluctuated between 118 and 122, which isn't all that much, but I always obsessed about my body, and I always had, but at some point that spring I started seeing myself in a new light. Maybe the bulb of self-acceptance had been changed, the wattage increased. And one day I walked home from class, checked the mail (nothing from NYU), ran upstairs to my room, took off all of my clothes, and pulled on a bikini. I was going to lie out on the roof with whoever else had gotten home already or whoever hadn't left the house at all that day. I pulled my hair up into a messy bun on top of my head, curls sprouting out everywhere like I was a small child, and I caught a glimpse of myself in the mirror over my dresser. And I stopped. And stared. And smiled.

It had taken me until the second semester of my sophomore year to realize that the key to getting my schoolwork done was to not go directly home after class. It was too easy for me to lie down, take a brief (three-hour) nap, watch soap operas, stare at walls—basically engage in anything but my required reading. One rainy day during my second year at school, though, it was pouring rain as I left class, the kind of teeming torrential downpour that you couldn't be outside in for more than a moment if you ever hoped to be dry again. The building my Biblical and Classical Literature class had been held in was right next to the Library, so I booked for its doors and, once inside, grabbed a coffee at the café on the first floor. With nobody around that I knew, I decided to take out my copy of *Antigone* and read. Two hours later, I finished the play and my work for the next three classes was done and so was the rain. I walked home; the streets and sidewalks were still damp and dark, the leaves on the trees glistening, and realized I had finally figured out how to be a good student. I called my mother that night to tell her about my new revelation, and I don't think she had ever been prouder of me, except perhaps for the day she managed to toilet-train me in just twenty-four hours by withholding bakery cookies until I complied with society's standards and hopped on the bowl.

The act of getting schoolwork done in a timely manner changed everything. I never went to class anymore feeling guilty or nervous. I didn't have to avert my eyes when a professor looked my way. I didn't have to bullshit answers when I was called upon, and that was a good thing since it scared me slightly that I could bullshit so easily and effectively. But now my grades were great and I found that I enjoyed knowing what my professors were talking about. And I liked the Library! It was warm in the winter and cool in the late spring and early autumn and there were usually cute boys all over the place who would sometimes look up from their heavy economics textbooks and smile at me and the cookies they sold at the café there were huge and had macadamia nuts in them. On the days I really needed to get serious work done, I'd go to the second floor and bypass the large wooden tables in the center of the room that sat under a gleaming skylight and instead weave my way through the dusty stacks and go to the mini cubicles that lined the walls. It was completely quiet back there, and I got a lot of work done, and then I would gather my books and feel really proud of myself for acting like a grown up. Then I would go down to the ground floor where the computer banks were and check my email and send a quick note to Clay or to Gwen, my best friend from high school who went to college in Connecticut. And even though we lived together or two minutes from one another, all of my friends at school and I emailed each other too. My inbox began to fill up with messages, including annoying forwards that often demanded that I continue the message or personally be responsible for an impending apocalypse, but I called the apocalypse's bluff and deleted most of them. But when Kim sent out a friend questionnaire one day, I had some time and I settled in to answer it and forwarded it to my girls.

From: JayeK@udel.edu

To: KimberlyM@udel.edu,
RachelS@udel.edu, ChristinaT@udel.edu,
LeeR@udel.edu, CarleyM@udel.edu,
CallieB@udel.edu, JessicaD@udel.edu,
EricaT@udel.edu

Subject: Secrets…

First celebrity crush:
John Travolta in *Grease*. I liked his
chin dimple, though now I can't carry on
a conversation with anyone who has one.
It's a really distracting physical
feature…Anyway, shortly thereafter came
Ricky Schroeder. I wanted him to ride me
like he rode that awesome train on *Silver
Spoons*.

Later celebrity crush:
Jon Bon Jovi. I really thought he'd be
mine one day. I used to sit in Science
class in 8th grade and figure out the age
difference between us. Thirteen years?
Please. That's nothing. More of an
obstacle was the severe gawky stage I was
in at the time and the unfortunate
asymmetrical hairstyle I was rocking.

First pet:
My collie, Brandy. She ruled. I learned
to stand by grabbing her belly fur and
pulling on it to raise myself to an
upright position. And she still loved
me. Apparently, my mother sent my father
to a pet store and told him to choose a
male dog that didn't shed. He came home
with a female collie. (Now that I think
of it, she might have had grounds for
divorce that I haven't previously
considered…)

Movies I can quote by heart:
I know that, as a Film major, I should
say *Citizen Kane*, but I fall asleep every
time I watch it—which is in every
fucking Film class I have taken since
freshman fucking year. But I could give
a dissertation on any John Hughes movie,
know every moment from *Tootsie* and

The Big Chill, every word of *Airplane* and
Caddyshack, and can scream "Plastics!"
with absolute precision when *The Graduate*
is on.

Movie that changed my life:
So many. Too many. But my recent two
viewings of *Pulp Fiction* are seriously
doing something to me.

Favorite word:
"Poodle." Love it. Best word. Also
like "apoplectic," since I just learned
how to pronounce it. Just learned how to
say "Proust" correctly too—but that's a
name, not a word.

Least favorite word:
"Moist." And fuck you all for making me
type it.

Book that has meant the most to me:
That's a tough one. Like movies, books
have meant different things to me for
different reasons, but a few have changed
me. I still don't think anyone has ever
understood what it means to be a teenage
girl more than Judy Blume. *Are You
There, God? It's Me, Margaret* taught me
that maxi pads used to be worn with a
belt! *Forever* taught me about what first
love was going to feel like, and it was
pretty spot-on. Recently, *The Things
They Carried* and *On the Road* have moved
me significantly. I like that they're as
much about the process of writing as the
stories themselves.

What do you look for in a friend?
Loyalty, which is harder to continually
pull off than it seems. Also, a great
sense of humor, the ability to handle
sarcasm, being able to sometimes just sit
in silence, and preferably someone who
wears the same size jeans as I do.

Favorite sex position:
Totally depends on the moment, but I do
like it from behind, and there are times
when a slap is more than appropriate.

Spit or swallow?
Like or love?

Favorite junk food:
Twix. But if the question had been
"favorite kind of dairy" or "favorite
ethnic food," I'd have found a way to
make Twix the answer to those questions
too.

*Boy band member I wanted to fuck back in
the day:*
Skipped that phase entirely and instead
entered the pseudo-metal phase. Think
it's that boy bands all wore coordinating
outfits, and I couldn't quite abide by
that choice of style. But I knew that if
I went down on any member of Poison or
Motley Crue, maybe whomever the lucky
recipient was would teach me how to do
that smoky eyeliner look I still have not
mastered.

Biggest luxury I've been given:
Getting to go to such a beautiful college
and being allotted these four years to be
here.

How many times have you been in love?
Twice.

Dream job:
Film critic for *Rolling Stone*. Also a
wedding cake designer. Actually, fuck
that. I want to be a wedding cake
tester. Does that job exist? Can I
patent it? Which one of you Business
majors knows about such things??

Prized possession:
My geriatric Cookie Monster that you all
think is disgusting because he's missing
his eyes, one arm, and is just a matted
blue blob. But he has character, and you
can all suck it. Also, the letters my
dad wrote me each year on my birthday
that chronicled each year of my life. On
my thirteenth birthday, we went to a
Broadway show, to the Four Seasons for
dinner where we ate Chocolate Velvet cake
and sat by the pool, and then read the
letters at home together later that
night. If I ever have kids, I'm doing
that for them. It was one of the most
special, significant moments of my life,
and not just in retrospect.

Recurring nightmare:
I have three. One: my teeth fall out.
I've researched that one, and apparently
it means I feel a loss of control in my
life. Two: I am running away from
someone, but I can't make myself run
faster. I'm guessing the interpretation
is the same as the teeth dream. Three:
I have to go take a test for my Evolution
and Extinction class, but I have skipped
class all semester and I don't know which
room the test is in. Now that I think of

it, that's also a lack-of-control dream.
Might I need therapy?

Biggest fear:
Losing my mother suddenly like I lost my
father. And I am terrified of Pegasus
for reasons I truly don't understand.

Best physical feature:
My dimples. They define me——I hope!

Worst physical feature:
I've been fighting with my hair for
years. More often than not, it wins.

Have you ever told a big lie?
Yes, but not to anyone who is reading
this email. Okay, that was a lie.

Most likely to respond next:
Rachel. She has a long break between
classes today and will definitely go
online soon.

Least likely to respond:
Carley. She told me yesterday that she
forgot her login password and tried so
many options, the system locked her out.
She has to go to Computer Services to get
the problem resolved. The reality of her
doing that in the next month is slim to
none.

Something I'm looking forward to:
Saturday.

   Saturdays at school. I would get up at around eleven
thirty and immediately run out of my room to see what I

had missed in the hours that I had slept. In that house of twelve girls, you never knew. I mean, I could take a shower for ten minutes, and when I'd get out, I would find out that Jessica had broken up with Danny, everyone was mad at Justine, and Rachel had quit smoking. So on Saturdays I had to move quickly. I'd usually go and brush my teeth and then trek up the creaky stairs to Kim, Rachel, and Justine's room. They'd be awake already, and if they were still in bed, I'd crawl in with either Rachel or Kim and we'd chat for a while or make plans for the day. Then we'd all go downstairs and eat breakfast, Rachel bustling around the kitchen, and Kim sitting at the table, leaning back on one of the wobbly kitchen chairs. I would be perched atop the counter drinking my first of many cups of diet hot cocoa with fluffy marshmallows that I ingested every day, whether it was two degrees outside or two hundred degrees. I had recently discovered that marshmallows were the perfect food, having no fat and very few calories, and they were yummily filling. Upon telling my friends this startling bit of information, and especially after they had seen me ingesting only marshmallows for days, they became convinced that I had an eating disorder. I shrugged their sweet concern off, but Rachel started to threaten that she was going to start cutting out magazine articles about scarily skinny schizos and that she'd paste them to my door if I didn't start eating and acting like a normal person. Normal? What was that? Didn't everyone think about food twenty-four hours a day and feel guilty after they'd eaten a Pringle?

Anyway, Saturdays, as I prepared my second cup of hot, sweet sustenance, we would decide what to do that day. Normally we would study for a while, or at least pretend to. I would go to my room and take out a textbook. Then I would lie down with my open notebook and start to read. But the mess that always surrounded me all of a sudden started to close in, and I would come to the conclusion that this pigsty just was not conducive to my studying. So I would get up off of my bed and clean like crazy, dusting, folding, straightening, sorting, lighting peach-scented candles, carrying my dirty mugs downstairs and leaving them in the kitchen before anyone caught me and made me wash them. Then I would go upstairs, and my room would be so clean, and I would lie down again and pick up my book and read the same line as I had before. But then I would hear footsteps above me, and I would see through my window that the door to the fire escape in their room was open and that meant they were smoking and laughing, so I would run upstairs to play. We'd all sit with our legs dangling over the fire escape, and we'd smoke Parliaments, ashing in a Diet Coke can that already had so many dirty butts in it that it looked like a nauseating science experiment. None of us had showered yet, and we usually wouldn't until we got ready to go out that night. Sometimes we would go shopping at the mall, all of us spending money that we didn't have, standing over the money machine, praying that our card wouldn't be snickered at by the cash gods. Or we might go to see a movie, if I could convince them to, but nobody liked going to the movies with me. They said that I was too critical of movies, worse than Siskel and certainly a thousand times worse than Ebert. They were right, but going to the movies was always my favorite way to spend any day, so sometimes they would come with me and I would eat Jujyfruits; they have no fat also and everybody else hated them because they get stuck in your teeth, so I didn't have to share. We'd come home and eat dinner and lounge around and take turns heading into the shower, Jessica always going in first, and then slathering herself all over with a thick cream from The Body Shop, making the entire house smell like an orchard. It took about three hours for all of us to get ready, trying on outfits, changing them, and then putting back on the jeans and tank we had on in the first place. Fluffing hair, perfecting lip liner, spritzing ourselves with perfume—I was wearing Calyx, a throwback to my high school days, Rachel wore Escape, Justine wore Angel, Kim wore Fendi, Jessica wore the orchard; you couldn't breathe in our house on Saturday nights. And at about ten, we would convene near the staircase, ID, money, and lipsticks in our pockets, chewing gum, and ready to face the world, the school, and the band.

The Assassins, the band that Jessica had recently had convulsions over, was playing at the Balloon, and a bunch of us from the house went to see them one Saturday night in early April. I was looking forward to seeing what they were like—I always loved a live band—but I didn't think I would start lusting after any of them. Jessica and I had very different taste in boys. But all of us were getting along so well, every moment a silly, crazy adventure, and I knew that even if we just sat in a small room not talking, we would have fun. We strutted on into the Balloon, the dark, dingy, massive bar that vaguely resembled a cavernous tomb but sold beers for fifty cents, so it was the coolest bar on campus. We walked in as a pack, the bouncer recognizing Jessica, me proudly flashing my document of legalization, Kim summing up counterfeit courage to show her counterfeit proof. We separated once we were in, a few of my friends going over to the bar to get drinks and the rest of us heading down to the stage area. The band wasn't on yet, and the place wasn't as crowded as usual, either because it was still early or because no one really knew this band yet. Two guys, one tall, one dramatic looking, saw Jessica and waved and came over to her. In her groupie glory, she introduced them as Jimmy and Chris and ran down our names to them; though they smiled politely, it was obvious that they wouldn't remember who we were, but they shook our hands, and I felt embarrassed because I knew that mine was sweaty. They were definitely cute, certainly friendly, and heartbreakingly ordinary. And then they got on stage.

Swaying and singing, bending and shaking my hair, holding tight onto the protective arms of my drunken, darling friends, I was conquered by The Assassins that balmy night. With the energy that they radiated, the enthusiasm of their show, the way they made us smile, and the way they brought us even closer to each other than we had been an hour earlier, they entered our lives with a loud cover song that we sang right along with.

"Ordinary" flew right out the window once Chris opened his mouth to wail, once Jimmy grinningly plucked his bass. Suddenly each was Adonis, coming to life with a reverberating crash. They brought us into them, beckoning us to leave ourselves, our inhibitions, our thoughts behind, and just grab our ponytail holders to tie back our sweaty hair and sail along for the dizzying ride. I went, hurling myself to the front of the line, leaving Dramamine and monotony behind.

Though he was electric onstage and hard to define offstage, it wasn't Chris that I began to dress for on our weekly forays to the Balloon. It wasn't Jimmy either, though he was sweet and hot as hell, and every once in a while we'd flirt ferociously. Instead, it was the little one. The first time I saw Tim was at the first show, and Rachel grabbed my arms in a clammy clench and yelped for me to glance to the right and see the boy looming in front of me, who she breathed, in a hot breath, was the spitting image of Luke, my first true amour. I looked up at the stage at the beautiful boy with long black hair, bright blue eyes, and lips twisted too wickedly for one who looked so young. He was playing guitar and dancing and prancing and gleaming in the glow of adoration. He smiled constantly and licked his full lips approximately every seven minutes. He did look like Luke, but he looked more open, less afraid, and like his soul was double locked with something special held inside. And though he didn't even look at me that night, and even though I didn't really give him a second thought after I left the bar, I think subconsciously I began window-shopping the next day for the key that would open him up really wide.

I hadn't even had time to investigate my newest boyfriend, the one who didn't yet know that I existed on the planet, when the biggest secret of all dropped in our laps. At the last show, Rachel had gotten charmingly chummy with The Assassins' manager, and he told her that Tim was *eighteen*! I was fantasizing about someone who had just been granted the right to vote earlier that month? It became the biggest joke of all time that if one of us went to the prom with him, maybe he'd come with us to our sorority formal. It seemed a fair exchange. It was crazily, privately acknowledged, however, that he was still something to hunt down and capture, despite his age, and though we all had a lot of laughs about this beautiful baby boy, we were all racing against each other to corrupt him first.

Then it was spring break, and Kim drove me to the airport in Philadelphia so I could catch my flight to Michigan and to Clay. I was totally not excited for my vacation, dreading having sex with him, knowing that it would last two minutes at most, as it always seemed to these days. As I sat in the plane, reading a particularly steamy Jackie Collins book to get me in the mood to copulate, I remembered when Clay and I had first started going out. I used to count the hours, the minutes, until I would get to see him, picking out my outfits four weeks in advance, popping my green birth control pills four hours early. I would be with my friends, be at class, be out, and all I could think about was Clay and how I'd leave everything behind if I only had the opportunity to lie in the crook of his arm and watch a movie from Blockbuster. I realized, sitting on that chilly plane, that he reveled in the fact that I was so dependent on him, and he adored my clinging. I used to adore it too, but now it just made me sick and made me feel like a stranger to myself. I had promised myself in my journal the night before to try to put the romance and the excitement back into our relationship on this vacation, but then I hugged my arms around myself, gulping in the artificial air until I was bloated, and knowing that the feelings and the smiles that I was about to project would sadly and needlessly be just as, if not even more, fake than my current surroundings.

At the airport, Clay ran over to me with a huge smile on his sweet face and gave me a big hug and a kiss that made me slightly nauseous, a reaction that had never happened before, and it instantly scared me. We got my bags and walked to his jeep holding hands, and with a soul-crushing ache, I felt his heart through his soft palm. Suddenly I wanted everything to work out between us. Memories of stable yesterdays poured around me constantly during my weeklong vacation in the Midwest; stuck in an environment for days where I had nothing else to do but coddle and be coddled, I immersed myself in my second true love. We had a relaxing time. We saw lots of movies, I dragged him shopping, and we ate out a lot. We cooed and laughed and smiled. We spent a lot of time with his friends, guys who were laid-back, sexy, intellectual potheads that I enjoyed spending time with. They always treated me with that "she's our buddy's girlfriend" respect, but they were also affectionate and most were hysterically funny. I sometimes admitted to myself that I was so much more compatible with Clay's friends than I was with him, and I fleetingly wondered if he'd hook me up with one of them if we ever broke up. Clay's girl friends were also sweet. They were all invariably anorexically skinny, undeniably pretty girls with long, straight, dark hair that fell to a few inches above their tight, used Levis, who came from Long Island, and who called Clay by his last name. And they all looked *exactly* alike, maybe only their eyeliner color serving to help in the differentiation process. I didn't think that I would pick to be friends with them on my own—they made me feel fat—but when I visited Michigan, I could deal with spending time with them.

On my last night in Michigan, Clay and I went out to my favorite restaurant in Ann Arbor and then came back to his room in his fraternity house and got into bed. I didn't cry when I left the next morning like I usually did, and on the plane, my cynical self again at last, the girlfriend role ten thousand feet below me, I realized that all week long the sex was as fleeting as it always was, and I had just hid my impatience, faking orgasms with a bored detachment. And away from Clay, I became angry with him because he was satisfied with our relationship, and it wasn't exciting at all anymore, and I wondered if it ever was. I was pretty sure that it used to be. And I was so annoyed that after almost four years, I so rarely had a real orgasm from sex, but I was even more scornful of the fact that my shitty, half-assed acting abilities, performed under his checkered, cotton comforter, fooled him every time.

Back at my sorority house, we all began to realize that we were graduating in less than two months, so we started confiding, laughing, going out, and telling secrets with a vengeance. We became like children in our intoxicating closeness, holding tight to each other so that we wouldn't be thrown into that snarling pit called adulthood all alone.

Days began to pass by in a happy blur, marred only by the fact that soon these soft days would end, and I still had no idea where I would be spending next year. The date that I was supposed to hear from NYU had come and gone with no notification and I knew that the smart thing to do would be to call the office of Cinema Studies and inquire about my status, but I was scared. I guess I knew deep down that I wasn't going to get in, and once I knew for sure, I wouldn't be able to fantasize anymore and I was beginning to believe that it was fantasy that kept me smiling these days and that it was fantasy that laminated these last months of school in a gooey, rosy glow. I mean, I went to sleep and woke up thinking about Luke, a boy who was in no way involved in my present life. I walked around campus dreaming about a school that I didn't have much of a chance of getting in to. I spent every night with a group of people that I probably wouldn't see much of in another two months. I didn't live in real life. None of us did. We just spent those blurring days acting out our own parts in our own movies and in each other's movies, and then we'd settle back to watch them just like Laura Mulvey and the lesbian theorists said that we would.

I let another week slide by, and a bunch of inane controversies started to swell throughout the house and the sorority, taking my chaotic thoughts off of myself and placing them into a clearly concocted hysteria. The biggest problem being whispered about behind closed bedroom doors and in hushed, huddled groups during Alpha Chi Omega meetings on Sunday nights was snarling complaints about Kim and her role as President of the chapter. She had been elected in February, and she'd won by a landslide. Everybody was excited about her being in charge because she was so crazy and funny and crass; and though the college as a whole and our chapter in particular had been targeted recently for hazing, we figured she'd probably let us get away with murder. And then she surprised everyone. She sat up straight in her wooden chair at her first meeting, and with her voice level she announced, "There will be no hazing with these pledges. No blindfolding. No forced drinking. No scavenger hunts in fraternity house basements. No sucking down goldfish. You will not make them wear ugly outfits. Nothing. Or the offender be punished severely." Now, Kim's proclamation was nothing new. All of the presidents and pledge trainers laid out the "official rules" to the chapter every time a new group of pledges came around. When I was President when I was a sophomore, I said the same thing. Then I went home and made a list of things for my little sister, Allison, to wear for a week. I remember recommending that her beauty would best be set off with stripes and plaid worn together. I bought her a bottle of Boone's wine to guzzle at her own free will while cute boys stood over her suggesting that she finish it, and I had her go buy a goldfish to nurture until Hell Night. She named him Dead. Basically, I just turned the other cheek to sorority mischief and nothing ever happened. (And I never made Allison swallow Dead. I mean, I had been a staunch member of P.E.T.A. during my early high school days.) Our chapter was known on campus for being the wild hazers, the big drinkers—I was often told jokingly that I was a disgrace to my letters—the fun girls, and we had fun by hazing. There was no harm meant in it, there really wasn't.

One night in particular of my pledging experience stood out in my memory, in blazing Technicolor. Seven of us were told to go to this house, a place I'd never been. We were told to tell no one and to bring bandanas; they were obviously not for us to accessorize with, but to wear as blindfolds. We all recognized the lack of safety in this sorority situation and I'd told my roomie, Alice, that if I wasn't back by 3:00 a.m. that she should come looking for me. She laughed, only I wasn't kidding. All of us walked the short distance to the designated address on that crisp fall night of my freshman year, taking hesitant steps and pressing close together. We knocked on the door, and some guy that none of us had ever seen before appeared, wearing an anticipatory smirk on his face. "Hi, I'm a piece of meat," went through my mind as this definite frat boy's eyes washed over my face and body. He told us to come on in and to sit down in the living room, a room filled with cheap beer and cute boys. We smiled at them, our eyes pleading with them to be kind, and they responded by ordering us to put on our blindfolds and to answer questions about our sorority's history. If we got the question wrong, we had to drink for disrespecting Alpha Chi Omega with our ignorance. If we got the question right, we had to drink for being sniveling wise asses. Then we had to stand up, and still blindfolded, we had to fake an orgasm for the attentive audience of degraders. I was humiliated oohing and aahing for these boys, but the grip of Dana's hand in mine and Jenny's quick breathing on my other side made the experience bearable. I knew that they were scared too and that later we would all laugh about this mini-moment, embellishing it to make it sound more fierce to others, and that it would bond us for quite some time. And I was right. So that theory that hazing made pledges respect the sisterhood was a bunch of bullshit, but it definitely brought us close to one another while we shrank and shriveled in fear. And now Kim seemed serious in her plans to stop hazing forever. She seemed stern, and a week later, when one girl made her little sister pick her up a pack of rolling papers and bring them to her apartment, Kim brought that girl up on misconduct charges and refused to let the girl go to the spring formal.

So Kim's name was officially changed in many people's minds to Kim, That Fucking Evil President, and the words "power trip" flew around so fast, it was as if they had sprung strong wings. To the majority, Kim had become a bitch. But she was also one of my best friends, and though I thought she was taking all this responsibility a mite too seriously, I defended her and her actions publicly and often. Privately, however, Rachel, Jessica, and I whined that she was starting to be no fun, and we made a pact that we had to find the old Kim before she buried her true self under sorority resignation forms and signed affidavits that solemnly promised that no sister would force a mere pledge to do anything so degrading and harsh as remember a sister's name or the date that the sorority was founded.

Alone in my cozy bedroom at the end of each day, I was writing in my journal constantly, for the first time since I was a senior in high school, and it was both wonderfully liberating and frustratingly disappointing. I loved feeling that I just had so much to say that I needed to share it with an extension of myself, but the brief bursts of poetry that I scribbled out in one long, heaving sigh were nowhere near as good as my high school angst pieces. Those had felt epic. My new poetry seemed a bit contrived and chop-chop-choppy. But it was still kind of interesting to read, because it seemed that I had always written in the past about *this* guy not loving me or *that* guy not needing me, and now when I went back and read my almost unintelligible scrawling, I realized that now I was writing about the future, my future, and my feelings about myself. For the first time in my life I was defining who I was based on me and me alone, and I didn't even think about how the guy in my life would respond. I sat up one night on the last week in April and heaved a big sigh of relief because I knew that soon I would be single again and that I would be just fine, thank you.

My video camera started going anywhere and everywhere with me, and everyone was getting a little fed up with always having to be "on" when I entered the room with that red light blinking, but deep down we all thrived on the whimsical attention of posing and preening, so no one resisted too much. I found I liked the power that came with filming. I captured Jessica and Lee giving each other hand massages and realized when I watched it back that if I dubbed in some music, I could turn that innocent moment into something that looked salacious. I didn't do it—pretend porn starring two of my friends didn't do much for me—but I was amazed by how I could change the meaning of a moment through editing. I figured my Film professors would be proud. I got Kathleen and some random guy in her Anatomy class sitting in the dining room during a study session, pointing at each other's legs, arms, and stomachs while rattling off the bones and muscles in the human body. I had about an hour's worth of tape of Rachel and Kim singing sorority songs and talking about what the voting criteria was for a rushee to get into Alpha Chi—"She could have fucked my dad, but if she made my mom watch, she's a mean bitch and she's out!" I had the entire house dress up like Guns N' Roses one Sunday night, lip-synching "Sweet Child of Mine," which they got into—Rachel tying a bandana around her blond head and putting on a kilt to be Axl, Jessica carefully drawing on an eyeliner beard to be Slash. I got the tryouts for all the major competitions for Greek Week, like Looking Fit and Greek Goddess. And the battery on my cute little camcorder kept stopping at the most inopportune moments, after everyone had finally let guarded guards down, but I did get funny stuff. When I would watch it later on, alone in my pink room, I would stare at myself as if I were seeing myself for the first time. I would watch myself laugh and smile and light cigarettes and roll my eyes, and I would be surprised by just how little my voice was, and I would finally understand why everyone always laughed at my laugh, and I would want to close my eyes and stay that happy forever.

Fleeting, happiness is. It was so ickily sticky outside that I couldn't lie out, and my cleavage was all sweaty and gross, and everyone looked like shit, and we were all carting around huge bottles of water, when I locked myself in my room, and hands trembling, dialed New York. The office staff at NYU was cordial and sweet, much like the director of a funeral parlor, or maybe a mohel. They were very sorry and very embarrassed that I still had not received notification about my status for admission, and would be happy to fax me their decision. Fax? They were going to fax me what I guessed would be a rejection letter? My tummy plummeted and rumbled as I gave them the fax number at Kinko's and then hung up the phone to dial my mommy to tell her that I was going to find out my fate. I heard in her soothing voice that she was terrified that I was about to never wake up from my no-from-NYU nightmare, but she told me to relax and to take a deep breath and to call her as soon as I knew. I pulled on a pair of old jean shorts and my black sandals, grabbed my car keys, and walked out of my house without telling anyone where I was going. I got into my car in a daze, not even feeling the scorching burning on my bare legs from the hot leather seats. The two-minute drive to Kinko's went by much too quickly, as deep in concentration, I prayed hard. Please. Please. Oh, my God, *please*. I pulled into the parking lot, walked through the swinging glass doors, asked the lady behind the counter if a fax had come in, and gave her my name. She looked, pulled out two sheets of paper, charged me four dollars, and clucked, "Have a good day" at me. I just glared at her. Holding those papers in my hands, with words on them that I had waited weeks (years?) to see, I just stood there like a lump. My heart was beating so fast and so loudly that I was certain a senior member of the Kinko's staff would tell me to shush. But no one said anything to me. I just kept standing there. And then I looked down. "We regret to inform you…" and the rest of the words on the paper blurred before my eyes, and all that I could see was a big black and white mess in front of me, and I knew that it represented my future. And as I went to leave the store, eyes bloodshot and a big ball of suffocation in my throat, two guys approached me and handed me an invite for their fraternity party that night. I couldn't read the invite, but both of them were wearing ZBT T-shirts and baseball hats, committing double-letter jeopardy. ZBT was the biggest bunch of losers at Delaware, and I just stood there with my NYU rejection letter in one hand and my personal ZBT invite in the other, and it had to be my lowest moment.

I walked into my house through the back door and cringed when I heard voices in the living room. I hoped that no one would try to talk to me. I just wanted to be left alone. I walked past everyone quickly, managing a super-fake smile that they all saw right through, and as they exchanged worried glances with each other, I ran up to my room, where I burst into a torrent of salty tears that got in my tangled hair and fell onto my Film paper that I had just gotten back earlier that day. I had gotten an A on it. I looked at myself in the mirror, at my swollen and ugly face, and I thought that I should get my video camera out and capture my misery; and then I thought that was just the kind of sick thing that women always did, watch themselves, and I wanted to murder those lesbian theorists because they were right and they had probably gone to NYU, and I was just this weak little girl who was now headed off to Miami, and I couldn't even stand a day of Delaware heat.

I stayed cocooned in my room for many hours, allowing nothing to permeate through my misery: no light, no fresh air, no empathy. I didn't turn on the TV, and my radio was bound and gagged, and just the sounds of my shallow breaths kept me company. Before I crawled into my unmade bed and brought my musty stuffed animals to my blotchy face to try to look back onto my now unattainable and optimistic childhood, I reread my essay that I had written for NYU, and I was so ashamed by how amateur it now seemed to be. So I kicked the folder containing that essay, the copy of my application, and my rejection fax under my bed, where it remained until I threw it out on graduation day.

I probably lost about eleven pounds in water weight from crying so much, and that alone made me cheer up slightly. And then I thought of the beautiful palm trees, and I remembered how romantic it felt riding around in a car with the warm breeze blowing my hair all over the place, and that in Miami, it was warm enough to keep the windows open all the time. And air conditioners were probably everywhere. And maybe the humidity would make my hair curl better. And Gloria Estefan probably wouldn't be on *every* station. I finally swallowed my scorching pain and admitted embarrassment and defeat, but I also allowed myself to recognize the fact that I wasn't such a failure. I had gotten into two very good schools. It wasn't like my future was a gaping pit of steaming emptiness. At least I didn't think that it would be. At least I hoped that it wouldn't be. At least I would be tan.

I skipped two days of classes and didn't shower for three before I grabbed a tight hold on my fleeting composure and forced myself back into my life, trying real hard to focus completely on my present and not bemoan my past or obsess about my future. And I went to my weekly screening for my film theory class, this week watching Dr. Harris's favorite movie, *The Texas Chainsaw Massacre*, for the first time ever, and I shuddered and sickened myself into a good mood and positive thinking. The movie truly repulsed and disturbed me. I mean, all of those movies, all of the *Halloweens* and the *Friday the Thirteenths* and the *Peeping Toms* were disturbing and slimily yucky, but in all of those, I was always able to hold tight to a level of detachment and enjoy watching the harlotty victims shrivel and shrink in fear. In *Chainsaw,* three quarters of the movie felt like it was a close-up on some girl's gooey eyeball, and her horror felt so tangible that I could even smell it, and I couldn't help thinking, "Why am I supposed to be enjoying this?" And when the movie ended, I sat in shock for a few moments and looked up into Dr. Harris's open and smiling face; and as I told him of my queasiness, I began to realize that he probably wasn't the right man for me.

We kept going to the Balloon to see The Assassins play, and we were always down front, leaning against the slimy stage, cheap, warm beer in our hands, our attention held rapt by our favorite local band. A lot of my friends started getting friendly with all the guys in the band, following them upstairs between sets to hang out and throwing them perfunctory come-hither gazes, really and truly believing they would bring one of them home afterward like a freshly polished trophy. I did like all of the guys, and I still thought Tim was so stunningly sexy, and I still stared hard at them when they were on stage, but I just couldn't find that detached level of groupiness in me to spend my time running after them on a personal level. Every once in a while, I wished that I could squelch my inhibitions or my uncommon common sense and just go with it, because it seemed to me that my brazenly cavorting friends always had so much more fun.

Then one Friday night the entire house decided to stay in and just hang out. When I woke up from my daily nap at seven o'clock, I walked my bed-warm body upstairs to Rachel's room and found everyone sitting on the floor playing blackjack with sticky old pennies. Madonna was belting out fluffy song lyrics in the background, taking us back to a time in life when we had finally outgrown those ugly beige training bras, and I hummed along to "Borderline" as I kneeled down and joined the game. They were all drinking beer, but I just grabbed the warm Diet Coke that was thoughtfully offered to me, the non-alcoholic member of the group, doled out seven of somebody else's pennies, and came up with twenty-two. Soon the game I had joined an hour late became boring, so we decided to move on to a good, intrusive game of "I never…" To play, someone makes a statement, starting with the words "I never…" and everyone who has been involved with the nasty, usually sexually-charged scenario must drink. As the game started, I looked down at my Diet Coke and wondered if I'd lived recklessly enough to wind up with a caffeine headache.

   "I never hooked up with more than one person on the same night." I remembered that sticky senior night in high school when I was at Ann's house, when I had majorly hooked up with Luke and then kissed Darrell a mere hour later and started slurping my Diet Coke while everyone else in the circle chugged as well. "I never hooked up with a married man." Ha, ha, frivolous, futile scenarios to even concoct, but there was one of my crazy friends, hysterically laughing and drinking away! Ooh…the secrets revealed during a good game of "I never…" Truly the stuff hush-hush memories are made of. Two of us drank to "I never tried cocaine," and three of us drank to "I never had an orgasm," while the rest of us murmured horror-tinged empathy. I realized that so far I'd had a pretty fun life and I'd had some pretty good sex. But halfway through the game, I found myself too aware that for so many of the silly questions, I had to go waaay back to high school to remember if I'd done it or not; when I couldn't drink to the "I never hooked up with more than five guys in the same fraternity" question, the relief I thought I would feel by not being a slut turned into a wave of depression. I was a tortured, twenty-one-year-old, claustrophobically kept girl/woman, and later on in the night, when I threw my soda can away and some of the remaining soda splashed into the garbage can, I knew it was infinitely past time to make a change.

Sometime during that night, the angel of congestion came to visit my locked bedroom, and I woke up the next morning sniffling, sneezing, and suffering away. I rolled out of my tissue-strewn bed, grabbed Mr. Gerber, my trusty teddy who always made me feel better when I was under the withered weather, and toddled my way upstairs to find Justine, who always had more over-the-counter medicine than a drugstore. She took one look at my swollen, crimson nose and my watery eyes and handed over the Benadryl. The drowsy kind. Score. I waved to everyone else as they lounged around watching a *Real World* marathon, turned on my slippered heel, and went back to bed.

Five hours later I stirred. My room was almost dark, and my television was still on, and so was *The Real World*. I still felt really phlegmy, and I figured that I would stay in that night and relax and watch movies and call my mom so she could commiserate with my ailments; but then I realized that she'd probably be out, so I got out of bed, wiped the gooey goo from my sleepy eyes, brushed the sicky smell from my teeth, and found everyone in Jessica's room. They were making plans for the night. After rejecting another Saturday night at Kate's and the Balloon, Rachel jokingly suggested driving down to Sea Isle City, New Jersey, to see The Assassins play at a bar there. And we all fell about laughing while I clutched my dirty tissues, and when we stopped laughing, we looked up at each other in silence for a classic "should we?" moment. Without a word we ran from Jessica's room to our closets to decide what to wear to visit the boys playing in the bar on the beach.

Kim, Jessica, Kathleen, and I drove down in one car, while Rachel and her friend Sara drove down in another. We listened to the radio the whole way down, singing along to the songs that we'd hear live later on that night. It took us almost two hours to get down there, and we had been carelessly carefree the whole way, but as we pulled onto the deserted beach road and saw the bar just ahead, the band's name spelled out horizontally over the illuminated marquee, we began to lose our nerve. What kind of psycho groupies were we going to look like? They knew how long it took to get down there; they were going to think that we were crazy! What if Kim's fake ID didn't work? And I was sick—I should be home all snuggle-snuggle in my bed! And why, oh why, were we all wearing little spring dresses when it was fifty degrees on the block next to the ocean where we pulled up? Rayon and chiffon and lightweight cotton flew up and showed our carefully selected undies while hitting us in our blushing faces as we threw caution and demure desires to the gusting wind and ran toward the bar for its warmth and the adventure that it was holding for us.

Our freezing nipples hit the bar ten minutes before the rest of us got there, and they paid our cover as we went in and walked straight to the bar. Jessica immediately ordered a shot, knowing she would have to be wasted to act natural while the rest of my friends ordered beers. Still woozy from the Benadryl, I got myself some water and sipped it slowly through the plastic straw while looking down into the cup crammed with ice. I still felt like my head was swimming, but I thought that maybe it was from the heady circumstances instead of from my fever. We heard the band playing, and as we walked over to the side of the bar to see them, we saw a startling sight. A bride in full wedding regalia was in the middle of the dance floor, a bottle of Bud Lite in one hand, a lit cigarette in the other, and she and her groom were dancing all over the place. I couldn't help it: the first thing that I thought about was the movie *Urban Cowboy* and how I had seen it as part of a double feature that also included *Grease* at a drive-in with my parents before they got divorced. I wondered if these two joined in matrimony were also named Bud and Sissy, and as I heard my friends scoff at the down-home wedding celebration in their midst, I thought about how lucky I was that my wedding day would surely be so different. I looked at my friends, and I knew that some of them would be there with me on that special day, whether it be five years from now or ten years from now, and I felt so lucky to have them. We were all so different from one another, and I know that they always thought that I was the stable, together one, but I felt that they had qualities that anyone should dream a warm dream of having. They were spontaneous and adventuresome and *alive,* and I had been like that once. I had. And starting from that night, I knew that I could be like that again.

The band saw us as they launched into that Beastie Boys song that we all loved, and they looked grateful to see people ready to have a great time in their midst. We all grabbed a high table and put our drinks down and most of us lit cigarettes, and then Chris walked off of the stage and right toward us. Wordlessly, he shook each of our hands, gave us a wink, and walked back onto the stage. I exchanged smiles with the rest of my sidekicks, acknowledging that it was cool of him to thank us for being there, and I guess that warm hand squeeze gave each of us a burgeon of confidence, because we all suddenly moved away from the circular safety of the table, out to the center of the floor, just a few feet from the band and the bride, and we all started dancing and laughing and whispering to each other. Everyone in the bar was staring at us, and I knew that we looked striking as we all fell into a strikingly great mood.

Halfway through the first set, I went into the bathroom at the back of the bar, but I didn't have to pee or anything. I really just wanted to see myself. I knew that one day I would so badly want to remember how I looked at the moment when all of my insecurities had blown away into the salty, sea-smelling air, when I had watched from afar as I detached them from myself like a psychotic angel from the real world heavens, and when I found myself feeling warm despite having shed my snugly secure skin. And I knew that my favorite film theorists would say that it was a classic "female" thing to do, to monitor my appearance; but for the first time in a while, when I looked at myself in the mirror, the band's music playing loudly just a wooden bathroom door away, I loved what I saw.

Back in the bar, the band had taken a break, and I found myself in a deep conversation with Chris on the troubles that beset a natural curly-haired person when he dared to defy nature and tried to straighten a head of hair. His hair, previously a mane smoothed to idyllic perfection, was now a mass of frizz and fuzz, and as a tortured curl victim myself, I chose to share a startling secret with him:

Bumble and Bumble hair serum. Just a little dollop of the sticky stuff combed through the precious coif, and whammo! Silky straightness. He seemed truly grateful for my beauty counseling, and when we moved away from each other, I felt as though I had found a new friend.

Then I saw Tim come from the back room and I saw Kathleen rush right up to him, throwing her naturally straight hair back in a practiced swing, and I found myself hating her. I also found myself noticing that Tim was looking past her and right at me. Hmmm…I walked over to him casually and asked him if he had a light, and accidentally on purpose, I touched his little hand as he lit my convenient Parliament. He then asked me for a cigarette and instead of using his lighter, he lit it with my smoldering one. Our hands touched again, and we looked at each other for a long moment while Kathleen stomped away to flirt with a more attentive audience. Then I smiled sweetly and looked carefully into his so-very-young face and said in measured tones, "You look just like this guy that I used to go out with." He smiled wide and his blue eyes hooded over. And then he came close enough to me that I could smell his sweet breath and he whispered, "See that girl over there? She hasn't stopped staring at me all night and she's with her boyfriend. That's the kind of thing that gets us in trouble!" I glanced smoothly to my right at the girl sitting on the bar stool with a big burly guy, who was indeed staring hard at the band member in my freshly woven web. I looked back at him, took a deep but lady-like drag on my prop, and as I blew out the smoke in a steady, seductive stream, I answered, "Cut off your hair and it won't happen." He laughed loud and he laughed deep, and the years between us melted at my swimming knees, and he gave me one last long look and got back on stage to play with his friends while I moved over to play with mine.

The bar had gotten really crowded and really hot, and there were some cute boys there, but the guys wielding guitars above us held our attention captive. They were talking to us from the stage and winking at us like we all shared some private joke, and it was apparent that we were now a vital part of the show. I always felt so self-conscious dancing, imagining myself as a rhythmless embarrassment to myself, but that night I didn't care what I looked like as I whirled and twirled and tapped my sandaled high heels to the thundering beat. My friends and I kept throwing our arms around each other in impromptu embraces, and the love was flowing even quicker than the beer, more profusely than the sweat, as our dreams ran toward each other at a hundred miles per hour, colliding without incident, meshing without needing to be stirred.

After the show ended, Chris came up to Rachel and me and asked us where we were staying that night, and we told him that we were going home, back into the vehicle for the two-hour trek back to school. Chris told us that we should just stay in Sea Isle for the night; the band was staying in the motel right across the street, and we should get a room and stay too. Since the night already reeked from non-blushing adventure, we gathered into a huddled conference near the back bar, much like a winning team planning our next practiced move, and we decided, hell, yes, we were gonna stay! At least some of us were. Kathleen wanted to go home; if she didn't get all of the attention, she was no fun. As a good, guilt-ridden friend, Jessica went with her on the long drive back to Delaware, as Kim, Rachel, Sarah, and I bid good-bye to the band, telling them we'd see them later. Tim was in a corner with a pretty, short-haired, blonde girl whom I immediately wanted to spit at, and it turned out she was someone he had been hanging out with a little, but he wanted to tell her that night that it was o-v-e-r between them. As we all left the bar, the rest of my friends hugged him good-bye, but I just waved nonchalantly over my shoulder at him, going for the playing-it-cool thing. And God bless this seductive little prince, but he reached past his jilted blonde princess, grabbed my hand, pulled me toward him while she glared at me, and kissed me good-bye on my cheek. I smiled sweetly at both of them, cheered with satisfaction and amorous delight in my head, and walked toward the motel.

There was no telephone in the motel room, no clock, and the sink wasn't in the bathroom. We were all in dresses, had nothing to sleep in, no toothbrushes, and we had to be back at school by nine thirty the next morning for the start of Greek Week. All of a sudden, it just seemed so ridiculous that we were there, in that dirty motel, the band nowhere in sight, freezing our scantily clad assess off. I had no makeup with me, but I knew this night was not about looking good. It was about feeling good and being bad, but I still thought longingly of my tube of Coffee Bean Revlon lipstick sitting on the edge of my dresser in my room, so lonely for my pouting lips, to say nothing of the compact that I relied upon daily to conceal any facial flaw that decided to spring up. Kim, Rachel, and Sarah were hungry for both pizza and band members, so we sauntered out to the pizza place right next door to the motel and ordered a pizza and some diet soda to go. The band was nowhere in sight, so we took the hot stuff back to our room and sat on the floor to eat. I didn't know why I wasn't hungry—I hadn't eaten a morsel of food all day—but I just drank some soda and smoked some cigarettes and wondered what the rest of the evening held in store for us.

Then Rachel, valiant sorcerer of our group, decided the time had come to find the band. And my spanking new confidence began to seriously wither and wane, and I just felt so stupid running around that motel searching for Assassins members. I put in my lone vote to stay in the room and hold tight to our fleeting pride, but I was seriously and quickly vetoed. We took the rickety elevator down the two floors to the lobby, where Rachel asked the old manager what floor the band was on. He gave up the information easily—Rachel had a way with all men, even the elderly—and we were told that they were on the floor above us, and I swear we were wasting our time. We should have been spending our time running after Pearl Jam or something! We got back in the elevator that I feared was going to break down, but it didn't and we arrived safe and sound on the fifth floor, the floor where the band was supposed to be staying. We walked to the rumored room number, and Rachel knocked while the rest of us giggled inanely, but nobody answered. I was convinced that Tim was probably in there with that blonde chick, and my friends agreed that I was probably right. We walked away from the room in combined relief and bittersweet rejection, and I thought about the probable salacious activities going on behind those thin motel room doors with the boy that I'd become entranced with; and as I broke into a run down the narrow hall with my friends in tow, I was sad and suspiciously let down.

But Rachel wasn't ready to give up quite so easily, and she decided that Tim may be swinging naked from chandeliers upstairs, but the rest of the band was probably still in the bar across the street and we should walk right in and hang out with them. I just looked at her, my brave, loony friend and laughed out loud at her voracious appetite for conflict and mischief. I admired her so much, and I realized that this night wasn't close to being over.

Back outside in the glacial ocean air, Kim suggested that we try the pizza place one more time to see if the guys were chowing down after the show, and when we walked in there for the second time that night, this time with no real reason to be there, who should be reclining in the front booth but the band, minus Tim. We didn't want to look like we were following them, so Kim played our stalking off brilliantly by walking right past them and grabbing a big bottle of Diet Coke, acting like we had come into that pizza place in great search of liquid refreshment to combat that thirst that always takes over in frigid forty-degree weather. While she paid for our embarrassing excuse, Rachel, Sarah, and I sat down with the rest of the band and spoke to them for a while. Jimmy was really the only extremely friendly one; his smile was so big and so bright, and he asked us for our room number and told us that he'd be by later to hang out. And we left the restaurant and went back upstairs to our rented shit hole and staked out our beds for the night. I figured that since Rachel was the only one of us who was close to Sara that she would sleep with her, but Rachel jumped into bed with Kim, so it was Sara and me. It felt kind of strange lying down next to a girl I didn't know well, but we crawled into bed, my skirt already moving to the top of my hips, and settled down for a night of uncomfortable sleep, unbrushed teeth, and a non-Noxzemaed face.

Five minutes after we turned the one light in the room out, someone knocked on the door. We flicked on the dim light between the double beds, and Rachel jumped up and ran to the door to see who was calling on us. Jimmy. He came in alone and took a look around at our pizza box, Diet Coke, and dirty ashtray-strewn room and sat down on the bed with Sara and me and started jabbering away. He was on an adrenaline kick after the show, and he talked a lot, telling us about his girlfriend that he was getting a little sick of, about those days that felt so long ago when he was in college, about his computer job that he enjoyed, and about his friendships with the rest of the band. It seemed he and Tim were crazily close, a big brother-little brother connection forged through a traveling cover band, and he said that Tim was the greatest kid who did not sleep around and was in fact not upstairs tying the lovely blonde to the bedposts, but driving her home after ditching the poor dear. I told Jimmy that Tim looked so much like my adored ex-love, and he told me that Tim had told him that I'd said that, and that he had also said that he thought that I was really cute. I smile demurely while my happy heart pitter-pattered urgently beneath my lacy black bra, and when Jimmy left the room an hour later, I jumped up and down on my shared bed with gleeful elation and immature abandon.

We left the sand and the scintillating sea very early the next morning, driving back to Delaware at eighty miles per hour, our hair in messy buns on top of our hung-over heads, our dresses still on and riding high above our goose-bumped thighs. I was in the backseat with Kim as Sara drove and they all smoked cigarettes, but I felt like my lungs were going to fall out, so I reluctantly abstained from a hefty inhalation at the crack of dawn. I kept my eyes closed much of the way back to school, but my imagination stayed propped majestically open, and as the sun broke through the dim pre-morning sky, Tim and I danced a tango through a field of daisies.

Looking Fit started at noon, and we had just enough time to shower, put on denim shorts and sorority tees, and tell everyone about waking up before farmers in Sea Isle City with a full bottle of Diet Coke. We drove to Harrington Beach, where the competition that kicked off Greek Week took place. As I stood in the dirt, staking out my spot for the day, I saw my freshman dorm through the glare of the sun, my old dining hall that I hadn't been in three years, and I thought I might have even seen my old self walking with my head down into my memories, while the new me lifted my face to the light and breathed in my stunning, luminous present.

Under a tree a few feet away, the brave participants of Looking Fit, the fitness competition that kicked off Greek Week, stood in their shaking splendor, oiling themselves all over with body lotion so that their popping muscles would be accentuated even further. The guys wore little shorts, and the ones wearing boxer briefs looked the best, and you just knew that they were on steroids. The girls were wearing teeny sports bras and spandex shorts with colorful thongs over them, and most of them had their hair pulled into slicked-back ponytails, matching their slicked tummies, and maybe I was biased, but I thought

Erica looked the best by far. She came over to the section where we were waiting to win, though Erica would be doing all of the work for our shared glory, and she looked nervous to flex for the entire school, but confident too. Her black shorts were molded to a body that hadn't enjoyed a morsel of fun food for a long time, and I thought of the night just recently when we had gone to dinner, and she had requested salsa to put on her baked potato instead of butter, and it seemed like such a sacrifice to for her to make for all of us. On the sidelines stood her two roommates, one with a Milky Way and one with a bag of crunchy cheese doodles that Erica planned to inhale immediately after she got off the stage. They were in different sororities, but they were rooting for their friend. And my video camera captured their pride, Erica's tremulous smile, and the opaque closeness that we all shared on that fine festive day.

The girls went first, and even though the purpose of Greek Week was supposedly to show unity among the lettered, being snide and envious ruled the day. The Phi Sigma Sigma sorority had won the competition for the past four years, and they had shirts made up that branded that fact across their Wonder Bra-ed chests. It made us hate them even more than we already did—it was like a rule— and while we all certainly hoped that Erica would win, it seemed even more important that Phi Sig lose. The girl from Alpha Phi went first, and she was awful, spending the entire aerobic routine opening her legs wide and wider, like she may as well get a full gyno exam while she was there. She was so dreadful that our nostrils flared along with our huge, happy smiles. When I saw who the Phi Sig contestant was, I felt badly for hating her on command. She was someone I'd had a bunch of classes with over the last two years, and she was sweet and smart. She performed her routine. Good, but not great. When our sorority's name was announced, Erica strutted purposefully onto the makeshift stage and looked everyone in that huge crowd straight and haughty in the face, and she was immediately mesmerizing. She was perfect, she didn't miss a beat, and when her song ended, she looked right toward us and raised her impossibly cut arms high into the air.

She got second. The truck-like, impossibly ripped girl from Kappa Delta snagged the blue ribbon, but it was okay. Erica looked so happy as she was lifted high into the air, a fresh dab of caramel on the side of her mouth. The guy from AEPi got first place, and since they were our partners for Greek Games, we applauded him like he was one of our sisters, and they gave it up fully and completely for Erica. Meryl, the Phi Sig girl, got fourth place, and she slunk away. I felt badly for her and wanted to tell her that it was okay and she had done well, but then I got caught up in the festivities. I stood with my friends, all of us shouting our sorority's name loud and then louder like we were participating in color war. And even though I knew I was behaving in such a pre-adolescent manner, I was having the best time.

It just seemed that the proclamation I had made to myself while I stood alone in front of the bathroom in the bar in Sea Isle was sticking, and I became more alive and carefree that week, much to my delirious friends' delights. Later on that night, after we'd all taken a much-needed nap, we went out to Kate's. It wasn't so crowded because it was Sunday, but we sat in a booth downstairs anyway. I didn't drink, but I loved being out on that typical night of rest and relaxation.

Back at the house at 1:00 a.m., I found myself on the phone with Clay, who seemed slightly confused that I had gone out on a Sunday night. Truthfully, it was something to be confused about, since it was something so unlike me to do, but I didn't need it to be rubbed in my face that was freshly covered in an acne-prevention mask that I had rarely taken advantage of these college benefits. I told him about going to Sea Isle the night before, since he was "worried" when I didn't call at all, and I told him the entire dizzy story, only leaving out the part where Tim had called me cute and I had melted in a muddled puddle at his size-eleven feet. Clay didn't seem to find the whole experience to be as wonderful as I did. I guess I would get a little worried if he was out driving across state lines to see a band of girls pluck their guitars, but it was all so innocent and still such a fairy tale that took place far far away, so I thought his lack of enthusiasm was in no way warranted and just further inclination that the time to lose the boy was now.

He was right, though. I had no business going out that Sunday because the next night I had to do my oral presentation with the rest of my group in my Social Deviance class. We were doing a whole report on homosexuality and about how something may be "deviant," but that may just mean that it's not part of the majority; it doesn't necessarily have to be a taboo, negative thing. My job for the group was to read three autobiographies by gays and report themes that came up between all three authors. I'd read all of the books, and they were all pretty interesting, and the rest of my group was nice, but I was graduating in a month, and I really just didn't care anymore. So, Monday at five thirty, after I left my film screening where I saw *Alien*, I ran to a corner of the building where my next class was held and sat there scribbling out notes on flimsy index cards for my presentation that started at seven. When the rest of the group got there, we all smoked a few cigarettes—I never knew that they smoked—and when we went in to do our report, the class was silent and probably bored to tears; but we did fine and when I got up to tell the story of Greg Louganis, I didn't even tremble.

On the way into Carpenter Gym the next night to see the Greek Week talent show, someone came right up behind me and said my name softly. I turned around, and it was Dave, my friend from high school who also went to Delaware, but I never saw so much of him at school. We had been pretty friendly all those years back, bonding on warm nights on suburban lawns when we were seventeen years old. He was really close friends with Luke, so I used to always try to get pertinent and pivotal info out of him to help push my romantic life along the bumpy track. In December I had taken Dave as my last-minute date to my formal because Clay hadn't been able to fly in. With his hippie blond curls and a face that looked to me like a lion, I knew he'd photograph well and we'd laugh a lot. The two of us had a fun time, but there were no kisses, which I guess made sense because I was supposed to be in a serious long-distance entanglement. But I kind of wanted him that night, and I was a little surprised that he hadn't tried anything. I hadn't hung out with him since then, but as we walked into the gym together, I told him that we should get together because I was in total and complete lust with his roommate, Andrew, who was in sight a lot this week as the programmer of Greek Week. Before every event Andrew got up and explained the rules while all of the girls in the audience fell to their bare knees in a swoony swoon. I took one look at him a few days ago and wondered where this extraordinary specimen had been all of my life. The answer was McDonalds. Before this school year, Andrew had weighed about three hundred pounds and was known as the sweet, fat kid in Sig Ep. When he arrived back in Delaware in September, the massive bulk melted off of him, a lot of people didn't even recognize him, while a bunch more went salivating after him. Most of the girls who were now stalking him were people who had blown him off for three years, girls he used to love who would only be his friend, girls he used to drive home after they'd been fucked by one of his fraternity brothers. And you could tell he liked the attention he was getting, but that he was deep down aware that before this year, none of those girls had given him the time of day.

But I had never known Andrew before, not even by sight. This year we'd been introduced a couple of times by different people, and he was always really friendly, but our meetings were too brief. I decided that night that I wanted him, and I hoped that Dave would come through for me and somehow get us together.

The next morning Rachel knocked on my bedroom door at ten o'clock and woke me up by plopping down on my bed and squealing, "I just got us dates for tonight!" Seems she bumped into Dave and Andrew on the street on her way back from class, and they invited the two of us over that night to smoke and then go to Kate's. Go, Dave! Way to come through for an old friend! That day two of my best friends who had graduated last year came to visit, and the three of us went to the mall, where I looked far and wide for a stunning, slimming outfit to wear that night for my much-planned seduction, something I was kind of out of practice in, having been a girlfriend for so long. I invited both of them to come over to Dave's with us that night, but both Nikki and Gina wanted to just go straight to the bars they had missed, so I told them I'd meet them there. We got back to the sorority house where we had all once lived together, and I could see in their faces that it was difficult for them to be in the place that used to wrap them in comfort and familiarity but now only blew wisps of memories at them, dangling days of ease before their eyes, but pulling them away before they could slip their arms tightly around them.

I showered and shaved almost every hair off of my body and got dressed in tighter jeans than I usually wore and my brand new tank top with the skinny braided straps. My hair looked pretty good, and I was really excited to go over to Dave and Andrew's and hang out with some new, very sought after friends. Before we went there, a bunch of us decided to make a detour and stop by the rehearsal for Airband that was going on over at AEPi. Airband was a huge deal during Greek Week, and every sorority and fraternity took it seriously, practicing every night for weeks beforehand, perfecting costumes and lip synchs and practiced enthusiasm. AEPi had given our sorority the use of their band room to rehearse in, and at that very moment, about thirty of my sisters were there, dancing around to the song "I Want Candy," impersonating the characters from

Willie Wonka and the Chocolate Factory. It was a clever, adorable concept, and I thought we had a good chance of winning. While we were there, the little pledges who had just gotten into the sorority about a month earlier all ran up to give me hugs and to squeal hello, and to be honest, I didn't really know who most of them were. So much for sisterhood, or maybe it had just gotten to the point where I didn't have much in common with freshmen now that I was a senior, and that was probably natural. We stayed for about half an hour, and I videotaped the rehearsals for the girl who was running the show, and then we said good-bye and dropped Gina and Nikki off at Kate's and headed over to Dave's.

Dave was pulling on a shirt and Andrew was chomping carrot sticks when we arrived, flushed and smiling. I was holding the video of the talent show in my clammy hands because I wanted Dave to watch himself sing the song he'd performed the night before. He was self-conscious and didn't want to watch, so he left the room, and Rachel, Andrew, and I watched some of the video. Rachel introduced Andrew and me again, and he smiled and said, "We've met before." And it always floored me that people I thought would never know who I was did know me, and I wondered how many more people who I thought had no clue I existed on the planet knew who I was, and I wondered if they thought that maybe I didn't know who *they* were. And the circle of pretending at college was so inflated, and I thought it was such a shame and that we all could have had so many more friends if we just had more confidence that we were all recognizable, noteworthy people.

I guess the reason I was thinking so introspectively was because I was high as a kite, because the second that we stepped into their apartment, they started rolling blunts and packing bowls. Rachel and I could not stop laughing. Andrew was telling us all of the stupid questions that fraternities and sororities kept calling with that pertained to Greek Week, like whether or not barnyard animals were allowed onstage during Airband. He was such a wise ass that he'd just act serious and tell the people, "I'm sorry, but I don't know the policy on farm animals. Maybe you should call the Greek Affairs office directly to inquire." The whole time I was staring at him like he held the solutions to poverty and celibacy in his slimmed-down face, but while I was so entranced with his beauty up close, there were really no sparks. The weird thing was, I felt all fidgety in front of *Dave* and I loved being around him and there was definitely something new crackling between the two of us. A few minutes later when Dave decided to run down to TCBY to get a soda, I went with him, and we stood outside having an in-depth talk about Clay. I told him how unsatisfied I was with Clay and how I was planning on breaking up with him after graduation. Dave asked me if I was interested in someone else, if that's what was causing me to feel this way, and I told him no because I wasn't about to tell him that I wanted him. I didn't know if I really did, and I wasn't going to tell him about Tim, because he was such a fantasy that just lived happily and fully beneath the everyday. Dave asked me if I still cared about Luke, and I told him that I would always care for Luke, but that he wasn't a part of my life anymore, and I was happy with that, and it was probably better anyway, since just the thought of him made me feel sweaty.

Back inside we smoked a bit more and then decided we should go to Kate's. I remembered that two of my best friends were there waiting for me and I had forgotten about them and I felt bad. Rachel and I went to the bathroom while Dave and Andrew prettied themselves up, and I was just about to tell Rachel that I wanted Dave when she announced that she wanted Andrew. I stopped short. I wasn't ready to give up on him yet, even though I was imagining his roomie and me tangled beneath his sheets on the top bunk, so I declared she couldn't have Andrew. He was mine. Or he might be by the end of the night. The next thing I knew, Rachel and I were shoving each other in the bathroom, almost pulling hair, almost having a full-fledged catfight over the boy just a few feet away who probably would have kicked both of us out of his enviable bed. After we'd knocked each other around for a minute or two, we came to our extremely amorous senses and realized what we were doing. We collapsed on the floor in laughter, holding our legs together so we wouldn't pee all over their bathroom tiles.

I couldn't find Nikki and Gina at Kate's, but some people said they'd seen them there earlier. I wasn't worried; I figured they had gone to the Balloon and I'd see them there later. It was right across the street anyway. Andrew bought us beer, and then the crowd of adoring females in his wake swallowed him up. Every step that boy took, carefully straightened hair and perfectly manicured fingernails wrapped around him, and Dave, Rachel, and I just stood back and watched the slaughter. I was trying to catch a glimpse of myself in the mirror at the far end of the bar to make sure that I hadn't gained ten pounds since eight o'clock; in the reflection I saw my friend Brian, and I snaked my way through the crowd and made my way over to him to give him a big hug. We had met on the very first day of school freshman year, and we had immediately launched into a most productive game of Jewish Geography, and it turned out I had gone on a teen tour three summers earlier with a bunch of his friends. And his roommate, Mike, lived in the town next to me at home. We found out that we all lived on the same floor, and we had been great friends ever since. Both Mike and Brian were adorable, fun, genuinely nice guys who thought of me as a sister. I thought of them as my brothers, and there was never any consideration of incest, so we all got along all of the time. We didn't hang out so much, but we spoke on the phone a lot, and both of them were friends that I knew that I was so fortunate to have. On this hazy night toward the end of college, I threw my arms around Brian and asked where Mike was. I found him a few tables away, and I gave him a hug also. I kissed his girlfriend on the cheek, and I told them I was lusting after Andrew and Dave tonight, but I'd call them tomorrow and maybe the three of us could have dinner sometime this week.

We decided to head over to the Balloon after being at Kate's for about forty-five minutes, and when we walked in there, I went in search of my friends. I found them near the back of the bar conveniently situated near where Andrew and Dave's fraternity always hung out, and I threw my arms around them. I smoked a cigarette with Nikki, and I told her I thought that the game plan was changing, and that I wanted Dave now; she said she'd always thought that he was so hot and she told me that I should totally jump on him. I looked around to see where the newest object of my affections had situated his stoned self, and with a self-affirming jolt of wondrous wonder, I saw him just a few feet away, staring right at me with a smile on his lips.

For not the first time, I wasn't disappointed that bars in Delaware are required to stop serving at one o'clock, because I wanted to see what was going to happen next with Dave, but it was obvious nothing was going to happen in the bar. There were hooded-lidded gazes and quick, shy smiles through the sweaty smoke, but those were starting to get boring, and the sweat was starting to dry, leaving me just feeling dirty. When the bar started to empty out, leaving the Balloon just a wet, cavernous tomb, a poor college student's dingy den of dishonor, we all went back to Dave's apartment. Once there, Andrew lit another joint, and he, Dave, Gina, Nikki, Rachel, and I smoked it. Nikki and Gina left soon after the second spin of our never-ending high, wanting to go wreak havoc on the town of Newark that they were supposed to have transcended above and beyond, but they actually slunk down in the reminiscing ditches long enough to slither their post-senior ways into a fraternity party, mingling with those not blessed with a birth date that made them twenty-one or an older sibling who looked uncannily like them. The ID-less. They danced and pranced their way through the night, while back at Dave's apartment, Andrew left the room to go telephone some girl who never used to glance his way, and Rachel and I tried not to laugh at Dave passed out on his couch, holding his guitar, and we also tried not to take off our clothes to the beat of the Fugees. Alive and high, feeling festive and ready for adventure, I wanted to wake Dave and tell him to hoist his way onto his top bunk, where I was languidly reclining, and then hoist himself onto me.

And into me. But still-functioning brain cells knocked with my newly broken synapses, and I clamored down from my possible-new-boyfriend's bed, shook him awake for a few minutes before he opened his sleepy and crusty eyes, and he stumbled his way to the door to walk Rachel and I out. What a gentleman! And Rachel and I found ourselves on Main Street on a beautiful post-midnight clear night in late April, running through the light breeze toward my big blue Caddy, laughing all the way home about our night, and trying to figure out how long it would take me to get Dave naked.

That night was the start of my Dave days, one of which I was always so sure would end with us having raunchy, very nasty, very sweaty, reeeally slow sex through the night and into my future. But it never happened. I refused to give up, though. It was made easy by the fact that I didn't really like him. I just wanted him to like me. And, truth be told, I just wanted to fuck him. I'd never just wanted to fuck anyone. It made me feel kind of like a grown-up. We spent a lot of time together, and the conversation soon stopped the annoying trend of always leading back to high school moments, and we started laughing about the now and creating a fun friendship. But I could never figure out what he was thinking. Some days I would be positive that he wanted me. He'd give me that look. God. I loved that look. But then the next minute, he was standing me up after he was the one who asked if I wanted to hang out in the first place! I always tried to look pretty in case I ran into him, and I made daily pilgrimages to TCBY, because he lived right next door. I knew what day was non-fat cappuccino yogurt day, but I was kept wrapped in the pitch-black dusk about how my new fickle prince thought about me. Or if he thought about me. I loved being preoccupied with thoughts of an unsure thing, especially because I didn't care nearly enough to get hurt. I also liked having a boy to obsess about to my friends, and I lapped up the advice that I used to spew out to them with a look of practiced sincerity on my face. Rachel told me to invite him to a movie, go back to his house, get high, and turn on some good music; the rest should come naturally, and we'd be cavorting like hedonists in not more than a jiffy. Jessica told me to look deep into his eyes and to say his name a lot. She reminded me that I was the one who had told her that the most intimate thing you could say to anyone was his or her name. I had also told her that when you couldn't sleep, you should just try to close off your mind and fill it with only the color of blue, which would soothe you to beddy-bye. Nervous to take my own advice, even if it came out of someone else's mouth, I just bided my time and trimmed my pubic hair every two days.

Part Two
May, Senior Year
The University of Delaware

Then it was formal time, and Kim and I went shopping for dresses. As we caroused the Christiana Mall, Kim and I spilled and respilled secrets to each other, getting closer each time we tried on another pair of strappy sandals. I told her I knew I had been saying it for a while now, but this time I was serious. I was going to break up with Clay. He was boring the living shit out of me. I wanted excitement. I wanted thrills. I craved flutters. I was choking back the bile that my stability was causing to rise. I was sick of pretending to adore. It took away energy that I would rather spend tanning so that I'd look good for every other guy on the face of the small planet called the University of Delaware. I guess I just wanted some me-me-me time, but I felt a little selfish coming right out and saying that. My wonderful friend didn't make me utter the damning words, but her do-it smile told me that she understood and supported my decision. And a little while later, as I stood in front of a large silvery mirror wearing an amazing little silvery blue dress that ultra-conservative Kim told me was atrocious, I realized with a rush that being selfish was a look and an attitude that I wore well.

But I still had to get through the formal. Clay's school had let out for the year, since Michigan always got out early, and he was planning to drive down that coming Friday to be my date. I didn't know what to do. Clay knew that I seemed kind of lethargic about him lately, but he thought that blahness stemmed completely from my looming graduation and my desire to spend all of my time with my friends. He didn't know that I had become an almost-conceited bitch with a roaming set of irises. I wanted to call and tell him not to come. I wanted to take someone else, someone whom I would want to touch all night, and someone who would brush my waist accidentally on purpose. I wanted a date that made my tummy drop hard. I wanted my beloved to stay home.

But since I was the ultimate chicken-shit with a clamoring shred of sensitivity that still piped up annoyingly, trying to get heard, I sat in my room on that Friday, dress on, hair straightened, and lips lined just right at four in the afternoon waiting for Clay to show up. The formal wasn't going to start for another five hours, but I figured that if I were all dressed, I wouldn't have to have sex with him by blaming it on not wanting to get mussed up. My knees were knocking with nerves and frustration as I waited for him to show up on my doorstep, and I knew when I heard his engine instead of the clitter-clatter of hooves that he was not my Prince Charming arriving on his great big pony ready to sweep me off my high silver heels. He was just a boy that I had pretty much grown up with, whom I deep down adored. But I had grown up and I had grown away from him—and yet I knew, even in my self-centered atmosphere where I only allowed myself the benefit of air, that I would miss him when I said good-bye.

As he rang the bell, I erased the message from Dave that told me to have a good time at my formal and ran downstairs, remembering to put on my earrings, forgetting to put on my fake smile. He was standing there, holding a single red rose, willing me to look happy to see him. I just couldn't do it. And when we went upstairs to my room, I fidgeted my way off of his lap and pulled away from his kisses. I felt nothing. Nothing but terrified that he didn't even have the teeniest effect on me anymore. Nothing but repugnance at the sight of his crotch straining its way against his jeans. Nothing but my life whirling out of control. I felt dizzy.

He was a virgin before we started going out. That soon ended. But he was still a drug virgin, never smoking weed, and as far as he was concerned, I hadn't smoked either cigarettes or weed in eons. I hated lying to him. I didn't know why I should have to act like he was my parent, but I guess I just didn't want to hear it. I knew that while he was visiting that my lungs would have a few days to regain their pinkness and fluff, instead of their normal state of being black and charred. But I wanted to get high. Rachel and her date, Randy, were smoking. I didn't join in. Then Lori announced that her date, Michael, had made a whole batch of pot brownies, and I thought, fuck it. I've never had one, I will tonight, he can deal with it. After we had our first fight because I looked decidedly disenchanted by the feeling of his tongue loping its intrusive way into my mouth, I left my bedroom so he could change into his tux and took my video camera into Kim and Lee's room, where Lee turned the truth on me, and I looked right into the red light and whispered, "I don't know what to do! Clay's inside giving me sad puppy dog looks. I'm a little nervous. All of a sudden I'm in love with Dave, Luke's best friend. And in this dress and these shoes and with this sparkly nail polish, I look like I just stepped out of the fucking *trend* awards."

On the way to the happy hour, I ate one of the brownies, and at the happy hour, not yet feeling anything, I ate another. I relaxed a little and posed for pictures with Carley, who looked beautiful in a white chiffon dress, and with Jessica, who was wearing the silver dress that we had shopped for hours and hours one Wednesday evening to find. Smiles genuine, alcohol flowing, eyes glistening with gratitude that we all existed at that stellar moment in time. Say cheese.

Say something. That's what Clay said to me when I refused to say what was bothering me on the way to the formal. But what could I say? Take your sweaty palm off of my leg? Stop joking around with Kim's date; he's not your friend? Don't yell at the bus driver to hurry up? Sit still and please cross your arms? I just kept quiet.

The pledges who were no longer pledges and who had never been called pledges and who had never been treated like pledges and who had only pledged for four weeks when I had pledged way back when for a full thirteen weeks were all dressed up. There were French twists everywhere, and the prom dresses they had worn last year were getting another shot and they looked so excited to be at their first big sorority function. They held their beers in one sweaty palm and their date's hand in the other, and they looked around desperately, their flitting eyes revealing that they hoped they'd remember all the sisters' names. I didn't care if any of them knew my name. All I could think about was eating formal food, those yummy cheese cubes, the carrot sticks smothered in ranch dip, and I wanted that food immediately. Nerves about trying to be happy with Clay had definitely set in, but munchies were quickly kicking nerve's ass, and I had to eat. So while everyone ran for the bathroom to pee out all the happy hour drinks, Clay and I joined forces for the moment and sought out some nourishment. Skulking about, we came across some rolls that were meant for dinner, and we smuggled them out of the ballroom like thieves. All the time that I was chewing, I could see Clay watching me, searching my eyes for dilation, my skin for loss of pigmentation, my lips for the words "I love you" to form, and my chest, expecting to see my heart burst through because of drug-induced hysteria. Whereupon, of course, I would clutch and clamber to him, and he could somehow protect me in the manner in which he was so accustomed.

I made it until the middle of the salad course, where I sat next to Clay and Randy, eating with the correct fork. And then Randy started telling the same story over and over again. And Kim sat down with her drink twice in ten seconds, and her smile started to drip. And colors blended and the music thundered. And I just tried not to close my eyes.

It was like that time in high school when my mom was out of town and a bunch of us sat on my back porch a little after ten one January night, inhaling to our lung's very best ability, and I just kept smoking and taking such deep hits that my friends started calling me "Iron Lung." It wasn't until a half hour later or so that I clamored down off of my flower-scented, floating high and stumbled on top of the turning, twisting, constantly climbing conveyor belt that was taking me nowhere good in non-time. I went upstairs, threw some cold tap water on my face, and looked in the mirror. "You're fine. You're fine. You're *fine*!" I kept repeating to myself, loudly, then whispered, over and over, slower, then even slower. My legs felt heavy and tingly. My heart had moved out of my chest and had run up to my head for safekeeping, where it was thundering in my temples. My back was starting to sweat. And then I started to taste my words—so salty and bitter and way too chewy. And right after I stripped out of my clothes and pulled on my flowered pajamas, huge winter coat, and slippers and ran out into the cold night, demanding to be taken to the hospital, my friends carried me back inside, smoothed my hair back, and tried to send me off into a dreamland that seemed layered with some strange kind of stardust.

I hadn't felt that out of it since, and I had not smoked for a long while after that experience, when I had felt such a loss of control that robbed me of my ever-conscious conscience. The only positive thing that came out of that experience was that I wrote a poem while wrapped in incoherence, a substance-induced masterpiece. A tricolored sugarplum coated with candy, dipped in arsenic, fried in terror.

And that night did something else. It made me realize, when I started freaking the fuck out at the formal table in my pastel blue dress and my high silver heels, when conversations started to melt and faces started to swim the backstroke before my eyes, that I would be fine. But I needed to go to sleep. Quickly. So I turned to Clay, buttering a legal roll next to me, and I said in what I thought was a deliberate, extremely practiced, and calm tone, "I don't feel well. I want to go home." He looked concerned and asked if I wanted to just try to hang out for a little while longer, upon which I lost it and hissed, "Now." I turned to Randy and Rachel and said good-bye and waved to Kim, who was sitting down for a third time, and got up and walked out. They all stared after me, disbelieving, worried, statues. Clay caught up with me to walk outside to get us a cab, and when Rachel came toward me to check on the status of my non-sanity, I started shaking, catching a dim sight of her hooves and her tail, and insisted that she not come anywhere near me.

Walking through the front hallway of my house, I stumbled out of my shoes. Climbing the stairs, I unzipped my dress. And in the middle of my room, I ripped my strapless bra and my thong off, needing to feel that I was not constricted in the least. I crawled into bed, holding Mr. Gerber for support, because if I was going over the edge, he was coming with me. In an hour I was asleep.

The next afternoon when I finally woke up, my head hurt worse than any hangover I'd ever known, my tongue was heavy and stuck to the roof of my mouth, and I was absolutely starving. Clay was up, watching "Sports Center," and he turned to look at me with hurt and disappointment and distrust in his eyes. Exactly what I needed to see just then. He asked me how I felt, and I shrugged and asked him to pass me the warm diet soda that was perched precariously on the Yaffa blocks next to him. I gulped the soda down in the way that makes me so nauseous when others do it, so loudly and gross, and then threw the empty can over Clay's head and onto the floor, missing him by an inch and my dress by two. I faced the wall and tasted the sick taste in my mouth and whispered that I was sorry.

I just felt so embarrassed that here I was, a senior, former President of this fucking sorority, someone whom people looked up to, the smart one, the normal one, the responsible one, and I had to leave the formal because of goddamn *hallucinations*? "I never had to leave a formal because of delusions…" And my goody-goody boyfriend was so disgusted with me, and I was so disgusted with me, so at least we had that one thing in common. Rachel knocked on the door and asked what had happened, and while she was in my room, Carley also came over and made sure I was okay. I realized that most people thought I had been fighting with Clay and that we had left in the fiery fit of a non-lovers tizzy. I felt better knowing that everyone thought that it was all his fault and that I was in no way responsible for what had happened. I couldn't deny what a selfish and unfair reaction that was for me to have, and I didn't feel right behaving so callously, but my head still throbbed terribly and I decided to deal with the truth later on, maybe tomorrow. Or maybe the day after that.

We got up and went to the Student Center for lunch, not showered and not smiling. We held hands and didn't talk, and the distance between us seemed so huge and sticky that it didn't seem possible to cut through all of that; it would just be too much trouble. We got chicken sandwiches and waffle fries and sodas and sat down. Clay leaned over to hand me his pickles, and I passed him the ketchup even before he asked, and he smiled and I cringed. Then he said that he just wanted to make sure that I thought that last night was such a waste and so stupid of me, and he just wanted to make sure that I knew. He just wanted to make *sure*. I tried to tune him out, and I tried to say the right things, but there was no hope anymore. We got up to leave, and he threw out our trash, and we bumped into Lee and her boyfriend on the way home. I expected them to ask me if I was okay and what had happened, but they hadn't made up from the fight that they had had on the dance floor yet, and they weren't exactly in the mood for conversation.

He'd now been at school with me for twenty-four hours, and we still hadn't had sex. A few hours later, while we were still lying in bed resting, he leaned over to me and kissed me. I kissed him back, my hand touching his hair, my fingers clutching his shirt, and for the first time in forever, I felt really excited by him. My arms got the chills, and it felt familiar but so good. But when the time came for the hooking up to naturally turn into sex, I lost it, and I pushed him away at the hip and told him that I was still too tired.

On the day that Clay left to go home, we woke up early and drove to the video store, where I had to rent a horror movie to write my final paper on for my Film Theory class. I had to take Laura Mulvey's view of "the gaze" in cinema and relate it to the lurid and grisly film I was about to shudder my way through. I wanted to get *Splatter University* in keeping with the festive theme of the class. Rumor had it the killer in that movie sliced up the flimsy sorority girls with a dagger hidden in a cross. Blending religion and violence in a phallic way? Yum. But apparently one of my fellow sick classmates had already been wooed by the psycho priest flick because it was out, so I had to settle for *Slumber Party Massacre*. Part 2. Not even the original. Part 2. God. My major ruled.

He didn't even come inside, because this paper was supposed to be fifteen pages, and it was due the next day, and I had to get to work. I was not just the Princess of Deceit and Drug-Induced Delusions, but the Queen of

Procrastination as well. I was so well rounded that May. We kissed good-bye on my front porch, and I held him to me and smelled his familiar scent, and I finished separating myself even as I pulled him closer. When I finally said good-bye it seemed more than slightly prophetic. Then I watched him pull out of my unpaved driveway carefully, and I waved to him as he sat at the light on my corner one last time, and then I went inside and upstairs and had a cigarette.

The movie wasn't even scary, but ridiculous and insulting and poorly acted and pathetically directed, and the killer wielded a guitar with a pointy drill sticking out of it. It was just *perfect* for a fifteen-page paper on sadism and masochism in schlock horror films. The movie that I really wanted to see was the very much talked about but very rarely seen *I Spit On Your Grave*, where the heroine, if you can dare call her that, is supposedly raped and battered in extreme close-up and then takes revenge on her attackers, mutilating, castrating in full color, right there on film. I really wanted to see it. I remembered reading a review of it in a movie guide, where the authors called it the most distasteful and irresponsible bit of filmmaking ever created. My gutter instincts were immediately piqued. My textbook from my extremely academic theory class talked as much about Freud as it did about *Spit*, and sometimes it talked about them in the same sentence, which was always a kick. On the first day of class, I sauntered on over to my beloved professor and asked him if he was planning to include this mysterious little film in the screening sessions for the class. He looked at me with a mixture of repulsion and regard and told me that the film may have come across looking glamorous in the text of *Men, Women, and Chainsaws*, but it was in reality an unbelievably disturbing and gruesomely violent hour and a half and that he just couldn't in good conscious require his students to sit through something like that. So one night I worked up my nerve and appealed to Rachel to watch with me, regaling her with information about the film on a strictly need-to-know basis, drawing heavily on the notoriety of the film until she agreed to watch with me. But when I went to Blockbuster, I was told that our favorite neighborhood video store wouldn't stoop to carrying such trash, so we got high and rented *The Doors* instead.

My final paper came out well, and it only took me about three hours to write it from start to finish. It would have taken even less time, but I had a rule of stopping after each page was completed to celebrate with a nicotine blast. Since I was working on Kim's laptop in the communal study room, I had to talk to everyone who came through the front door. (I rationalized my actions by telling myself that college was not only about hard work, but also about socialization.) But when it came time to proofread and punch up the paper, I forbade anyone to talk to me and gave my paper the consideration that it was due. The next morning, after I stopped at Purnell Computer Lab to print it out, I stapled the corner of the completed work carefully, and I delivered it to my hero with pride.

Jessica's birthday. This crazy housemate of mine was finally due to turn the majestic age of twenty-one, which shouldn't have been any sort of big deal because the girl had had great ID since just about birth; but now there was no way she could end up in jail on any given night, unless she peed on the street or something, so we all gave her birthday celebration a ton of attention. Rachel, queen of underage bossiness that she was, followed Jessica around for days before, making her promise to do twenty-one shots on the big day. Not one to let anyone down in the least, always taking her word to mean more than anyone else ever did, Jessica started the day with a big bagel, shoved down potato chips and a sandwich for lunch, and dove into a trough of pasta for dinner. She ate bland and she ate a lot, and when she was all set to go celebrate at eight o'clock that night, she looked straight into the red light of my video camera and clapped her hands and crowed with delight that she was stuffed and legal.

Since it was a Tuesday night and no bands were playing at the Balloon, we decided to go to Kate's. We picked up Christina on the way and piled into two cars to take us to the other end of Main Street to the bar of the evening. We snapped pictures the whole night: Jessica posing with the bouncer who had let her into the bar illegally for the past three years. Jessica doing her first shot of the night bought for her by some people who always pretended to be her friends, but called her a slut behind her back. Jessica holding a Three Wise Men shot in one hand and a pitcher of water in the other. Jessica and me. Jessica and Steve. Jessica and Christina. Christina on the stage, singing "You've Got a Friend" to her birthday buddy. And just a few hours later, Jessica facedown on a table strewn with empty glasses and other people's cigarette butts.

Getting her home wasn't going to be easy, because when she jumped the line from absolutely, unbelievably, can-you-believe-she's-even-still-alive wasted to dangerous oblivion, she was in no mood to cooperate, and none of us were in any mood to get thrown up on. When shot number nineteen raced through her bloodstream, and her blood alcohol count reached far past the crescent-shaped moon, she slumped forward and hit her head for the first time that night. The bouncers suggested that we take her home. Then they said, "Now!" so it wasn't much of a suggestion, I guess. So there we were, Kim, Christina, Rachel, and I carting Jessica down the windy wooden stairs, through the throngs of friends and acquaintances who didn't offer to help hoist her through the crowd and onward to the outside, where we would try to fold her body into my car's backseat.

As soon as the cold air hit her numb face, she just fell and started laughing, a loud, free cackle that came from nowhere and had no idea where to return to, so it stayed out and about for the next few hours. After taking some pictures of her falling from Christina's arms to Kim's to the pavement, we got her into the car, where she sat with her face in Kim's crotch while I drove home with the emergency brake on the whole way. I had other things on my mind. Like getting her home before she got sick. We careened into the driveway and parked at the bottom so that it would be easier to get her to the railing way and inside. The girl smelled nauseating and weighed a ton. Every inch of her had gone limp and she was five feet eight inches of dead weight. It was heave, ho, heave, ho all the way up the stairs, through the hall, into her room, whereupon I ran to my room to grab my camera and pointed it right in her face, asking her to say something to me while they stripped her out of her jeans and shirt and tied her long black curls up in a knot. She fell on the floor, her bra wrapped around her forehead, an old sorority rush T-shirt on, and opened her chapped lips. The light on my camera went on since the room was fairly dark. A trail of saliva ran from her tongue to her front tooth. She smiled her wide smile, hit her head on the corner of the dresser, knocked down the roses that her boyfriend had sent her for her special day, and shouted, "I'm wearing a thong, and it is so far up my ass that I can taste it!"

It went on for a long time, Jessica laughing that loud, shrill laugh that none of us had ever heard her utter before. She didn't sound human. Kim wanted to put her to bed on her belly and sit with her to make sure that she was okay, but I was insisting that we get the girl to the bathroom and make her stick her finger down her throat, because nineteen shots could have sent anyone into a permanent kind of snooze, and she was so drunk that it scared me. We fought back and forth for a while on the best way to care for our slobbering friend, until she yelped, "Uh, oh!" We all tried to get her to the bathroom quickly, pulling her, pushing her, pleading with her, but she just cocked her head and chided in her loudest voice, "Anyone with any intelligence would just get me a plastic bag!" It was classic Jessica, and we all ran about searching for a proper throw-up receptacle, laughing our asses off at our friend who was obviously going to live.

She didn't puke then, and Christina finally took my side and helped drag Jessica into the bathroom, where she hit her head on the sink, then on the toilet, and kept falling face-first into the bowl. We stayed with her, talking, taping, and congratulating her until we heard some guy in the hallway. It was Randy, the guy who had been dicking Rachel all semester and who, when he spoke to her, stared only at her boobs. Very classy. Rachel left all of us in the bathroom and went upstairs with Randy, while the rest of us shook our heads and made faces indicating how stupid Rachel was being and how much Randy sucked; but when we tried to tell Rachel to her face that she was being taken way advantage of, she fought until we would get blue from our efforts to make her understand, and it just stopped being worth it. The battery sign on my camcorder started blinking, indicating it was about to shut off, but I wanted Jessica throwing up to end my little segment, so I prodded her along and when it all finally started coming out, brown and liquidy and horribly smelly, I knew I had in my possession something unequivocal for posterity or great blackmail potential if she ended up running as a republican for political office.

Turned out that as we were putting Jessica to bed for the first time that night, when it was finally safe for her to lie down, Rachel and Randy were sitting up in her bed for the last time. He had come over to tell her that he had another girlfriend and that this one was serious. He might even love her. And he was so sorry that he had hurt Rachel and that she was such a great girl and so cool and so pretty, and he kissed her good-bye on the forehead and left quietly while she just sat in bed and hugged her knees to her chest, crying softly.

Rachel took the breakup harder than any of us ever expected she would, especially herself. She moped for days, speaking only when spoken to, eyes glassy and flat. Sometimes I would walk into her room and catch her dialing the phone, and she would hang up suddenly, so I guessed that she was eventually going to break down and call him, but she was strong, and she always ended up not giving in. Then one Sunday night at Kate's, I saw Randy near the bottom stairs while Rachel was in the bathroom, and I was planning to ignore him or maybe just throw him an evil look, but I decided to be mature, so I walked over to him and said hello. He turned to me with a shy smile and looked into my face instead of at my chest and gave me a tentative hug and asked me if Rachel was out that night. I told him that she was, and his face lit up almost genuinely, shocking me. I searched his face through narrowed eyes, looking for deception. It wasn't there, and I realized that yes, he was definitely in love with the new girl, the one we had tried to run over on Main Street a few days before, the one who looked an awful lot like a duck. But he also did care for Rachel, and he had just made some mistakes just like the rest of us, and maybe, just maybe, if he never hurt my best friend again, maybe I could forgive him.

Out of nowhere, Kim had started hanging out with this boy, Rob, an AEPi brother with a steep top bunk bed and a penchant for giving bright magenta hickeys. She came home from his fraternity house one midmorning, covered with the purplish welts and smiling a huge toothy mouthful, wearing the widest fraternity T-shirt and elastic waist shorts imaginable. "Look!" she yelled. "I'm wearing Andrew's clothes from last year!" This Rob kid was a little slow on the calling-the-day-after bit, but he was still a fun guy, and we started spending a lot of time with the Pi boys.

There was this one that I considered hooking up with. Jason. I'd known him since I was a sophomore, and one night at a Greek mixer, he had walked across a crowded and smoky room to tell me that he wanted to talk to me because he thought that I was very attractive. He wanted to make quite certain I knew he didn't waste his valuable time talking to those he found average. I had sneered at his pickup, but I also thought he was kind of funny and I guess I was kind of flattered, and he quickly became a good friend. We flirted madly, constantly, and I knew it was one of those things that should just happen once and then never happen again, and he did try, often, but never too hard, never hard enough. And when he did make a move, I would laugh and push him away and tell him I had a boyfriend and remind him that he had a girlfriend. When we were in a room together, it felt like a huge game that went nowhere that nobody won, but we would both come out of it all flushed from the repressed exertion of it all.

The AEPi house was right on the edge of East Campus, next to Russell Hall, the dorm I had lived in as a freshman. Even back then I questioned the university's wisdom of allowing a fraternity house to be in such close proximity to a dorm filled with impressionable and often-drunk young girls who were away from home and curfew-free for the first time. But besides the mattress that the guys prominently displayed on their sprawling front lawn on the first day of school that they'd spray-painted, "Welcome freshmen girls!" there had never been too much of an issue. I hadn't spent much time at that house over the last few years, but in May I started going often to hang out with Kim and Rob, the guy she was into, and I found being there was a good time. The house was near where my Film Theory class was held, and I'd sometimes go over there after and spend the two-hour break I had before Physical

Science lounging around someone's room. Each bedroom that I was in was a different size. It seemed that seniority meant something significant in a fraternity, at least as far as allotted space was concerned. Most rooms had lofted beds held up by sturdy cinderblocks and, underneath, there were ragged loveseats and mini refrigerators. Nothing matched, but every room I was in had a huge television set, and every guy there had at least one video game system set up, the controller ready to go on the stained and chipped coffee table that was topped with empty cans of beer and half-filled mugs of coffee gone cold. There were appliance cords all over the floor and most rooms smelled like bong water, but the guys were welcoming. Sometimes I would visit with Jason if I was in the mood to do some mild flirting, but the relationships I formed with the rest of the guys were completely innocent. There were days I even went over in sweatpants, my hair in a ball on top of my head. The guys would smile and invite me to play a video game, and I would kick their asses at old-school games like *Tetris*, but lose miserably at *Tekken 2*. One of the fraternity pledges would usually stop in and politely inquire if I would like him to prepare me a bowl of Fruit Loops, which I sometimes accepted. It was known that I had a boyfriend in Michigan, and the guys respected that. They seemed to appreciate having a girl around that they didn't have to act slick in front of, and some began to ask for my advice about girls they liked or girls they desperately needed to cut out of their lives. I started confiding in a few of them, too, saying it out loud that I wasn't sure a twenty-one year old like myself should be in such a long-term relationship, that maybe it wasn't healthy in my growth process. Most of the guys agreed with me. I found myself being able to be absolutely honest with my new male friends, and it felt really nice when, one day, as I sat next to one of the boys on his threadbare couch, he leaned over, touched me on the knee, and told me that I was different from other girls, that he meant it in a good way.

Two weeks of school to go, and all I wanted to do was be with my friends, see The Assassins play, get an A and a smile from Dr. Harris, attack Dave, maybe get a kiss from Jason, and eat all of the Salad Works salad I could get my hands on. I was loving life to the absolute fullest, loving my surroundings, swimming through my environment with my eyes open and my hands clenching those crystal days to my grateful soul. On the days that I didn't have Dr. Harris's classes, I wouldn't even leave the house; a bunch of us would just lift open the bathroom window, crawl out onto the silver roof, and lie out all day long, smoking cigarettes and telling the same jokes that were still funny and only ours. Christina, Carley, and Erica would come over, and I was even feeling okay enough about myself to wear a bikini, and when the time came when everyone got quiet and read magazines or John Grisham, I would take out my folder of film theory articles and read for hours. I was constantly amazed by how stimulated that stuff made me, and I attacked those readings with gusto, sometimes reading them aloud to everyone like they were the daily horoscopes. My favorite article was the one about ideas of the apocalypse in *The Texas Chainsaw Massacre*. It totally made sense, and I couldn't wait to get to Miami and to film school, and I just knew that one day I'd be as good a professor as my father or Dr. Harris, who in my whirling mind had almost morphed into one extraordinary person.

I was enjoying those days too much to deal with any sort of depression, so I had decided to myself and aloud that I would wait until I got home to break up with Clay. Why ruin my last few weeks with crying and long, drawn-out discussions via AT&T? We spoke for less time each night, and I always pretended that everything was fine, and everything actually was. For me, anyway. I had moved through the stages of ending the relationship and dealt with them as if I were working through a death, until finally the pain and the shock had faded, and all that remained was a dull ache in my stomach that, thanks to my diet, was getting smaller every day. By the time that I decided to regale Clay with the fact that we should end our relationship, I had already reconciled the whole thing and couldn't have been more content. But I did know that if karma existed, the callousness that was feeding me would come back at some point in my life and destroy me.

One week and three days until graduation, and the sun was always shining, and those loud birds that always sat outside my window in my air-conditioning vent waking me each morning had flown away. I had lost those few pounds that always made me crazy, and I had bought some new cute shirts that weren't black and that made me happy, and I had handed in my article for my Journalism class, and I had finished my Sociology class, and all that was left was my Film final and my Science final. I was going out every night and getting tanner each day, and my skin was clear, and my hair was long, and I didn't even have to look in the mirror during those days to know that I was happy.

But the nights were different. I spent a lot of time that last week sitting outside alone on my fire escape at around three o'clock. I would smoke or read or just listen to that Tracy Chapman song, "Fast Car," play on repeat, over and over. I would talk to myself during those times, in my head, sometimes with my lips moving. I would imagine that I was an older me, a more beautiful me, secure with my world, secure with my nights, attaining my dreams, and being loved constantly and completely. Sometimes I would pretend it was Luke who was talking back to me, and he'd tell me how great I was and how glad he was that he was back in my life. Or I would glance soulfully at the illusion to my right and tell Tim that I thought that he'd never ask. And sometimes I would just sit quietly, not imagining anything, but holding tight onto the cool railing even as the rest of me burned, letting my eyes fill up slowly and fully, knowing that this part was on the verge of ending, and I wasn't able to do a thing to hold on.

What was bizarre was that even while I was about to jump over the threshold into the next stage of my life, and I felt ready for it and excited by it, voices from the past started paying visits to me. Men from my past. I was thinking about my father almost constantly during that week, playing Springsteen in my car and in my room to bring him right to me. I stared at his picture and could almost see the wisdom clouding his glasses. It had been seven years since he had died in front of me on that East Hampton beach, seven years since I had lived without cynicism, seven years since I had felt whole. I always thought about him, and he remained one of the biggest influences of my life, but he had been creeping up more and more lately, begging to be heard while I would plead for him to scream. I think what pained me the most was not that he wouldn't be there on that coming Sunday to watch me get my diploma, but that had he dropped by for the day, he would have been seeing a stranger. Because the last time that he had seen me, the last time that I had said the words "I love you, Daddy" to a face and not to the cold air, I had been a child. Fourteen. Gangly. Braces. Insecure. Never really been kissed. And now here I was, verging on certified adulthood, without stars in my eyes and without trust in my heart. A pretty picture, a budding intellectual. With friends never met and a mind not explored. Confident at times. Enthusiastic. A tangle of inconsistencies. Never sleeping soundly. Walking the line alone.

And when I was able to sleep, dreams of my mother's second husband came to me more than twice an evening, and I always found myself greeting Bill politely in my dream state and then beating the living shit out of him seconds later. I would kick him in the mouth and search for the blood. I would punch and tear and pull and grip. I would smack until my hands turned blue. Then I would wake up and stare at the dark ceiling above me, and I would feel out of breath and ashamed, and I would hold Cookie Monster's fraying arm and talk to Luke out loud:

So you think you've moved on, and you look at yourself and you know you've grown. Taller, prettier, a little heavier, but at certain times you know those pounds look lovely and settled. You sometimes flounder in your new skin, and sometimes you revel in it. And you try to understand why you feel so different when you really do look the same. It's strangely liberating to see how the years can change you, and it's almost frightening how much you have changed, because you don't realize it until part of you has altered. Sometimes it feels like it's too late to save what's gone, so you feel like a failure, then you feel like a child, but you know you've grown. But why do you still feel so much for what you told yourself was the past, so far gone it's become hazy and too rosy for it to be real? And you admit to yourself in bed at night and in the shower in the morning how low you really felt then. Perfection becomes fantasy and fantasy rules the daylight hours, the nighttime dream state. The unconscious seeps upward, and you intrinsically know that changes must be made. But what can you change when you are in a different state and you're a new person, and you understand reality in a way that never existed? The future is almost here—and you still feel the pulling from the past. There is just so much unfinished business that has translated itself into feelings that you don't want to acknowledge in the light, but they're there. It's so painfully obvious why they're there. Only a child would ignore them. But a grown-up wouldn't have them in the first place. And the future in your fantasy is thick and it's sweet and it moves so slowly, so languidly. The gloss covering those days shimmers in your mind, and your beauty shimmers in his mind. And you've become beautiful. And comfortable. And your questions get resolved. And you retain the silliness and the awareness of childhood. And you blend it with the clarity of finally being all grown up.

I was wearing awesome new underwear, pink and white with the lace around the sides, and my bra was white satin and made me look like I had a ton of cleavage, even without padding. I put on Justine's tight Seven jeans and my cream V-neck with my little hoodie over it, because even though it was almost June, the air had a chill to it. I lined my lips very carefully, hoping so much they'd get smudged later. I was so happy that my period had finally ended for the month, since I just knew that tonight was going to be The Dave Night, the night it finally happened with us, and I didn't want to leave stained sheets for him to remember me by. A wet spot, maybe. I was going over to his apartment, supposedly to help him proofread his final paper on Iroquois villages, but I was contemplating bringing my toothbrush over there with me instead of my thesaurus. A spritz of perfume here, another coat of mascara there, and five more wet and soapy Q-tips to help remove it from all over my face since my hands were majorly trembling. A quiet prayer and a good luck from Jessica with another reminder to say his name a lot and to remember everything so I could relay it back to her, word for word, later. I grabbed my keys and my gum and I left.

It wouldn't really be cheating, because as far as I was concerned, Clay was just bittersweet, ancient history by now, musty, faded, smelling kind of stale, even with all the cologne. And I wanted Dave so much. I felt it everywhere through my body when he said my name; and though I didn't want to acknowledge it, it had been a long time since I had had a purely physical draw to someone, and I loved how primally female it made me feel. I mean, I had never been so aware of the power of my sexual senses until I looked at Dave holding his guitar, rubbing his palm over the curves of the wood, his fingers moving rhythmically, plucking the strings, gently, then harder, faster, slapping them almost.

I was shaking when I pulled my blue car into the parking lot behind Dave's house. I wished so badly that Rachel or Kim or anyone was there with me so that I didn't have to make my entrance alone. I wondered if I should start with a smile. A joke? Did I have lip-gloss on my teeth? Deep breath, in through the nose, out through the chattering mouth. I decided to just go for it and not worry so much about what the reaction to me would be.

He kissed me hello on the cheek, and we sat at the small kitchen table. I went over Dave's essay with a puffy red marker, no good for making corrections. His writing was pretty atrocious. The ideas were good, and he'd obviously done a great deal of research on the Iroquois, but there were no transition sentences, the spelling was infantile, and the structure of the essay was fractured at best. I wondered how we had gotten into the same college. It became clear I would be there for a long time and that all of my attention and devotion would be administered to his needy paper and that would be that. He made me chamomile tea and Andrew offered me kiwi slices. We finished the second draft at around two o'clock, and Dave walked me to my car, thanked me over and over again for my help, and hugged me good-bye. It was a good-bye devoid of flutters, but when I saw him watch me until I pulled away, I knew and felt fine with the fact that we were just going to be friends.

It was a Wednesday night, and we were in the middle of a five-day heat wave. The heavy humidity had not let up; it was excruciating. Most of the classrooms were stifling, so for a few days a bunch of us hadn't left the comfort of the house. That evening, Carley drove over to hang out with us. The house she lived in didn't have air conditioning. We were all lounging around in Jessica's room, the air on full blast, eating barbeque potato chips and mini Mounds bars—a delicious combination of flavors and textures that we had discovered one night while exceptionally high. At one point I went into my bedroom down the hall to find a band to put my hair up, and Carley came in as I was attempting to construct a non-bumpy ponytail on the top of my head. She leaned against my door and told me she had to ask me for a weird kind of favor, and she looked uncomfortable. I thought that whatever she was after, perhaps she'd be more comfortable talking to me in total privacy, so I suggested that we leave the house for a bit. I walked back into Jessica's room and said that Carley and I were off to make a 7-Eleven run, and who wanted what? Kim and Rachel put in orders for cigarettes, Jessica wanted a Big Gulp full of Sprite, and Kathleen asked for some Tylenol P.M., saying she hadn't slept well in three nights because of her anxiety about looming exams. Carley and I collected money and left the house. We got into her car since it was parked at the bottom of our gravel driveway and two other cars out back had blocked in my car. We pulled out of the driveway, immediately got stuck at the red light at the end of the street, and Carley, still staring straight ahead, finally spoke.

"I want to go to a psychic, and I want you to come with me."

I just stared at her. Carley and I were a lot alike, and one of the things we shared was a deep level of cynicism for most things. It was one of the qualities I loved most in her, and I had always just assumed that cynicism included anything in the mystical family.

"I know it sounds strange, but I've been feeling kind of lost lately. At first I thought it was because some of you guys are graduating and I have another year and it feels weird to think of being here without you, but it's more than that. I feel like I'm losing my way. I don't have any more of a clue about what I want to do with my life than when I got here three years ago. And I know it sounds crazy, but I feel like my grandpa's presence has been surrounding me lately. It's like he has something to tell me. I can *feel* him. I'm not even sure I believe it's possible, but I need to know. I can't go alone; I'm too freaked out. You're the only one I feel comfortable going with. You're the only one of us who has lost somebody too."

We pulled into the parking lot of the store, but we didn't get out of the car. I thought about what she was asking of me, and it was strange because, all of a sudden, the idea seemed right to me.

"I'll go with you," I said. "I'm feeling out of sorts too. I'm not sure what a psychic can do, but, if nothing else, it'll be a damn good story."

"Maybe your dad will say something to you during your reading."

I laughed at the idea. It had always been kind of my joke that all these people had felt my father's presence after his death but I never had. My mother claimed she felt him around her a lot. My sister swore that once when she had been walking alone on her college campus at night soon after he died, that she heard his moccasins squeak behind her. When she turned around, no one was there. It wasn't that I didn't believe what my mother and sister had told me. It was that, out of the three of us, I was the one my father had been closest to, by far. He and my mom had a contentious divorce. It had gotten to the point that she asked us to tell him to wait on the stoop when picking us up for a visit, that she didn't want him inside the house. It was a lovely thing to ask your child to request of her father; it seemed unlikely that he was hanging around her. As for Cathryn, she and my father had a complicated relationship, and I could see him wanting to offer her some kind of comfort through a drop-in visit, but I just wasn't sure I believed in any of that. First of all, I just kind of always subscribed to the belief that when you died, you died. That was it. No ghosts. No afterlife. Certainly no bright, shiny heaven. I was too logical and not nearly religious enough to buy into any of that. But if, on the off chance, that spirits *could* visit, I just always believed my father would visit *me*. Back in high school I had a conversation about this very subject with my best friend Gwen. She had known my father well. She was also more religious than I was, going to Hebrew school and having a bat mitzvah and fasting (sort of—once she ate some toothpaste and an entire pack of green tic tacs without telling anyone) on Yom Kippur. But she told me that the reason my father didn't visit me like he did other members of the family was that he knew I'd be terrified by that kind of mystical manifestation, and she was right. The only time in my life that I ever prayed on a consistent basis was after my father died, and it was always the same prayer: "Please let my mother stay safe. Please don't let me lose her or my sister. And please let my father be watching me from a distance." That "from a distance" was included every single night. I never forgot to say it. I was so afraid that I'd wake up one night and he'd be standing in my bedroom. When I got up to close my blinds, I would avert my eyes from the lawn below because what would I do if he was looking up at me? Gwen's theory made sense. But I was curious. Could my father talk to me from the beyond? *Was* there a beyond? What would he say to me? I had done some things to make him proud, but I knew that I had also made so many mistakes and I had hurt people along my path. I had never wanted to disappoint him in life. Now I was going to perhaps hear about how he viewed me in death? The thoughts jumbling were frightening, and when I looked over at Carley, I realized exactly why she didn't want to go to the psychic alone, and I smiled at her and told her to go ahead and schedule readings for two people. She reached over and took my hand and looked down at the steering wheel for a moment, and then we let go of one another and went into the 7-Eleven to buy cigarettes, soda, and sleeping pills for our friends.

Carley worked fast. She had a roommate who was from Delaware who made a few phone calls to some family friends, and three days later, we were whizzing down I-95 to the psychic who lived in Wilmington. I'd asked Carley to ask the psychic if we should bring anything with us, thinking maybe a family photo or a meaningful piece of jewelry might help, but the psychic's response was that the only thing we needed to bring was "an open spirit." Frankly, a family heirloom would have been easier for me to grab hold of, but I was trying to be open to this experience, and I felt honored that Carley had chosen me to accompany her. We laughed nervously on the ride down and I told her that she had to go first. I had brought with me my copy of *Men, Women, and Chainsaws* to read during Carley's appointment. Ironically, I had an exam on the possession film genre pretty soon, and I wasn't sure that a psychic would have magazines to peruse in a waiting room.

The psychic lived in a regular house. I don't know what I expected, but it wasn't a yellow house with a little wooden porch and a polished brass knocker on the front door. Carley pushed me ahead of her and I rang the doorbell and the next thing I knew, a pretty woman, maybe in her thirties, answered the door. She smiled, introduced herself as Cindy, and invited us inside. She told us she was just finishing her lunch and would Carley or I like something to drink, some iced tea perhaps, but we just shook our heads and watched her eat the last of her turkey and avocado sandwich. I looked around the room. There were two floral couches and a high-beamed ceiling that contained a skylight and photos of her family members in polished silver frames on every surface. It all looked so normal, and I began to calm down.

Carley went in first for her reading. I watched them walk down a short hallway and turn into a room on the right, and I settled down on one of the couches and took out my book, but it sat unopened on my lap. I couldn't hear anything coming from the room where Carley's reading was taking place, and I wondered what was going on in there. I had visions of drippy red and black candles and crinkled tarot cards and lace tablecloths, and I hadn't told anyone that I was going to see a psychic, and I couldn't stop wondering if anything that she would end up telling me would be true.

Forty minutes later, the door down the hall opened and Carley and Cindy came out. Carley's eyeliner was slightly smudged, so I could tell she had cried a bit, but we didn't have time to debrief, because it was my turn and Cindy ushered me down the hall to that room. Inside was a bookcase filled with regular books, not books on psychic phenomena like the ones I used to see advertised on television late at night when I couldn't sleep. There were no crystals, no drippy candles, but there were two clocks, and those threw me for a second, because it seemed that this session was going to be timed to the millisecond, and I felt like a customer, not someone who was asked to arrive with an open spirit. We sat down. My chair was comfortable and leather, and my legs stuck to it as I pulled my skirt down a bit so it didn't ride up. The table we faced did have a lace tablecloth, and it looked like the giant doily I had made in my junior high Home Economics class, and on the table were indeed tarot cards. Cindy asked me to shuffle the cards and lay eight of them out, face up. It was like the most intense hand of blackjack ever played. I shuffled and dealt, and when I looked at the images that had come up on the cards I'd chosen, so many of them looked frightening. Before she read the cards, she looked up at me. I stared back, and the moment felt long, but strangely comfortable.

"You lost someone in a car accident many years ago," she said. "She is still watching over you. Do you know who I'm referring to?"

"One of my best friends from high school died in a car accident right before our junior year."

"Do you miss her?"

The question was odd. The truth was that I didn't miss Jackie. I had loved her and I had mourned her and I had been stunned that her death occurred literally one year to the day after my father's death. I thought about Jackie still, especially when I would hear songs by Bread or Edie Brickell, because she had liked those groups, and we had all listened to a lot of their songs after she died, but I couldn't sincerely say that I actively missed her. I was on edge. I had to tell a psychic that I didn't miss my dead friend? And furthermore, wasn't that kind of an easy guess for her to make, that I had lost someone in a car accident? Hadn't most people lost someone in a car accident? It's not like she asked me if I had lost a friend or relative to a bungee jump gone wrong. Either way, I decided that if any of this was authentic, I'd better just be honest.

"I still think about Jackie, but I can't say that I miss her. She was a good friend, though, and her death brought a lot of us closer together."

Cindy nodded. Then she looked at my cards and asked if I felt like I was going through a series of transitions lately. I nodded. She pointed to one of the cards, the one that seemed to my untrained eye to be horrifying in its imagery.

"This card shows a rebirth," she said. "You're about to experience a new life, not just as far as graduating, but also as the woman you are becoming. You're changing. You're making difficult choices. These choices must be made for you to move forward. It may be painful, but the death of this part of you is necessary to get you to where you belong."

The card she was pointing to showed what looked like a man being hanged by a thick black noose.

"Are you telling me that the violent picture on that card is saying something *positive*? Because, to be honest, it's scaring the shit out of me."

She laughed, patted my hand, and suddenly asked me how old I was when my father had died.

"I was fourteen."

"You were with him when it happened?"

"Yes. He died in front of me on the beach in East Hampton. He wasn't sick. It happened suddenly. A heart attack."

"Your father wants to know if you remember the last thing he said to you before he died."

I could feel my chest swell, but not in a good way. I felt like I was suffocating. I felt like I was the man on that tarot card. I had pushed down the majority of the experience of the day of my father's death in my psyche for so many years, and now here it was, and both the psychic and my father seemed to want clarification.

"He said, 'Be careful because I won't be here.' Then he walked down the beach to fish."

"Your father wants you to know a few things. He is telling me that he is with your grandmother. She's not coming through to me clearly, but she is beside him. He is telling me that he loved your mother very much, but he had blinders on. He regrets not working harder on their relationship. Do you have an older sister?"

"Yes. Cathryn. She's four years older than I am."

"He says that you need to tell your sister to 'cut it out,' but he's not clarifying what that means. And he needs to let you know that his biggest personal regret is that he didn't make more of his writing career, but that you have a book inside of you and it's important to him that you move forward with that. He is also telling me that he's a very handsome man, but that doesn't seem to be as relevant as the other messages he's passing forth."

It was the last comment that got me, that made me believe that Cindy might be for real. My father always used to tell my sister and me that he was a very handsome man. It was a weird quirk. He just stated his vanity as fact. He *was* handsome. He was incredibly tall and he had a nicely trimmed beard and two deep dimples in his cheeks that I had inherited, but Cathryn and I used to laugh because it seemed an odd proclamation to make out loud. But here he was saying it to the psychic, and I felt it was his way of making me know that these messages were authentic. I took a tissue from the box on the table and dabbed my eyes.

"Is he saying anything else?"

Cindy was quiet for a second. It looked like she was listening intently to something. Then she looked me dead in the eye and said, "He told me to tell you that he nicknamed you 'Tuffy' for a reason."

The readings had each lasted less than an hour and had cost fifty dollars, and when Carley and I said goodbye to Cindy, she hugged each of us, and we walked down the front steps to Carley's car. We got in, shut the doors, turned to one another, and we both started crying and laughing at the same time. On the drive back to campus, we told of what our sessions had entailed. Carley's did not begin with a question about a car accident victim, but Cindy had spoken to her grandfather and he had told her to be more kind and compassionate and, most importantly, to live bravely. I told her that my father had mentioned that he had really loved my mother. We talked nonstop, and then we were back at school. Before I got out of the car, I turned to Carley and asked her if she was okay keeping this experience between us, that I didn't want to have to tell this story over and over, and I didn't want to answer questions, including my own. We pinky swore that "The Cindy Experience" would be our little secret.

But I did have to tell two people what I had done. I started with my sister. Cathryn was living with her boyfriend in a tiny studio apartment in the city and I looked at the clock and realized she might be home already if the traffic from Long Island where she worked hadn't been too terrible that day. The phone rang and was picked up on the third ring.

"Hey, Cath, it's me."

"Hey! I just got home! It's so fucking hot in this apartment. Hold on; let me take my shirt off. Okay. I'm literally standing in front of the air conditioner in my bra. What's going on?"

"I have something very strange to tell you, so I just need you to go with it, okay? I went to a psychic today. I went with my friend to keep her company, but I got a reading too."

"You went to a *psychic*? I don't mean to sound judgmental, but that doesn't seem like something you'd do."

"It's not. Well, it's normally not. Your reaction makes sense. I did go, though, and, well, daddy came through. I have a message to relay to you from the beyond, which, by the way, is a sentence I never thought I'd utter."

I started laughing. How could I not? The entire experience, from watching a psychic eat a turkey sandwich to calling my sister with cryptic information seemed crazy, and the longer I was away from the actual moment, the less I felt inclined to believe in its truth.

"Look, he said that I should tell you to 'cut it out.' I don't know what that means. Do you?"

"I have no idea what he could be referring to. What else did he say?"

"He said he wished he had gotten his writing published. He said he really loved mommy. Do you remember him loving mommy?"

"Sure. You don't?"

"I can't even picture them living in the same house. I remember almost nothing of when they were married, let alone them even liking each other."

"I'm sorry you don't remember those days. There were some wonderful times. Don't you remember how mommy and daddy would go walking through the garden and pick the vegetables we'd eat at dinner?'

"We had a garden?"

Cathryn sighed.

"Did he say anything else to you?"

"He said he's a very handsome men."

And at that, Cathryn laughed.

I got off the phone with my sister and called my mother. I dialed her work number, and she answered immediately. I told her breathlessly about my experience earlier that day, and that daddy had made sure to tell me that he had been around my mother often, that he had loved her once with all of his heart, but that he had been "wearing blinders." My mother was silent for a moment, and then told me that she felt his presence frequently. She said she had adored him as well, but that the two of them had been so young and foolish back then; she wished they had both been better equipped to handle the difficulties of what a marriage entails. She said "wearing blinders" was an expression she and my father had said often in the seventies. She knew exactly what he was talking about. And she told me how much she loved me and how proud she was of the person I was becoming, and I felt so close to her and I believed every syllable that came out of her mouth. I hung up the phone feeling calm and content and when I went to bed later that night, I slept like a baby.

One hundred and sixty-seven hours until graduation, and instead of doing the responsible thing, like packing up my sweaters that I hadn't worn in two months or studying for my Physical Science final that was being given on Tuesday morning, I was running around the third floor of the house searching for something white. "Does it have to be *all* white?" I heard Jessica yell from her closet, her raspy voice tinged with panic. Pulling a cream-colored tank top out of Justine's middle drawer, messing up the entire pile of shirts in the process, I looked at Rachel, pulling on a pretty black dress, and at Kim, searching under her bed for her other black shoe; and I realized that this was almost it. The end of the sorority journey that I had always made light of, that I had always downplayed, and now it was over.

I finally settled on white wool pants, so practical for the arctic gusts of May, and Justine's top that sort of matched. The pants were really long because I had always been too lazy to get them hemmed, and the last time I had worn them was to my mother's wedding party in December, so they still smelled like brie. I ran out the door, still pulling on my shoes, and I got into the back of Kathleen's blue Saturn with Jessica and Lee, who were making fun of Mindy—not because she was wearing Keds, but because she had Keds. The last time I owned a pair was when I was in eighth grade, and I was so cool then, wearing them without the laces. Kathleen started her car, following Lori's and Kim's car, and our caravan arrived at the Oratory in less than five minutes.

The last time I had been in the back room of the Oratory for any significant period of time was when I was a pledge, about to take the much-suffered-for step over the threshold, toward a sisterhood I wasn't sure that I wanted to belong to, run by friends that I sometimes felt I had written a check for. I had waited quietly in that small room, huddled on the floor next to my pledge sisters, all forty-three of us wondering what was going to happen next, if the next three years would be filled with the laughter and the closeness I had seen in the slide show that had been shown to us during the third rush party, and maybe I should have pledged Phi Sig instead? We had heard bustling in the other room, where the sisters were with the secrets of what was next. I couldn't believe that pledging was about to end; what was I going to do about the sisters that I had never interviewed, whose names I still didn't know, and would I have to smile so widely at everyone once I was no longer a pledge? Our Pledge Mom came into the back room and told us to get into bond order, a lyrical way of saying to line up alphabetically. I saw Teri's smooth blonde head in front of me, calm, frosty as the moment when I'd first met her when she'd snarled, "You're only *seventeen*?" I felt Elizabeth fidgeting behind me with nerves and excitement, so small, too small. My bare feet felt cold, and my eyes were heavy, and if I'd been permitted to wear my watch, which I wasn't, I would have seen that it was only a little after seven in the morning when initiation began.

Now it was three years and three months later, and I sat in that back room of the Oratory again, nervous, my heart feeling urgent and my hands feeling clammy and my stomach tight with feeling. This wasn't initiation. It was the good-bye ceremony for the senior sisters. Kim came into the back room and handed out the red candles, giving Jessica and I white ones to signify that we were past Presidents, and she tried to usher all of us into our pledge class bond order. I couldn't believe how quickly we all remembered the order. I smiled at Mindy and Celia as the three of us lined up quietly, while I thought about Nikki's quick smile and Teri's cold eyes and Jenny's southern drawl and about my big sister, who was long gone now, and about my little sister, who still had another year to go, and I had been on the other side for three years. I had worn black, and I had stood silent, and I had cried real tears and waved slowly to the higher branches of my family tree and to my forty older pledge sisters as they spoke about what the sorority had meant to them. Now I was decked out in senior white—or close to white—and I heard the younger sisters in the other room start to sing "This Is My Sorority." The first time I had heard that song was when I was a seventeen-year-old rushee; everyone who had made me want to be in Alpha Chi Omega had graduated, and the only people who had been there as long as I had were the two girls behind me. My past was lined up carefully in a single row, which I stood at the front of, and my past sang a simple and beautiful song as Kim opened the door and led her oldest sisters into the darkness.

We formed a circle, one much smaller than the younger sisters had made surrounding us, for there were ninety-seven of them and twenty-two of us. As President, Kim lit Jen's candle and stepped back into the outer circle toward Rachel and Allison and Carley, allowing Jen to have the flickering spotlight to herself. Jen had only been in the sorority for two years, but she revealed that college before joining was just a blur and that she had never been as loved or had loved as much as she had during her moments as a sister. I looked across the circle at this girl I had not known so well, though we had been friendly, and I saw in her face something that I never had before; she seemed more real, quieter. Swathed in white, she was finally bathed in color.

Kathleen started crying as soon as the lighter lit the first wick, her body shaking furiously in the darkness, but I didn't start to feel that void open up inside of me until Christina began to speak. She stood beside Erica, and Christina was so very tall and Erica was so very small, and they were an odd coupling, but they were close as could be and they were both so dear to me. Christina spoke about her friends and her family tree and the day that she got into the sorority. I remembered the last night of rush when Christina was a rushee, trying to make her decision, and she was standing with my friend Dara. I walked over and Dara introduced me as the President of the sorority, and Christina looked at me with a wide-eyed respect. The moment and the memories began to fuse, because now she was no longer a looming name tag, but a part of my every day; I saw her in a millisecond singing to Jessica and sitting on our roof and driving me to the Taco Bell at three in the morning and standing before us in her black satin toga at the Greek Week talent show and passing me a lighter in her living room and holding my hand when she found out about me not getting into NYU. And when I closed my eyes to wipe away the memories and to bring me back to the now and what she was saying, the first tear fell.

The candlelight was being passed within our little circle. The room was so hot, even in the darkness, and I had a wet face and one soggy tissue. And then it was Jessica's turn. Even before she opened her mouth, she was hysterical and I was too. I saw her progression like a movie, fast and full of flash frames. Meeting her at rush when she still had bangs. Nikki taking her on as a little sister. Getting together in the Scrounge for lunch so that I could tell her about being President, trying to convince her to run after me. Jessica bringing me water and a bagel while I lay half-comatose after my twenty-first birthday and me filming the lunacy on the night of hers. Handing her a tissue when she broke up with Danny. The drive down to Sea Isle to see The Assassins. Shopping for her formal dress. Talking to her as she got dressed to go out for the night before I got into the shower. She was a girl so flawed, so imperfect, and yet so special, whole, real, and quickly the images came to me then, while her voice and her story were a sweet serenade somewhere in the distance. Then the sound of my name brought me back to the circle, and she turned toward me and told me that she admired me so much and that I just seemed like the perfect person to her, so together, so smart, so pretty. Then I felt like maybe she didn't know me at all.

The light was passed to Celia and then to Mindy, the only other members of the twenty-first pledge class still remaining, and then finally it was passed to me. The last one. My hands were trembling, and the candle didn't seem at all steady, and my voice sounded like a high-pitched flutter. I told everyone that when I was a freshman, which was the last year there was fall Rush, so I had only been at Delaware for two weeks before becoming a part of the sorority. I knew nothing of this school without it. It was the most defining part of my four years, and it was because of the people in this room. I looked at Jessica and Lee and Kathleen and told them how much I appreciated and adored them. I looked across the circle at Christina, who was smiling at me, and I just said her name. I looked out and saw my little sister, Allison, holding Rachel's arm and crying softly, and I relayed how proud I was to have gotten her as my little sister. I remembered how everyone had wanted her, but we put each other's names down first, and when I went to decorate her dorm room door with balloons and candy, I was so happy. I thanked her for getting us Carley, her little sister, a girl more like me than anyone that I'd ever known, someone I cherished and thanked my father for daily, because her trust and her loyalty and her brutal honesty was without competition, and I loved her so much. I forgot to speak about Carley's new little sister and about my memories as President, but I was just trying not to cry until I was done. I realized that I had two more people to speak about, so I took a deep breath and said, "Kim and Rachel." I looked over at them; it seemed as though they were standing so far away as I watched them hold onto each other and cry together, their bodies shaking like my voice was. I just told them that I had never in my life felt so close to anyone, and I just wanted to thank them for being the best friends I had ever had and that I knew that their senior year would be even better for them than this year was, if that was even possible. Then I looked around the room and with a quick breath, I blew out my candle, and the room went dark.

A non-Bill dream that last week: I was walking through my old sleep-away camp, and old friends that I thought I'd forgotten from high school were standing in straight rows of five singing the lyrics of Joni Mitchell's "The Circle Game" in a drawl that sounded super slow, almost like they were drugged. The rocks under my feet felt bumpy and huge, pushing through my white sneakers, and the dirt was heavy and so dry, my skin felt tight and flaky. The sun was warm, making my throat feel sticky and swollen, but I wasn't sweating. I stopped in front of my best friend's older sister, and the voices of the singers got louder as I told her that I'd decided to have my baby. Tracey placed her cool and delicate hand on my flat stomach and leaned forward to kiss my cheek gently. And in amazement I realized that her hand looked just like my mother's.

I went to an office hour session of Dr. Harris's that last week to find out if a film I wasn't quite confident with, *Peeping Tom*, would be on the final. I walked down the steep staircase to the basement of Memorial Hall, heading toward his office with a lighter knapsack than usual, but still getting lost on the way, since the numbers marking the professors' doors followed no sense of order for this world. I passed the soda machines where I used to arrange to bump into Dr. Thomas, my other favorite film professor, and I thought about the time that I'd stood there with him for over an hour one winter afternoon when he didn't even have office hours telling him about my *Showgirls* experience, how my friends and I were the only girls in the theater, how Elizabeth Berkley couldn't utter a syllable that sounded true, and how when her character husked to Kyle MacLachlan's, "I liked watching you come," how the big guy behind me who had been kicking my seat the entire time muttered, "Why the fuck can't I meet girls like that?" I walked past the stairwell, and I thought of the time that I had to dodge Dr. Cosell since I hadn't gone to his Victorian Fiction class in two weeks, but it had been during that icy, slippery winter. One time when I had been wanting to be a conscientious student, I had ventured out, bundled up in layers like a cased-in sausage. I had walked so carefully, keeping my eyes planted on the glacier-encrusted earth, trying my mightiest to stay afoot. Then I bumped into a tree. So class became optional after that and besides, the O.J. trial was on, preempting *Days of Our Lives*, but really, if you thought about it, that was America, *that* was culture, and it was really so sick and twisted that I had to examine the noise that had become news. It had felt like a defining moment.

That winter session I had been a junior, and my cash flow had been a little low because I had missed Clay so much, I'd flown to Michigan three times in one semester to see him. The only thing I could afford to eat was mashed potatoes made from those chalky flakes, and I ate them five or six times a day, telling myself since that was all I was eating, it wasn't all that bad for me. I got puffier and unhappier each day, and for a few weeks there I only wore sweatpants. That's what I was wearing when I did a screeching U-turn to avoid Dr. Cosell in Memorial Hall, and I definitely lost some sleep and had some anxiety-ridden dreams worrying that I'd fail his course, but the final paper I turned in was pretty good and probably too long for him to even want to read anyway. I'd written on Dickens' *Our Mutual Friend*, a text that he'd edited an edition of, so my A was secure. Memorial was like my house for four years, a place where I felt comfortable but not too comfortable, filled with people I knew and felt as if I needed to know better. But the floor in Memorial was dirty, thick brown dust, leaving trails, while my own home boasted of a floor so spotless it could be eaten off of, and if I ever dropped a cookie or a good snack, I often did. My mom used to yell about it. She used to yell about a lot. But it was all quiet inside Memorial Hall that last week, students staying either in the library or in bed, hung way over, so I just walked the halls silently and thought about how much I loved this place, and I just told myself to remember.

I had two finals left, but since I didn't give two shits about my Physical Science final that was being given in four days, it was as if I only had one more academic thing at school to get worked up over. Since it was my Film final, I got very worked up indeed. I got up very early Friday morning, pulled on shorts and a faded old Pink Floyd T-shirt. I grabbed a hoodie and set off to Morris Library with my notebook, lots of pens, and pretzels for nourishment. In my pocket was a supply of some dirty, some brand new and fresh tissues, in case an allergy attack tried to level my concentration midway through my cramfest. I had gum in case I ran into anyone of consequence. I had a reliable hair band. I was ready.

The library was a seven-minute walk from the sorority house, ten if you didn't make the crosswalk light. Some days when I would walk there, I would jump over the many cracks in the sidewalk like I did when I was a kid, making bets with myself that I could never live up to, like if I stepped on a crack, I would quit smoking. Sometimes I would search for leaves to step on that were really wrinkled up and extra crunchy so they'd make that *chrchh* sound when I stepped on them. Other times I would marvel at how strange the idea of college was, a place where the only people there were between the ages of seventeen and twenty-two and parents just left us all there, bye, be good, learn about who you're going to be. All of us, eating starch in dining halls, drinking, having sex, walking from laboratory to classroom, only acknowledging a small percentage of those walking the same routes. In the wintertime I would walk those roads quickly, eating the hair that the winds would blow into my chapped mouth, praying that when I got home, there would be a thick letter from NYU, and my future would thus be secure. Some days I would feel really pretty, and I would smile as I walked along, knowing that boys were looking at me, counting the beeps I got from old, rusty Subarus. But sometimes I would feel so fat and shlumpy, and I would have a bad zit or two in an area of utmost prominence on my face, and I would walk with my head down, especially past the fraternity houses, even the bad fraternity houses, hoping that the guys in big groups on the deck wouldn't say anything rude as I walked by.

Outside the library, I ran into Matt, Carley's older brother, who was in my film class, except he never really was there. Too early, he said. The class started at noon. He gazed up at me with his always-hooded eyes and asked if he and his friend could come study with me that night as kind of a last-ditch hope, and I was feeling charitable, so I said sure, and then I went inside and checked out the humongous folder of theory articles that Dr. Harris had put in the reserve room for us. I took a seat in one of those wooden cubicles in the back of the room and stuck my pretzel bag between my shorts-clad legs and ate them as I reviewed the semester that was all about gazing.

A few hours later, and I had just about had it with feminism and theories about the phallic symbols in Dario Argento movies and how in *Alien* the spaceship was modeled after a big, austere womb, so I gathered my books and my snacks. I went down to the basement to the computer site to check my e-mail, typing in my password to get into the system: "happy." Sick. I had a letter waiting for me from Rachel, commiserating with me about my lack of success in getting Dave naked, but she advised me to keep my spirits up, my pubes clipped, and realize that it wasn't anything to do with me; he was just oblivious to my feminine wiles. Either that or I didn't have any. I wrote her back that if I didn't hook up with someone soon, I was going to burst from all the pent-up estrogen in my body, leaving a big mess on the floor and walls of the house, which may end up being an improvement over the Pepto Bismol-pink walls. None of my frustration was all that accurate—I really was perfectly content having Dave as just a friend, but I fed into the drama willingly. Drama made every moment feel more real and lately it was making me feel more alive, so I signed off with hugs and kisses, logged out, and went back upstairs to tackle some more articles.

Saturday. The second to last Assassins night at the Balloon. Rachel's ex-boyfriend, Justin, who had been her boyfriend for six years and who was still kind of her boyfriend despite her dalliances, was coming up from UPenn, where he went to school, to hang out with us. He was bringing one of his friends, who Rachel promised was pretty cute. I showered early, at four o'clock, and put on Allison's jeans and my short-sleeved navy shirt, but I couldn't decide if I liked the way it looked or not. I went upstairs to Kim and Rachel's room to see what they thought. As I was obsessing in front of their full-length mirror while they tried their best to ignore me, the door opened, and Justin and his friend walked in. His friend *was* pretty cute, and when I went out onto the fire escape to have a cigarette, he came out also. We started talking, and it turned out that his favorite movie was *The Graduate* also, and he was from the town next to me at home, and he also loved Pearl Jam, and he seemed very cool. From the way he was smiling at me, I could tell he thought I was pretty cool too. It made me feel good. We lounged around the room and smoked a little bit, and then I went downstairs to dry my hair and change my shirt. I plowed through my dresser drawer, looking for something cute and flattering to put on, and I came across my white and orange Calvin Klein baseball shirt. When I had seen it on the rack at the store, I wasn't so sure about it. It was just so trendy. And it was just so *orange*. But I bought it anyway, and that night, when I finally took the tags off of it and put it on, it looked very cool, in a yes-I'm-wearing-orange baseball player kind of way.

At her big house down the street, Christina was having a party that night, so we decided that we would head over to her house early, drink there, and then move on to the Balloon. We hoped she wouldn't be mad at us for bailing out of her soiree early, but even if she were, she'd have to just deal, because it was an Assassins night. And Assassins nights were sacred.

We all went to Bennigan's for dinner. Jessica, Kathleen, Jen, Lori, Justine, Rachel, Kim, Justin, Evan, and me. We ate a lot. I kept looking over at Evan, and he was just so laid-back and talkative, and we seemed to have so much to say to each other. He asked about the band we were seeing tonight, and Justin said that we were all such psycho groupies over these guys and had any of us ever hooked up with any of them? We said we hadn't, though we all had a favorite band member that we'd love to ravage if given the chance. When someone mentioned that the object of my devotion was only eighteen, Evan looked over at me with shock and with one eyebrow raised. He asked me if I'd actually ever hook up with an eighteen-year-old. I looked down at my charbroiled chicken salad and smiled and said it didn't matter, because it would never happen.

The music from Christina's house hit us while we were walking there. When we arrived, she and her four roommates were already wasted and Callie was trying to light a joint off of the stove. There was a big bucket of grain punch in the corner near the back door. We all paid five dollars for a plastic cup and dipped them into the thing of grain, our fingers turning crimson in the process. I sat on the railing of the back porch and spoke to Jessica, who looked pretty in a striped Gap shirt and her blue short skirt. I felt a stillness in the air and I smelled the summer through the trees and I whispered that it just seemed like it was going to be one of those nights.

Ten minutes later, I heard girlish squealing, which either meant that a huge toothed rat had gone scampering across the floor or that one of my friends had just arrived at the party. It was Carley. She ran over to me to give me a hug and told me that she loved my shirt. I thanked her and introduced her to Justin, whom she had already met at some formals, and then to Evan, and I whispered that I thought he was cute. She got a big cupful of the strong punch, and we all hung out and played silly drinking games. The party was starting to get crowded with lots of cute fraternity boys, and people were starting to dance in the living room. At about ten o'clock we left for the Balloon.

The bar was much more crowded than it usually was on Saturday nights, and a whole slew of people were standing near the stage, ready to nod their heads to the music that was about to start. We pushed our way through the throng toward our designated spots in front of Billy, the guitarist. Jimmy saw us and waved, and Chris did also. The music thundered. I was already a little buzzed from Christina's party and the red stuff I'd drank there. We were all dancing like crazy to the familiar music, and we were getting extremely sweaty. Rachel had taken her camera out with her for the night, and she kept taking pictures of us and the band and us with the band. Justin and Evan seemed to like the music a lot, but during the break between sets, they went out onto the back patio of the bar and found a table and seemed content to stay there for the rest of the night, drinking pitcher after pitcher of cheap beer. Rachel felt she should stay with them, and Kim said she'd stay also. We had lost Jessica and Lee and Kathleen long ago in the crowd, so just Carley and I ran through the throng toward the opening beats of the final set.

It was steamy hot near the stage, and Carley had short hair that got wavy but let her keep cool. I had forgotten to wear a hair band on my wrist, so I couldn't put my hair up. I just kept twirling it away from my face and I kept trying to pull it back into a makeshift bun, but it kept falling out. I had never hung out with Carley at the Balloon. She had just turned twenty-one a week before, and she hadn't had a fake ID before then, so before tonight she had been an Assassins virgin. She was so incredibly into it, and with her and her newfound enthusiasm, I enjoyed the show even more than I normally did. Everyone kept commenting on my shirt and how tan I was, and when I paused from dancing to light a cigarette and try to catch my breath, Tim moved over to the spot right above me and stood there until I looked up. His Fugazi shirt was soaked with sweat, and his black hair was damp and starting to curl, but his skin was luminous and his smile at me was a mile wide.

The set list hadn't changed much since I had first seen them play; they were still closing with *Pride,* but it wasn't getting boring to me, and Carley kept exclaiming that they were amazing. After the show we pulled our shirts away from our bodies so that they wouldn't stick to us, and

I pulled down my hair. We were going to leave and walk across the street to Kate's, because that's where Rachel said she was taking Justin and Evan. Carley took my hand, ready to lead me through the still-thick crowd, when Tim came to the edge of the stage and motioned for me to come over to him. I hesitated. I thought maybe he was gesturing to someone behind me and that I'd look like an asshole if I went over, but Carley pushed me forward. He crouched down, leaned over, gave me a kiss on my cheek and thanked me for coming. I said no problem and introduced him to Carley. Tim looked at her for a second and then told her that he had never seen her there before. She told him she had just turned twenty-one, and Tim looked her straight in the face and said, "Yeah? Me too." I knew there was this whole rule with the band that they couldn't let out that he was underage, but I had never heard him lie out loud, so I just bit my lip. Then he turned back to me and took my hand and said, "Your friend told me about a party that you're all going back to at some girl Christina's house. I'm gonna try to get the rest of the guys to go, but if I can't, do you want to hang out after our show on Thursday?" I felt my head start to swim. I didn't even remember how to laugh. I felt my legs beginning to buckle. How was it that this kid who hadn't even experienced a prom could be calm and ready enough to experience me? I looked into his blue eyes and saw the daisies that I wanted to roll across with him. For a moment the Balloon even got cooler, because my sweat turned icy. But I outwardly kept my cool. I just smiled softly and said, "Sure. That would be great." And then I leaned over and kissed him good-bye on his smooth cheek, and we walked away.

But as soon as we had gotten away from the view of the stage, Carley and I looked at each other and screamed really loudly and jumped up and down like lunatics. We went running, holding hands, through the bar and out into the night that seemed so sweet, it was as if it were coated in gooey honey. We didn't see the people we pushed out of our path; we just ran, screaming, laughing, and we crashed our way into Kate's, where I just had to tell everybody the crazy news. I knew the first person that needed to be regaled with my stupendously promising story had to be Kathleen, who always made it quite clear that she lusted after Tim—who was now my new boyfriend. Just that evening, as a matter of fact, she had come up to me before the first set, and had made me come with her to talk to Tim. I'd rolled my eyes at her junior high school ways and said, fine, let's go, hurry up. When she'd cornered him near the stage door, telling him about this great picture she'd taken of him the last time they had played, I just stood a few inches away, aloof while she melted, standing up straight as she hovered. And though he was friendly to her, he had looked past her rehearsed animation and leaned over toward me to touch my stomach and whisper, "Hey."

Needless to say, Kathleen didn't get too worked up about my Tim anecdote, though I noticed a slight twitch come to her cheek. But Carley still couldn't stop screaming, and she ran over to tell Rachel, who just looked up at me and shook her head at me slowly with a disbelieving smile on her pretty face, and then she started to laugh. They were all sitting around a big leather booth, and their pitcher was more than halfway full, so we told her we were going back to Christina's house and they should meet us there when they finished their drinks.

We walked back onto Main Street. It was a little after one. I was not tired in the least, and Carley and I asked this AEPi kid on the corner if we could please bum a cigarette from him. He gave us two, and we smoked them as we giggled our way down the street. I wondered aloud if anything would happen with Tim and me, and we laughed about his straight-out lie about his age. Then I got a little quiet. I had never really pondered the thought before—I had never really had any just cause to—but now here it was. He was only eighteen. Could I really hook up with such a youngster? Then I remembered that the blonde he had ditched in Sea Isle was also twenty-one, and she seemed normal. I had even liked her pants, brown jersey ones, and I figured if she could do it, so could I. Because my new motto was going to be that "It was all about adventure." Certainly a little more optimistic than my old motto, which was "Nothing is ever as bad as it seems." As we walked along, passing Salad Works and Sig Ep and the new Student Center and many other drunk and stumbling kids, Carley told me that I was so lucky. I laughed and told her to stop and that nothing would probably even happen with Tim and me, and I wasn't lucky. She said it had nothing to do with that. But I was so aware of who I was, and I was comfortable with who I was; cute boys liked me, and I was pretty, and everybody looked up to me. And I swear, as she said the nicest things to me that anyone had ever said, I couldn't completely concentrate on her words because I couldn't for the life of me understand how someone could be so disillusioned as to think those things of me. I wanted to tell her I was so insecure that I couldn't even get dressed without someone's opinion of what I'd be wearing. I thought that she should know that while I truly acted as if my future was all planned out, I had no idea what the fuck I was doing or why I was going to Miami to do it. I wished she could see through my cheery facade and realize that my mother didn't always seem to remember that I existed anymore, not since she had gotten married to her newest husband, a man I literally met maybe seven times before she told me they were engaged. She hadn't even called me after I had taken my GREs. She'd forgotten. And then blamed me for being hurt. I wanted Carley to know that I sat awake each night clenching my hands, trying to get used to the feeling that soon I'd be on my own. I wondered if she knew what it was like for me, leaving the one place in the world that had never involved my father or my mother or my stepmother or my stepfather or my childhood shadows or the corners of punishment. I wondered if she thought that since I was pretty, I would feel the pain of leaving my one safe place less vividly.

I pushed the pain out of my head, and I pushed it out easily with just a sharp shake, side to side. I didn't take the time to pause and worry that I'd been doing a lot of pushing pain away lately. The only time I stopped to acknowledge my decisions were late at night when I was by myself and I couldn't escape; but though now it was pretty late, I was surrounded by people, and I didn't let myself care.

The night was still sticky-warm, and this twilight evening was the brightest that I'd ever remembered. Christina's house seemed lit from within from a rosy and flattering source. I perched with my legs straddling the white wood porch, flicking my umpteenth cigarette of the night between my smelly fingers, waiting for Evan, waiting for Tim, waiting for me to recognize myself in this strangely fizzing scenario.

Rachel came up the driveway then, Justin in tow, Evan straggling behind with Kim and Justine, all drunk, all loud. Rachel pushed me to the side of the porch, close enough to the screen door that I could smell the sweat of the dancing bodies inside. She told me she had just passed Dave outside the Balloon, and he had told her to tell me to call him. Hmmm...Dave? Evan? Dave? Evan. It was now two in the morning, and while I had for a time wanted Dave really bad, I'd known him for far too long to lower myself to being a very late-night hookup. I figured friends was the closest we were going to be, and we could end up being good friends. I didn't want to ruin that. Evan, on the other hand, meant absolutely nothing to me, was only the briefest source of lubrication, and I saw nothing wrong with taking off most of my clothes with him in rapt attendance. Well, I was in a relationship that was supposed to be monogamous, so I guess there was something wrong with it. But I had geared myself up for excitement, and I had convinced myself that at this stage in the game that excitement meant boys, so I proceeded with my evening's expectations. Rachel and I moved from the door to the driveway, where Jessica said she'd had enough and was going to go home and order herself a sandwich from Daffy Deli, and the rest of us decided that we'd leave with her. Walking down the tree-lined street to our house, Evan walked between Carley and me, and I looked closely at his profile while he spoke to her. I knew nothing of the crevices, slopes, the meaning of the rapidity of his blinks. I knew Clay's pores by number. *Just put it out of your head.* When we got to our house, I went to my room to check my machine, and Evan accompanied Carley upstairs to get some weed. My machine was blinking rapid green, and Dave's seductive voice was persuading me to come on over. I punched out his seven digits from memory. Then I sweetly told him that I was occupied at the moment with one of Rachel's boyfriend's friends and I'd speak to him sometime, maybe tomorrow.

I didn't know they'd kissed. There were no traces of Carley's Iced Mocha lipstick on Evan's full lips, and I saw no flicker of clandestine glances between them. But I guess I wasn't really looking either. All I know is that we all picked Jessica's room to hang out in, and while I was trying to act nonchalant about what was going to happen and oh, shit, what if it didn't, I took Jessica's flowered pillow from her bed, placed it on Evan's lap, and nestled my head into it. Evan started to rub my back. Up and then very slowly down. There were beads of conflict forming on my skin. Part of it felt kind of good. I mean, I'd done it. In just a few short hours, I'd made a cute boy like me the best out of a houseful of girls. And yet…there was this intrusive sort of twinge that I recognized, and I knew that it was because some strange hands were moving so knowingly. He worked my back so well. I'd hoped that I would have been a more difficult study.

We ended up back in my room, and it didn't take too long. I went over to my CD player, which sat atop the mini fridge that I prayed Evan wouldn't open because I hadn't thrown away my two-week-old grilled chicken sandwich; the smell the fridge gave off was past revolting, on to that of flesh decomposing. Not exactly the mood I hoped to inspire at the moment. Evan didn't reach for the fridge. He reached for and got me. He grabbed me by my shoulders, studied my face from the bottom lip up, and started to kiss me. I twisted and withered in his arms, liking his kisses and pulling my shirt up over my head. The rest of our clothing came off quickly, and I didn't know which one of us had removed what, but I found myself standing totally and completely naked in front of him. I pulled him on to my bed and straddled him. Tried and true lines came out like lyrics formed from his mouth: "I've wanted to do this all night long." "You're so beautiful, so erotic." "I love your hair." He loves my hair! Those curls fell along his shoulders and swept down his broad body and I saw his tummy quiver as I brought myself low and then lower while inhibition faded to nothingness and I opened my mouth. Using my hand too, I stroked here. Using my tongue, I licked there. And I did *awesome*.

Afterward, we talked like old pals, trading anecdotes about our significant others, who all of a sudden were these wonderful, tender people with smiles that made any hurt go away. I felt weirdly close to Clay after rolling around with Evan, in light of, or perhaps because of, my betrayal. I was proud that I had pushed Evan away earlier and told him that I wasn't about to have sex with him. He was cool with that, but knowing that he'd even expected to helped me realize that Evan was in actuality probably a scumbag at heart, who had come down to Delaware for the night expecting to get laid. And he almost had. He'd had to settle for some good head, and it was while I was lying in Evan's arms that I knew for sure there were a million scumbags gallivanting around a world that I'd been able to distance myself from by being a girlfriend. My role may have left me bored, and it may have gone on longer than it should have, but it may have also kept me safe.

In the morning, light shined through my windows and woke Evan and me up just before Justin and Rachel came pounding on the door. Justin and Evan needed to leave to drive back to school, and so Evan and I exchanged numbers and kissed each other chastely on the cheek to say good-bye. Rachel walked them to the car and then came running back inside to my room to find out what happened with us. I sat up in bed and hugged Mr. Gerber to my chest and told her all about my evening like I was any other girl.

And I guess I was just like any other stupid girl who got herself fucked over by a hookup that she pretended not to care about, and I got myself fucked big time. Rachel told me that Carley had left the house early that morning, and she didn't say good-bye, that they had all been sleeping, so I called her after Rachel left the room to tell her what my night had turned into. I was so excited to have a story of my own to tell the morning after, but it seemed Carley had a story to tell as well. First she apologized. "I'm sorry. I am so sorry. Promise me you'll still love me. Promise me you'll still be my friend." I had not a clue as to what she was talking about. "Carl," I ventured. "Did you hook up with *Tim*?" I don't know why his name came to me, but I couldn't figure out anything else. It was then that she told me it wasn't Tim, but Evan that she'd kissed. I was so completely confused and just asked her when it had happened. He'd spent the entire night with me! Carley told me they'd kissed before we hooked up and that she was sorry—she knew I'd wanted him, but it had just happened. That time. But she had no excuse for the time they'd hooked up at five in the morning when he had come upstairs to where she had been sleeping and crawled into bed with her. I remembered that he'd left my room for a while in the predawn. He had said he was going to go to the bathroom, but he was gone for a long time. I was going to go look for him, because it was kind of weird that he'd take so long; but then I thought, what if he had clogged the toilet or something, and it wouldn't flush, and he was trying to plunge it? How embarrassed would he feel if I questioned him about it? So I just stayed in my bed awaiting his return. He came back after fifteen minutes or so, and then we hooked up again.

So. Not only had a guy dicked me over big time, but one of my best friends had too. I felt like such a *girl*, the kind that I always made fun of, and loudly. I didn't know what to say to Carley. I didn't want to get mad over a guy I'd probably never see again, but more than that, I didn't want to show that the night had meant anything to me. That's what I told her. I told her to relax. It was no big deal; the night and Evan were meaningless to me, so she shouldn't worry. I kept my feelings buried as she told me that he had told her he'd been wanting to kiss her all night and that he loved her short hair.

Out came the journal. Flooding came the ramblings. I wished something besides fucking pain could, just once, inspire me.

I went upstairs and found Rachel on the phone with Justin. I moaned the story to her; Justin asked to speak to me, and said that Evan really had liked me. He thought I was so great. He found me beautiful. He just didn't think about what an asshole he was being, and he murmured his disappointment with himself all the way back to UPenn. I found that "apology" highly unsatisfying. I went back downstairs to my room and sat on the floor in front of the full-length mirror behind my door and felt this overwhelming confusion surround me. I didn't know if I should forgive Carley, and I didn't know if I should even care about Evan. I wasn't sure that Rachel wasn't upstairs laughing about this sorry situation with Justin, and I wasn't sure whom else she'd tell. I didn't understand how I should feel or if my feelings were real and justified. I didn't know who to go to for guidance. Jessica, who had been dicked over so many times that she must have formulated some authority on the subject? Rachel, whose friend had done this in the first place? Carley, who had betrayed me, and knowingly at that? Since I didn't know what to do, I just sat there until I heard footsteps at my door.

It was Carley, coming over to apologize, since she said that my voice was all wavering and quivery on the phone. I accepted her apology quickly because I was so glad to have the decision made for me.

Cameras were everywhere those last few days of school. Plain and ordinary occurrences like going to 7-Eleven to buy humongous cherry Slurpees for twelve sweaty girls on an eighty-degree Saturday, or Sunday trips to the stores that lined Main Street were captured forever with a zoom and a click. Whether we wanted to or not, we were required to smile those last few days. If we were caught off guard in a pensive or sullen moment, we would forever be branded as pensive or sullen. We hid our anxieties and buried tomorrow and lived totally and completely in the moment alone.

Years later, someone asked me to pick out from a song or a poem a quote that said something to me, made me feel a sense of inclusion. I spun inward and my mind immediately brought me back to the frenetic close of college, a time in which I lived as I had never before and never would again. The full immersion in only what was current had felt false and dangerous to me back then. How could any day not fit into the grand scheme of things? How could any decision I made be protected from the undecided whirrings of life? How was I able to black out the future since the very essence of those days hinged on the immediacy of "what's next?" Fake, hiding, and doing it consciously, and yet there was something undeniably beautiful about the time. For the first time, I didn't analyze each word, each glance. I laughed unabashedly. The forced smiles weren't really so forced. They came easily. The future was scary, filled with what if's, and the past was somewhat disappointing, filled with should haves. But the moment. It was only about can be's. And years later, flashing back to those floating days, Bob Dylan's stunning lyrics from *Mr. Tambourine Man* swam into my head and I imagined myself living out his words: twirling across the sand of a moonlit beach, one arm waving free, trying desperately to forget about today until it turned into tomorrow.

I shopped a lot before college ended, putting all of my outfits on my Visa card, praying softly each time I was up at the register to hear the whirring sound from the machine that meant acceptance. I spent and spent and figured I'd worry about payment later on. As finals started to wind down, we pretty much ran a shuttle service from the sorority house to the mall, and each night that we went out, we wore new clothing. I was going out every night, getting to the bar earlier than I ever had before, usually somewhere around eight. I didn't often drink, but the bartenders started to know me by name, and toward the end of the night, I scored free Diet Cokes, an accomplishment of sorts. I spoke easily to the people around me, both boys I had never met before, but everyone else seemed to know well, and girls I'd always been slightly afraid of because of their beauty and their confidence. These girls glided across campus, their jeans tight and their hair perfect, even if it was tucked beneath a baseball hat. They sat near me and my group in cafeterias and bars, and their laughter tinkled like ours, and yet they still seemed foreign to me. These girls went out every night and had for all four years of school. They were always tanned. They had names that ended with an *i* or a *y*, and I had often said unkind things about them when they owned a room. They were everything I publicly spat upon and everything I privately wanted to be. I was shocked to find out through silly interactions up against a wooden bar at Kate's or leaning against the dirty stage at the Balloon that these girls knew me, my name, and that they were very nice. I started to look forward to hanging out with these previously unknowns as much as I enjoyed sidling up to new boys or talking loudly with my friends. I went to sleep each night wishing the next day was here so that I could get back to squeezing into one lone week the years of college I should have had but had denied ever wanting.

I called as frequently but spoke to Clay for mere minutes a day. Something was always demanding my attention—screwed-up tan lines, news of a finally nailed hookup, a picture to take—and I was obsessed with missing nothing. Had the situation been the other way around and Clay kept getting off the phone with me to find out who had eaten four slices of pizza on the way home from the Balloon or some other bit of enlightening trivia, I would have been furious, confrontational, and extremely hurt. He may have been all of those things, but he reeked of understanding. "Go have a good time, sweetheart, and call me when you have time." Never, ever would that thought come to my head, and even if it had, I couldn't imagine uttering those words through clenched lips to my love who had zero time for me. Appreciation for understanding moved from the backseat to outside the car, and Clay went with it. I was finally ready to see that my relationship with Clay was a microcosm of the life I had made for myself at school, and I knew I had to make a last-ditch effort to save one from oblivion. I chose school.

He called back as soon as he received the monotone message on his answering machine, asking him to call me. Springsteen was playing on my CD player to give me strength as I first begged him not to hang up on me after I had said what I had to say. I made him promise and then forced a swear. As I spoke, I doodled hearts and stars and zigzags on lined paper with a marker, and I told him that I just felt now and I had felt for a while that something was missing. I didn't know what that something was, and more than that, I didn't know how to get whatever was missing back. It had been gone for too long to reclaim, and though I loved him, I thought we should not be together. As often as

I'd thought it, as much as I said it aloud to my friends and myself, I couldn't form the words, "Let's break up" to Clay. It would hurt both of us. I instead said every variation to end things, and he got the picture more painfully than if I'd just come right out with it.

I cried soft tears as his voice caught, and he told me that he understood; but I was in a very transitional time, and he thought I should take some time to consider things before I grabbed onto finality. I told him I was sure this was the end. The silence between us hummed, and my heart hammered, and the doodling increased to include three-dimensional boxes. He broke in to say that he didn't want to talk now and that he'd call later or tomorrow. I hung up the phone and felt a crash of pain that I wasn't prepared to feel. I felt utterly alone and rolled back onto my bed, curling into a tight ball, holding my face in my hands as "Jungleland" played. I tried to imagine where in his house Clay was now and what he was feeling, what words were plummeting around his head. I was pretty sure he had locked himself in the bathroom to ensure some time alone and to ward off parental questions. From my ball on the bed, I could see him staring at his face in the mirror, wondering what had just happened, trying to figure out what he would tell people. That I had inflicted this hurt onto the person I had always counted on to assuage my own made me sick to my stomach, and I felt like I had period cramps from what I had done. I rolled out of the ball I was in, and walked slowly to the full-length mirror on the back of my door and examined my face. I looked the same. How was that possible? How could I surround someone I loved in such misery, uproot my whole existence, change what course my life would take and come away with the same bone structure as before? I pushed in toward the mirror for my extreme close-up and turned around and around as the camera panned. I looked down on myself standing near my door, and then I watched myself walk outside of it to my friends waiting downstairs to hear what had happened.

I sat outside with Kim and Jessica on the wooden porch swing, and, as we swung slowly, I told them what had happened on the phone with Clay. I cried as I spoke, and they kept their arms wrapped tight around my shoulders, sympathizing, empathizing, somewhat enthusiastic. I didn't expect to feel so shell-shocked after doing the dirty deed. I'd had the conversation with myself at night and in the shower often, practicing wording, experimenting with where to place stresses, and I knew what I was going to say and why I was going to say it. It was all for the best. It was all for the best. It was all for *my* best. And still my insides felt hollow and talking with my friends did not fill me and smoking many cigarettes did not fill me and eating a lot of appetizers later on at Kate's did not fill me. I had this awful vision as we walked home from dinner of myself as a gaping form, forever searching to feel whole, and what if I never would?

The good detractors from reality that they were, my friends carefully instructed me to go out that night and keep the trend going—that staying home and mourning would be the wrong road to take. Each girl I lived with visited my room at differing times throughout the day and early evening to offer guidance, to ensure that I'd be joining them for the evening, and to find out what I would be wearing. I listened to them like the student I had turned into fully and went to take a shower fifth in the bathroom. I sang in the shower, bits of Carole King's "Will You Still Love Me Tomorrow," and some of Concrete Blonde's "Joey," the only song that Clay said I could sing on tune. The rest of the time, he said, I resembled a dying cat. Another reason not to love him. I counted and alphabetized the ways.

We started off the night at Christina and Callie's house down the street, the same one that on the Evan night had seemed lit with a rosy glow. Tonight it was just another house filled with cardboard boxes with "Christina's stuff" scrawled across it in firm, black marker. Four more days. Almost time to just count hours, the way I did when I was little and anxious for some event to arrive. We hung out in the living room as Christina, Callie, and Kim took deep bong hits and I sipped at a beer, willing myself to hang tight and make it through the night and not run home and get into sweats and order food and go to sleep—the way I always had before when the minute got rough. Each second I smiled was my own victory, but I couldn't hold out. I mean, four years. Four. I had to respect them and Clay enough to go home and reflect on the damage I'd inflicted. I needed to write in my journal about how I was feeling, so years later I would have evidence of truth, so that Clay would never become the unflawed fantasy creature that Luke had. I wanted Clay to never visit my dreams with his smile, to never make me a believer in the past being the best part of the puzzle, to never make me question the choices that I had made. When things with Luke had ended all those years ago, when I was still a high school girl, his unflinching hands had cocked the pain toward me, and the pain had been all-consuming. I hadn't been able to share those feeling with anyone, least of all my journal, so I never spoke and I never wrote anything down. What was real had faded and what remained was a golden boy, lit from within by a fluorescent bulb for many years. Everyone I later met was compared to the created Luke—and it was unfair to all of us. But most of all, it was unfair to me, and Clay's influence would never morph into more than it truly was. I told my friends that I felt like being home and being alone, and Christina told me I was doing the wrong thing and what I needed to do was stay out, get wasted, and hook up. I laughed and wished it were that simple and walked back up the quiet street alone to my house. I got into sweats, ordered food, wrote in my journal, curled back into a ball, and willed sleep.

I drifted off in little more than an hour from sheer exhaustion, but the rest wasn't sound, and I awoke a short time later sweating. I got up and turned on the air full blast and pushed open the window to get immediate results. It was just after ten thirty, and everyone was out. I was alone, the way I had wanted it, the way that made me swallow hard. I looked at the phone next to my bed and debated dialing Clay to talk, but I knew that it would only make him feel worse and me feel justified, so I turned on the TV instead. An old Nirvana video on MTV and a *Saved By the Bell* rerun on TBS. I stared at the show for a while and debated getting up and dressed and meeting my friends out. Even though I wasn't certain which bar they were at, there were only a few choices, and really, even if I didn't find them, it was impossible that I wouldn't find somebody I knew if I walked into Kate's at this hour. I got up to check out my hair to see if it was okay, but the hair band had ruined it, frizzed it out, and I got back into bed and wished that I had some Tylenol P.M. to help me out. I considered raiding Justine's stash, but I instead decided to watch some of the videos I'd been making. I slid the small square cassette into the converter and settled back to watch the memories of a few days and weeks ago, smiling at what I smiled at then and really and truly checking out the people that I had ended up with as friends.

Kim: Always willing to do anything for a laugh, praying for it and willing it. A mouth like a gutter; for a short time after New Year's, she tried to convert herself with her resolution not to say the *C* words anymore—*cock* and *cunt*. That resolution stuck until the blizzard on the eve of my twenty-first birthday, January 6, but we had all been impressed by her ability to hang tough for a while. Kim had longish blondish hair, straight or wavy, depending upon the humidity or the time to blow-dry; in the winter months she had put on some weight because many meals were the number 2 at McDonalds, super-sized—with barbeque sauce. She was graduate of a Catholic high school and still the proud owner of her kilt that Rachel had donned to play Axl Rose for Guns N' Roses night. Kim's parents believed she was a virgin and she let them. She didn't really sleep around, but her freshman year, she had kissed or been felt up by two thirds of Phi Kappa Tau's pledge class, a record she was at first proud of and later on ashamed of. I was personally jealous of her list of boys, the recognition she got when she walked down Main Street or into a party, and though some mean-spirited people said she had been slutty, the stigma never held and she was pretty much loved by most. She had another year of school—Allison, Rachel, and Justine were the other juniors in the house—and I tried to imagine them next year, living with all new people but having much the same experiences, and I wished I could stay. Kim told hysterically funny stories of her family, her days with ruler-snapping nuns, and of her evenings' thrills, but while we laughed each time and begged for more and countless retellings, no one could be sure if all of what she said was true, as she had always been a storyteller, though nastier people called her a liar. But part of the fun was figuring out after she had left the room the real thread of truth running through the wonderfully outlandish tale. She was always the center of attention in a room, the cornerstone of silliness, and my best friend.

Jessica: Acted like she was everyone's best friend, but I always kind of doubted her loyalty to most. She was in it for herself, and yet I never resented that about her. I found her fun and instinctual and I liked that she could peg anyone's personality in less than a minute. I also knew, even then, that she was just going to be a college friend, a fun-for-now friend, not someone who would be involved in my life in a long-term way. She knew a lot of people, and she always knew the place to go at night. She was risky and pretty and also a former Catholic schoolgirl who had spent her sophomore year kissing every member but one from the Sig Ep pledge class. Jessica was usually in a good mood, except when the boy that she wanted didn't want her back, and especially when that boy wanted somebody else in her presence. She had crazy ex-boyfriends everywhere, and her throaty voice reminded me of a phone sex operator. She had previously kept her almost black hair naturally curly, but around January had straightened it into a hairdo resembling a helmet, but she liked it and we all pretended to. One night when she wore it curly, we oohed and ahhed and hoped she'd get the message, but the next day the helmet reappeared, and we realized our opinions meant little. Jessica was a Business major, and she always had presentations with cute fraternity boys and those beautifully cool girls I envied. She did well in most classes and had hired a resume writer early to get prepared for the *future*. She got ready first every night, getting into the shower right after dinner to beat the rush; when she came out, I was always in her room to chat as she applied her peach lotion to her arms and her legs. I think that's when she would have liked to be alone and fully naked, but I enjoyed our after-her-shower chats, and she put up with me. We gossiped ferociously about most and were serious about the same things. However flighty she tried to be, she was deep down kind of serious, and I valued her opinions when they weren't masked by alcohol. She thought I was smart and I let her. She was the only one of my close friends who didn't smoke cigarettes. Christina and Kathleen fought over her. Her room was where we gathered.

Rachel: Always considered the bombshell, the Madonna look-alike, back when Madonna was platinum, fake blond, and surrounded by a smooth layer of baby fat. Guys loved Rachel. Many girls hated her, and not simply because she was considered competition, but because she was considered difficult. Anytime she was annoyed or hurt, she told you so. Her candor astonished me. I wondered from where she'd had it burned into that carefully dyed head of hers that she should always voice her opinions and feelings, and screw whoever resented the bluntness. Many a time I defended the underlying sweetness I often prayed lay beneath her steely exterior to others who weren't into searching for possible goodness, but I felt I owed it to her. To me, Rachel was a loyal friend, a partner in crime, an honest critic, a supportive rallier, and a constant presence. I had found her pretty late in college. We got to be friendly during the last semester of my sophomore year, but it wasn't until I was a junior that she began calling me, seeing if I wanted to get together, and making me feel fortunate to walk by her side. Her confidence swelled and was graciously extended, and from Rachel I learned the benefits of speaking my mind. And from the problems that sometimes ensued when she did speak her mind in no uncertain terms, I learned the benefits of sometimes just keeping quiet. Rachel knew how to straighten my curly hair into a sleek look, spending forty minutes or so pulling and pulling on my head, applying serum to tame the frizzies. She was adept at applying shimmery eyeliner and drawing a perfect lip liner pout. She had great jeans that she shared, a high grade point average since freshman year, and a loud giggle that reverberated around the halls of our home. I felt safe having her around.

My video transmitter continued to hum with my recent memories. My forever friends danced across the screen, and I put the sleep timer on my television set and drifted off to sleep, secure at least that my friendships weren't sources of failures. But before I finally slid into dreamland, I couldn't help wondering about how my friends that I had just pointedly evaluated would have evaluated me if the situation were reversed. I couldn't fool myself entirely into thinking that only good things about me would be said. I tried to do it myself, to put myself in the spotlight.

Me: The introspective girl in the group, so much so that many took this silence as supreme intelligence, which made her feel both pleased and misunderstood. Almost always in a happy mood on the outside, dimples denting and indenting further and a loud, tinkly little laugh that inspired laughter in others. A voice that alternated between childish and almost sophisticated. Spent a lot of time alone in her room; her favorite part of the day was going-to-sleep time, when she curled up with a mug of herbal tea and watched *Seinfeld, Cheers*, and *The Mary Tyler Moore Show* reruns. Always went to sleep with the television on and woke up around four o'clock to turn it off. Sometimes couldn't remember getting out of bed to turn it off and wondered how it had turned off in the morning. Wore mostly black and gray, both because it was slimming and also because it was habit from the days in the city. Shopped more than she should have on her budget, usually for clothing and very high-heeled shoes. Had long brown curly hair, unless there was no humidity in the air and then wore it straight, and eyes that people commented on but for a reason she didn't understand. They were brown, boring. Probably the least risky of all of the friends, and the lack of risk was due to pure unadulterated *fear*, but she was never sure what she was fearful of. Not a big going-outer, but wanted to be, and since the end of April was making up for lost time. Felt like lately she had been trying on different personalities like they were different styles of dresses, trying to figure out just who the hell she really was, but knew deep down that the party girl outfit didn't fit well. Still daydreamed about high school sometimes. Dreamed about the future always.

I went to see Dr. Harris one last time before graduation, arriving unannounced at his Memorial Hall office, taking it for granted that he'd be there. He was. I knocked firmly on the door, and he bid me a warm welcome; I pushed the messy pile of test papers off his extra chair and sat down. He congratulated me on a fine exam, and told me that my grade would be an A in the course, and the news made me swell with pride. I felt special and complete from my head to my pink polished toes that what I loved learning about and doing, I was good at doing. *Find something you love to do*, my mother, a college Dean of Students, had always said. *Try to be inspired every day*, my college professor father used to tell me. As I discussed with Dr. Harris the fact that I was considering not going to Miami in the fall for film school, but taking the summer course at the film academy and reapplying to NYU for January admission, I felt sure that I was making the decision that would be best for me. I needed to try once more to get what I had always wanted to attain. Dr. Harris nodded his haloed head in approval, and my decision was solidified.

I wanted Dr. Harris to know the impact he had made on my life, and I planned to tell him that day in his office how much I wished to one day emulate him, how much admiration I had for his craft of teaching, how his class was one that I replayed in my head countless times after I left for the day, how what he talked about in class was done in so fascinating a manner that I went often to the library after class to do additional reading on the subject. I wanted to tell Dr. Harris that he made me want to be a student forever, if not in the literal sense, then in the figurative sense. I wanted to let my eyes well up with the utter gratitude I felt for simply existing in the same time and place as he did. But I didn't tell him these things. My mouth couldn't form the words, and I don't know if maybe it felt too final to tell him that or maybe it would be inappropriately revealing if I said those personal words. Instead I sucked in the air-conditioned office air for memory's sake, smiled up at his familiar face, and said warmly and very simply, "Thank you, Dr. Harris. For everything."

And now the Miami decision was made, but neither my mother nor the Film department at the school was aware that such a dramatic choice had racked the inside of my head. Who to tell first, I wondered, and I knew that the right thing to do would be for me to tell my mom, because really, she deserved to know what was going on in her daughter's life, right? Well, yes, but even I couldn't hide the right-there knowledge from myself that I had better tell her first, because if she said no, I knew my ass was off to Florida, so I shouldn't prematurely burn my bridges with the Miami people. I just needed to figure out how to tell her of my decision so that she would agree that it was for my own good and not a stupendously foolish move. I got home from Dr. Harris's office, armed with the inner strength that my mentor's smile had given me, and settled down to release the news.

You can stay home, she said. Calm. Quiet. Kind of frosty. *You can stay home, but you had better have a plan. What do you expect to do if you're not in school?* and, oh shit, I had never thought beyond the mother-daughter confrontation about the issue! What *would* I do really, because I had to sound affirmative and secure, like I'd been using my newfound, almost-graduated maturity to choose this path. "Work in the field" were the words that popped into my head, and as they swirled through my muddled brain, the words slurred from my muddled mouth. We spoke for a few minutes about what "the field" could encompass, and I told her, "Look, Mom. I could work in a production company, with a magazine, in an agent's office. I know what I am doing, so trust me. Please." For some reason she voiced her assent, and I got off the phone and tried to deal with the fact that I had just fucked up in a major way, because the only thing I'd always had was a plan, and now I was basically just twirling in circles, getting dizzy, not knowing where the circle started and where it would end.

It truly sucks when the glitter fades from the glamour of the moment, the big decision that you can fool yourself into thinking is the route to coveted adulthood, maturity, really knowing yourself, and you get to the second, often by stumbling upon it, when avoidance can no longer work. I so badly wanted the true reason about why I wasn't going to graduate school to be that I wanted to get into the field of film, work, get my hands dirty, have my cuticles bleed, and then and only then reapply to the school of my choice and get myself in by way of my steeped-in-experience credentials. That was the story I'd somehow created and relayed to everyone, including myself, but around seven o'clock one evening, I was sitting on the porch swing by myself, waiting for Rachel to come downstairs and for Carley to come over so that we could head out to Salad Works for dinner. I was just sitting there, swinging slowly, not in a bad mood, not in a good mood, not anything but there, and it was then that I realized that soon I just wouldn't be there. I wouldn't be in Delaware. I wouldn't be in Miami. I thought I'd be in Manhattan, but who knew? But I wasn't going to a new school right away.

I wouldn't have to meet new people, other students like me, get competitive, kiss professors' asses, buy notebooks; and I was relieved, because while all that was like second nature to me, it was only second nature as long as I was doing it in Delaware. Once I went somewhere else I would have to start over, and the thought scared the daylights out of me.

I guess I knew that I would be terrified to start over all alone. If I were in New York, at least I would be around people I knew and could fairly trust. In Florida, who was there? My nana? The swing kept moving beneath me, and my mind was traveling faster than I could keep up with, and I knew what a coward I was. I was giving up the chance to really pursue a goal I had always wanted to because I was afraid of making new *friends*? Really, if I had the power to convince everybody including myself that the reason I was taking some time off was because my bravery and dedication was so utterly steadfast, certainly I could have convinced myself to stop being such a wuss and return to my previously best-laid plans. But I couldn't do it. I couldn't make myself. No way, I knew, would be the easy way out. On the one hand, I could do the Miami thing. Or I could do the sketchy New York deal, where plans weren't set in stone or even in dirt and were just voiced blandly and nothing was permanent or sure. I'd gone from right on time and always on target, with a boyfriend in flannels leading the way to hesitantly setting out on my own, toward an I'm-just-not-sure-anymore kind of future.

Wearing all white—white pants, white tank, white sandals—Carley came driving up in her beat-up Honda and tooted the horn and waved as she pulled in. *I am starving,* she screamed at me, and I told her that I was too, and that she should go inside, get Rachel, and then we could go. She ran through the creaky door, her black hair shining in the late-afternoon sun, and I stood up and stretched and tried to clear my mind. It was pretty useless. I just wanted to go forward in life to where I'd be secure with everything, the decisions already made as successful and bright choices. If that forward march wasn't a possibility, how about I could move backwards, to a time before I'd fucked up the chances for opportunity and success that had seemed so distant and far away then? The world was wide, and the sky shone down on my squinted face; I had never appreciated how free I had been, and I felt like a big mess of chaos, standing on my front porch steps in jean shorts and a light-pink shirt. I needed, seriously needed, to make up an adventure for myself to get my thoughts to someplace far less significant.

Extra black olives, chopped please, and sun-dried tomato dressing on the side. Thank you. After three years of the choices in cuisine at college being regular or curly fries, Salad Works was like a gourmet meal served on Styrofoam for easy transport and convenience. Every time we went there, I got the same thing. It had become my favorite food place at school, not just for the food, but also because the entire front wall of the place was a huge window that looked right out onto Main Street, and you could see who was about to come in and all those just walking around the shopping district of the school during the afternoon. Being in Salad Works put you literally in the center of things, and you could feel as though you were part of it all too.

Graduation in two days, on Saturday, and I realized that I didn't have anything semi-fancy to wear under my gown. Lee didn't have anything either, and Jessica wanted something new, so on that final Thursday morning, we went off to the mall in search of something unique and hopefully on sale. The mall was cold, but artificially so, and I wished I had brought a cardigan to wear. The three of us kept talking about how we felt it would be after this weekend when our lives would change. None of us were in any way sure of what we were going to be doing next year or next month or, really, next Tuesday. I had just blown my self-assured persona with this new why-don't-I-dabble-in-the-filmmaking-field-for-a-bit thing. To make us all feel a little better, we spent the time shopping and talking about upcoming graduation parties, hours we were sure we'd all get to be together. Lee and I, who lived about fifteen minutes apart from each other at real-home, planned to go to the beach and to lunch on Thursday of next week. This planning was necessary. It made us secure. It made time go slower. It even felt real. And in Bebe, when I found a beautiful, short lavender dress and the size small fit, I felt that the second to last day at school was going to be an excellent bunch of hours.

I was right.

The evening's plan:

Setting:	The Balloon
Entertainment:	The Assassins
Refreshments:	50-cent beers, gum, and all the cigarettes you could bum
Time:	10:00 p.m.—arrive fashionably late, but not late enough to miss The Assassin's first set

How twelve girls managed to get ready and out the door at the same time with dry hair never ceased to amaze me, but there we all were, walking the few blocks to the bar. The air was slightly oppressive, but the humidity wasn't that severe, and my hair had curled well. I wore a short jean skirt that I had borrowed from Justine with a low black V-neck tee and black sandals, and my ID and money were in Kim's pocket for safekeeping. I had already decided that I was going to drink that night, and we had started slamming beers at the house. Even though it took me twice as long as everyone else to finish mine, I did get it down and my face felt fuzzy, but in a cool way. I couldn't wait for this night. Jessica was a few feet ahead of me, speaking in her loud voice about this finally being the night that she would hook up with Chris or Jimmy and that she would make it happen, and that none of us should be surprised if one of them showed up in the kitchen in the morning. I wondered whom I should go after that night. It hurt sometimes to realize that all the girls I had always made fun of and judged so ruthlessly for only going out to get a guy and finding the night to be a total failure if she didn't get laid were just like me, the new me, the Clay-less me; and I got dressed that night with the hope that someone else would take those same clothes off of me. I wasn't sure which boy I wanted. Someone coveted, I knew. I wanted waves of attention showered upon me by everyone that night, and it was a little weird and exciting to know somehow that I looked good. That knowledge gave me so much confidence, I probably swaggered down the street.

Usually if you got to the Balloon before eleven, even on a fifty-cent beer night, it wasn't that packed. Often people went to Kate's or the Down Under or someone's house to hang out and drink before the Balloon, and the Balloon was where everyone just kind of wound up. If you were scoping someone out, chances are you could locate him after midnight, standing near one of the crowded bars inside the Balloon. It was almost a given. But that last Thursday night, the bar was teaming with people early. We had to wait in line to pay the cover change to get in. The aura surrounding the place was amazing: enthusiasm, recklessness, caution thrown to the light, smoky wind. I flashed my ID at the bouncer, paid my five bucks to the girl at the door, and was stamped. Validation. I led the way to the nearest bar and decided that I would drink beer that night, not Captain and Diet Coke, which I'd recently developed a tolerance for. Beer was cheap, beer was quick, and beer it was. I swallowed my first mug deftly. Everyone around me was impressed. I lit a Parliament, unwrapped a piece of Trident, popped it in my mouth, and ordered beer number two. That one I sipped slowly. I didn't want to get too out of it; I had plans that were not about to be ruined because of unplanned vomit, so I chose to take it slow. I ran into some people I knew as I made my way with Kim and Rachel toward the stage. My roommate from freshman year, Alice, stood near the steps to the stage. It was always nice seeing her out. We were definitely not the perfect roommate matches. She was an always-drinker, a strange kind of girl who brought home many strange boys. We didn't hang out so much when we lived together, but we sometimes went and got dinner together in the dining hall. She never rushed a sorority, and I did, so she mostly spent time with and got close to people in the dorm, while I went out with my sisters who lived all across campus. We'd get home around the same time and tell each other what we did that night, and that worked. No major friendship, but no hard feelings either. A nice arrangement while it lasted, and when we ran into each other over the next three years, it was always just and only that: nice. That night, on our last Thursday, we gave each other a hug hello, and I told her the Clay news. She was shocked, absolutely shocked. She had long since broken up with Christopher, her boyfriend from freshman year, but I'd stuck it out longer, and she thought that Clay and I were close to engagement. *Too close*, I told her. I hugged her good-bye, and we went our separate ways.

Jimmy came out first and walked to the side of the stage where we were and drank some of Rachel's beer. He told us that the set list for that night was filled with new stuff, including a Springsteen song, and told me I needed to guess which song, but I should remember that The Assassins had a sax player, so I should think of heavily saxed Springsteen. I guessed "Rosalita," and I was right; the night was off, I felt, to a rather fated start.

Tim came out next, walked right over to the stools we were perched on, and told us he had gone to Christina's party after the last time they played. "I went there to see *you,*" he almost shouted, and it literally took every sense of reason not to break into a grin so large, my gums would have bled. I told him I was sorry, that we'd been there but left, and then said maybe we could hang out later on that night. He told me he'd love that, and I told him I hoped he was in the mood to pack, because I was leaving forever in two days and my room was still loaded down with my stuff. In the back of my head as we flirted with our words, I realized that I was making definite plans with a boy I'd lusted after for almost six months and by God, I had almost gotten him. He left our small circle and went up to the stage to play, and I got myself a new beer and gulped quickly. I was a little freaked; crazy when fantasies start coming to life.

When I finally got the busy bartender to hand over beer number 4, the music rocked the place. Suddenly everyone to the left or to the right of me rushed toward the stage to watch the band, and my friends had the coveted spot up front, in front of the guitarist. I wound my way down the stairs, moving carefully toward the stage. I was mesmerized by the moment of everyone that I cared for at school in the same place at the same time, singing the same Top Forty songs. I was getting drunk; the fuzzies had entered the sides of my face, and I felt so much love for everyone next to me. When I looked up at the stage, I felt more love.

Talk about feeling special. Midway through the third song, Tim walked all the way from his side of the stage to the opposite side of the stage where we were, the cord connecting the guitar to the amp *s-t-r-e-t-c-h-i-n-g* to its limit, and in the middle of the song, leaned down to ask if we were still hanging out later. Every element of my environment became ultra-clear at that moment. I could smell the beer in the glass next to me. I could hear conversations taking place many feet away. I could see the curious and envious glances directed at me at that particular moment, and I had to shout up at him in order to be heard over the chaos, and my answer to his question was but one simple and loud *yes*.

I was so excited for whatever would be coming later, but I was nervous about it. Like, what would we talk about? Would he stay over? I had picked up yesterday's undies from the floor of my room, right? He was only eighteen! Would I have sex with him? Was what we'd do be considered cheating, since it fell within a forty-eight-hour period since The Clay Breakup? Questions swirled, and as they did, so did the beer in my belly, and I started to feel sick. But there was no time for pain of any kind, psychosomatic or real, and I knew I needed to stop drinking, stop dancing, definitely stop *thinking*, and get air. I tapped Kim on the shoulder and told her I'd be right back and pushed my way through the throng of sweaty people toward the doorway leading to the outside patio. I did need some fresh air, but it was starting, even in my almost-smashed state, to become so clear that I had this weird tendency to have to separate myself physically from "moments" in order to process them. Like in that bar in Sea Isle…I left my friends and went into the bathroom to think over what and who I was at that moment, looking into the mirror for clarification. And when I broke up with Clay and was all depressed, I left Christina's house and went home to be alone and evaluate myself through viewing tapes of all of us. And now here I was, shivering in a short jean skirt, outside a bar on a clear May evening, trying to chop it up into slender pieces with no sharp edges so I could swallow it all down in one big gulp. I looked down at the cement of the patio. Why couldn't I just go with moments? Why couldn't I trust in who I was? Why did every unprecedented incident require such careful analysis? It wasn't even *fun* to divvy parts of myself up for inspection. And it was at that moment, outside a dirty, cheap Delaware bar, as drunk as I'd been in forever, that I gained clarity and the confidence to just go with it. I went back inside.

By the end of the night, my hair was pulled up in a bun, fastened with a long strand of hair that wrapped around it, holding it in place. Carley was still by my side, but Rachel had disappeared. Jessica finally turned up, reporting that Rachel was beyond wasted and Justine had walked her home to sleep and puke or puke and sleep, and since Kim shared the room with Rachel, she wished out loud that the puke would come first, hopefully in the bathroom. I hadn't had a beer in over an hour, and I was just buzzing nicely but not nauseously, when Tim came over and sat with me on the edge of the stage. I noticed Carley had walked over to Mike and was talking with him happily. She fit in with him. She fit in everywhere. I asked Tim if he wanted to meet up later or hang now, and he offered to drive me home. At least he was old enough to have a license. I went to Carley's side and asked her if she would need a ride home. Just as she began to hem and haw, Mike saved her pride by telling me not to worry about my sweet little friend. He would escort her home. All right, chivalrous band member, I thought, and left the bar with Tim to start part two of the evening.

He had a nicer car than I did, a burgundy Jeep Grand Cherokee. I opened the door for myself and smiled at Tim, who was starting up the engine. I told him the way to the house: left out of the bar, straight up Main Street, over the railroad tracks, through the light to the big white house with the large green sorority letters on it. Impossible to miss. I kept up a steady stream of chatter as we drove the short minutes home, so nervous inside. What was going to happen? Why did I seem to like him more when it wasn't just him and me? He pulled in the back parking lot, and as we walked up to the front steps, we were no longer alone. Kim and Justine, both clad in boxers and sweatshirts, were swinging on the porch swing. Kim had her cordless in her hand and was waiting for Rob to call and come over or have her go there. They looked a little stumped to see Tim, but we sat down and hung out for a while, and it all started to seem normal. Had to lose *that* feeling, so I told Tim to follow me up to Rachel's room so we could check to see how she was feeling and make sure she was still alive. I felt acutely aware that he was right behind me as we headed up the creaky wooden stairs, and swayed slightly in a manner that Clay used to tell me looked sexy. I inched the door of Rachel's room open and whispered her name. She gave a shuddery moan and opened one eye and saw Tim's face. Laughing, she pulled a pillow over her head, and I jumped into the bed with her so she'd wake up. Tim sat on the bed with us, and before I could find out if she'd gotten sick or not, the room was crowded with people. Kim, Justine, Kathleen and her boyfriend. There was some sophomore Sig Ep guy I'd seen once and, of course, the Assassins band member on my left. A random but festive bunch. Tim and I lay back on Rachel's pillows and talked quietly about harmless subjects: packing, Memorial Day plans, the best ways to treat a sunburn. Stuff we were both up on. Our arms were getting closer and closer by the second. The upraised hair on mine was just starting to touch his, and our feet started to twine as though by magnetic force when Kim's cordless finally rang, sending me down to the spinning earth with a thud. Rob was on his way over, Kim reported. He was about to leave, and his friend Jed would be coming too, which meant we should wake Lee up since she'd been flirting with him for four years. But first there was someone who needed to say hello to me on the phone. I got up and took the phone. It was Jason. The same Jason I had wanted to seriously look at me for a long time. The guy that I flirted with shamelessly, the one who'd flirt back with panache, the one I'd never so much as held his hand, and now he wanted to come over. Now? I took the phone out to the fire escape and told Jason that I would love to see him, but I was kind of busy. I knew he'd think I was a huge slut, and I was pretty disappointed about that; but human nature couldn't deny that my walking out to a secret location to have a phone conversation would send an all-together separate impression to Tim. The message: I was wanted, in demand, a catch. It couldn't have worked out better to my advantage if I'd orchestrated it.

Downstairs in my room a short time later, Tim lay on my bed as I tried to figure out how to get into a pair of sleep shorts and a tank top without doing anything lame like walking into the bathroom to disrobe. I pulled the shorts up under my skirt, squeezed the skirt down past my legs and just kind of quickly ripped off my shirt and put one over my bra. All done really quickly, but my knees were knocking. Tim didn't seem fazed at all. I sat down next to him, and he asked me if I was excited to graduate. I spoke surprisingly freely about being excited and nervous, but worried also to be alone after spending so many years as part of a group. What I had with my friends was a different kind of family, one that I hoped would sustain, but who knew? I was starting to feel comfortable with him when he started talking about his friends at Seton Hall, his college family.

"Look," I said. "I know."

"Know what?" he asked.

"That you do not go to college because you are a very young person! Very young, but quite cute, which is so to your advantage right now."

"You know?"

"I know. So bullshit me about something other than your age, because I know the deal on that one, and you're still lying on my bed now."

He laughed a young laugh, a giggly laugh. The most uncensored laugh I'd heard in weeks.

We didn't kiss until an hour or so later. We were lying on my small single bed, facing each other and I was telling him about my family, both real and now from marriage. I told him my dad had been my favorite person, the most unique, intelligent, brutally funny man I had known, but that he had died when I was fourteen. I was so used to getting the sympathetic head tilts and the "I feel your pain" nods when I brought up my dad. The empathy thing was played out, and somehow Tim knew it. He squinted his eyes and touched my hair. Then he changed the subject. We talked and talked while the music that I'd put on played. I told him about college life and the time we'd spent running after his band, and it all seemed so silly, but talking about it made me realize how fun the last few weeks had been. He held my hand and told me about his older sister whom he adored and how his family was supportive of his dreams, and that they believed in him fully, and that's exactly the kind of father he wanted to be. He told me my hair smelled unbelievable. I told him about my film classes and Dr. Harris and how being in those classes, thinking analytically, had opened my intelligence and taken me to a new level where I challenged myself mentally; and I worked so hard sometimes that I left the classroom winded, but exhilarated. I told him I was kind of scared to be graduating in two days because I was nervous to go to a new home and leave the cushions of familiarity behind for someone else to decorate with next year. He told me he had just broken up with his girlfriend, a blond bombshell named Jamie, who was also eighteen years old, earlier in the week. She was wonderful and special, but they just didn't excite each other, he didn't live to hear her opinions, and she never commented insightfully or passionately on his. I found in his voice the embodiment of mind and soul that I'd always felt, cynically, couldn't really exist. And, amazingly, there it was, lying down in front of me and happy to be there. I leaned over and kissed him softly on the lips, and when I pulled away, he smiled at me.

That was the first time I had ever taken the lead and kissed somebody first, the first time I hadn't just sat waiting patiently, hoping I still looked good and my breath was still fresh. I had been known to excuse myself and rush to the bathroom to pop a Tic Tac and check my reflection to see what might be accounting for the physical holdup. But that time with Tim…I just felt so me, so free, and I did what felt as natural as sighing.

We stayed up all night laughing, whispering, sometimes comfortably silent. At around three I crept quietly into Jessica's room where I had left my video camera and brought it back to my room so that Tim and I could get a technological memory of our encounter. I pointed and shot and he emoted. The songs playing from my little CD player had not ceased since we had gone into my room hours earlier, and the same songs had started to play, over and over again.

At around four he was lying on my bed in only his plaid boxers and I was on top of him, kissing his sweet, full lips and touching his face. He was pushing his fingers through my curly hair, bunching clumps of it into his fists and holding on.

At around five we tiptoed down the sorority house steps and walked outside to sit on the porch swing and have a cigarette. I sat on the right and swung my legs over his. I was wearing a white V-neck tee and boxer shorts, and my hair was in a ponytail. I had worn black strappy sandals to the Balloon earlier, and my toes, now bare, were discolored from the dirt of the bar's floor. They were really disgusting, and Tim made comments about how gross my feet were, but we just shrugged it off. There were only a few hours left, and I wasn't going to take time out to scrub my toes and we both knew it. We sat outside on a morning that was already light and crisp, the wind moving slowly and steadily. The yellow marigolds that surrounded the front porch that I had helped plant when I was a pledge smelled delicious and strong. There was no traffic, no people, just us together and realizing that we had missed out on something incredible and now it was too late.

At around six, we went back to bed and finally fell asleep for a short while. I had drifted off heavily, and he woke me by hugging me so tightly and telling me that he loved the way I breathed, very irregular.

At seven thirty he had to leave. The band was rehearsing at four and playing at nine in Pennsylvania somewhere, and the next night they would be down the Delaware shore at the Bottle and Cork. My graduation night. He asked if there was any way I could come to Pennsylvania with him, but I told him it would be impossible. My whole family was driving up for my graduation, and they'd be there at almost the same time the band would be loading the amps into his Cherokee for the trip. My sister, her boyfriend, my parents, my stepbrother, my aunt, uncle, and cousin were all coming to Delaware, and I had to be in the same state to welcome them. I wished in a way I could forgo the whole commencement thing and just ride off toward the next show with him, but I was excited about graduating and being with my family and my friends and being proud of myself and each other. Then I thought quickly and told him that maybe I could get down to the Bottle and Cork on Saturday night after graduation and see him then. I was just pondering and problem solving out loud, like I used to do in math class, but he jumped on that thought and begged me to go, to please go, with a cherry on top, and I swore to both of us that I'd try.

At eight I walked him through the foyer, the living room, the kitchen, and on to the back porch, savoring the moments, the seconds, we had together. He had in one hand my miniature Cookie Monster that I had given him, and in his other hand, mine. We weren't speaking, but somehow everything that had to be was said. I was still barefoot and messy, but I didn't care how I looked because I finally was sure that the only thing that mattered was how I felt, and for the first time in forever I knew. I felt sad and content and comfortable and tense and relaxed and sure of myself. I felt it all, and it was all okay. Tim stopped me when I went to walk off the porch, telling me not to since I was barefoot, and kissed me good-bye on the cheek. He checked his pocket again to make sure he had my phone numbers, both at school, where I would have service for forty-eight more hours, and on Long Island, where I would be thereafter.

Tim headed over to Carley's house to pick up Mike so they could head home and get some sleep before it was time to perform again. He followed my scribbled directions to Carley's house on East Park Place, just a few traffic lights from my house. He entered the house, which was never locked, and knocked on what he hoped was Carley's door, and found her not amused, sleeping roommate, who growled to him that Carley was on the second floor and to get out. He backed away quickly from the scary, angry girl and found Carley and Mike upstairs, half clothed, where they were indulging in an early-morning hookup and were more than surprised to see him. Tim apparently was pacing around her room as they got dressed, telling Carley and Mike that they didn't know, they couldn't know how our night had been, but it was special, so special, and please, could Carley make me, force me, *drive* me to the Bottle and Cork on Saturday, please? All of that information came to me via Carley, who called after they had left, but the first phone call I got that morning was from Tim, who asked Carley if he could just use her phone for a minute, that he wanted to call me and talk to me, and Carley said sure. And in my messy room, in my disheveled state, where I was sitting next to my silent video camera, the phone rang, and it was Tim calling, just to say hello again.

Explanations and descriptions were demanded a few hours later when everyone else woke up, but I was at a loss for words. I had a hard time making people understand, and it was almost like I didn't want them to understand because they couldn't possibly. I had taken Tim home like a shiny prize, but that glow had worn off of him, and what was left was a person that I had almost missed knowing. I was kind of in mourning, mulling over what had to end before it could even start. I remembered how I had wanted so badly to nail Dave and then report ad nauseam all the yummy details, to be a girl, to be like the others. But that sun-drenched morning, I realized that being a girl was also about just being myself and holding things dear and not needing a press conference, not needing to share.

The day passed slowly as families started to arrive, and there was cleaning and packing to be done. Rachel, Kim, Allison, and Justine moped around as everybody else rushed around to get everything ready to go for good. I hadn't eaten since the day before, but I wasn't hungry. I was restless and settled and tired and bounding with energy. At about four I got a phone call from my mother and my stepfather, telling me that they were at the hotel and that I should come over for dinner, so I finally went into the bathroom and took a shower and washed my feet.

Rachel went over to the hotel with me to see my family. The whole time she was speaking to me slowly, as if she spoke slowly, I would definitely comprehend what she was saying. She said that this Tim and me thing was unreasonable, impossible really. I lived in New York starting on Sunday, and Tim lived in Southern New Jersey. I was twenty-one, and Tim was eighteen. I had just ended a relationship, and so had he. We were transitions for each other, necessary lessons that taught us there were others out there, fish in the sea, oats to sow. We should look at the night we'd shared as an experiment only, not the start of something permanent. I listened to her as I drove to the hotel, nodding at her words, but felt differently inside and chose to keep those feeling to myself, because she was on a roll and wouldn't have listened anyway.

My family was staying in three separate rooms, one for my parents, one for my sister Cathryn and her boyfriend Rich, and one for Danny, my new stepbrother, which I thought was kind of ridiculous, since he was eight years old and didn't need his own hotel room. They were happy to see me and Rachel, and we all went out to an Italian place for dinner. I ate like I hadn't in weeks—Caesar salad, chicken marsala, chocolate cake. We spoke about safe topics like finals and friends and left after-college plans out of the discussion.

Rachel and I left right after dinner and went home, where we had all planned to stay in together. I decided that I needed to record the evening, so I called each person into my room one at a time and asked them to do a "confessional," like on *The Real World*. I taped their words and their images so I could be sure to take them with me as they really were.

Kathleen spoke about being afraid to leave her boyfriend, Clint, the same guy none of us had ever trusted because we always saw him flirting and being way too touchy with other girls. But Kathleen was lucky in one instance, because she knew what was next for her: she was heading down to Atlanta to go to chiropractic school starting in August.

Jessica ran down everyone in the house and told my camera who she'd miss and who she wouldn't and why, and then afterward asked if anyone besides me would see this. I told her it was just for me. I didn't know if that was true, but I wanted good stuff. She spoke about Danny and their breakup, all the boys she'd kissed last night—which I think totaled out at seven—about how I had changed in the last few weeks, and that she hoped my new going-out-every-night-drinking-beer-or-whatever-was-there-hooking-up-with-boys-and-laughing-constantly thing was credited to her, at least a little bit.

Rachel cried as she spoke. She was just sad, plain and simple. She didn't want all of us to graduate. She didn't want new people to live in our rooms next year. She didn't know what she was doing for the summer. She didn't know if she should break up with Justin. She didn't know why she still thought about Randy. She just didn't know.

Kim cried too. She just cried and cried and sniffled loudly, and when she spoke, it was to say she had learned so much from me. She took from being my friend strength and kindness and fairness and intelligence; and she seemed so sure about it, she even convinced me.

Allison was too busy trying to track down an entire pile of white laundry that was missing to give a confessional.

Lee was excited to graduate and get on with life, even though she'd had the best year ever. Lee already knew she'd be teaching Special Education at a Long Island high school come September; she knew that she and her boyfriend would make up like always; and she knew she and I were going shopping at Roosevelt Field Mall on Tuesday, so she felt confident, content, and happy.

Justine didn't cry but said she was bummed about us leaving, and who had taken it upon herself to put her in a room with Kristen next year; she didn't even know Kristen, and if that strange girl thought she would share clothes and be her best friend, she was sorely mistaken.

Carley came by in the middle of Lee's confessional, and I put her on standby so I would be sure to get her on tape. After Justine's ranting and complaining, I ushered Carley into my room for her turn. She told me once the red light went on from the camera that she had good news for me. She would be going with me to the Bottle and Cork on

Saturday to see The Assassins, and I was so happy to hear that, I almost exploded from expectation and exhilaration. And *gratitude*. She jabbered on about how she would miss all of us and how she wished she were graduating too. She relayed juicy Mike information and giggled that Tim had seen her half naked that morning and imitated his gushing over me. While that was all good stuff to hear, all I could wrap my mind around was that tomorrow night I was going to see Tim again and I could, for another day, prolong the end.

And that was the last night I slept in that house as a college student. I was aware as I walked up the steps for the evening that I had completed a huge stage in my life, and I was proud of myself. But given the opportunity, I couldn't deny that I wished I could go back and do it all again, because I would make such different choices since now I knew better. I said good night to Jessica, who was washing her face in the bathroom, and good night to Lee, who was tying her short blond hair up in a little knot. I found Allison asleep in her room on top of her covers, her hunted-down laundry in a neat pile at the foot of her bed, and I pulled a throw blanket up around her so she wouldn't be cold in the middle of the night. Then I went into my room, closed the door, changed into the one old sleep shirt I hadn't yet packed, and got into bed. Even in the still darkness, my room felt different. The pictures were no longer tacked to the white walls. My clothes weren't falling off hangers in my too-small closet. My television had even been unplugged. Tim's smell was mashed into the pillows. My stomach knotted, and my head swam with so many memories and thoughts and ideas and words, and I didn't sleep.

I was up and dressing in a surprisingly enthusiastic mood early the next morning. It had been almost two full days since I'd had any sleep. Jessica, Lee, Lori, Kathleen, and I were getting a ride in Lee's parents' minivan to the stadium, where we'd graduate, and there were bagels downstairs to eat as we pinned our caps to one another's heads. Some of my friends had the sorority letters taped to their hats and some had "Hi, Mom!" on them, but I went for the blank slate look.

It was so hot outside, my sunglasses kept slipping from my nose, and my dress stuck to my sweaty back. I should have sat in the English department section, but I didn't have close friends in my major, and I felt that I should be with someone I cared about during the festivities. Since many of my friends were Business majors, I sat with them. I didn't see my parents before the ceremony, but I knew they were there, and I sat tight and listened to the soothing, amazingly resonate voice of Maya Angelou, who was our hired speaker. She said we were all rainbows, soaring, blending, having no limits or boundaries. I guess I liked the message she passed, and I know I loved the way it sounded when she said it, but it was so hard to concentrate. I kept looking all around me to search in the stands for my parents by trying to track down my mom's curly blonde head. And right across the aisle was Randy's disgusting, always drunk roommate, Les. He and his low-class girlfriend were drinking beer out of shiny metal cans; and then there she was, peeing, right there on the ground, lifting her gown to crouch in front of the stadium seats. It was still so incredibly hot, the sun beating down on my shoulders, and I wished I'd brought water with me. I thought of last night with all of my friends, and I was glad we'd stayed in to talk and remember, because really, we were like keepsake boxes of one another's memories and college youth. We had over a few short years supported dreams and wiped away tears and pushed one another until we pushed ourselves. We had bet on each other's successes and celebrated when the bets were won. We were all excitable and bounding with energy and luminous in any room, and sometimes we were too careless and too trusting. And we would never in our lives be as open again.

The music played, and we all switched tassels from one side of our hat to the other like we had at high school graduation; and then it was over, the years as a student, the rushing, the procrastination, the professors, the dining hall. We filed out of the stadium quickly, and from the end of the field, I looked up into the bleachers, once again searching. This time I saw them, all of them, my family waving frantically to me. I waved back with my entire arm and pointed them out to Jessica and she waved too, and my mom looked radiant in a light-blue dress, and her smile was so big and real. We had made arrangements last night to meet after the ceremony at the big metal Blue Hen statue in the main parking lot, and I left the congestion on the field to get there. I wanted to see my family right then in the worst way. And on the way to the mascot, I saw so many people I knew. I saw sorority sisters and old friends from my freshman dorm and cute and almost forgotten fraternity boy crushes; everyone looked different in caps and gowns—mature, older, serious, even with sneakers poking out from under their hems.

There was a delicious flurry of hugs at the meeting place, and my mom smelled so familiar even as she stood next to my stepfather, who was still so unfamiliar to me. And my father's sister was there, and she took a ton of pictures of everything, and I couldn't stop smiling, and the moment felt so good. I unzipped my gown so that much-needed air could find my sweaty body, and I drank some of my mom's lukewarm Diet Coke. I felt special in my costume, like I'd achieved something all on my own, and like I did that morning when I walked around Memorial Hall, I told myself to remember.

We drove back to the sorority house after the pictures, and I rode with my mom, my stepfather, and my stepbrother in the black BMW. My stepdad kept looking back at me in the rearview mirror and smiling at me and asking all sorts of questions about school and my classes and my friends and my opinions. I knew he wanted to be a part of my life, that he wanted that badly, and I guess I wanted that too. I mean, he was kind and funny and good to my mother, but I didn't know much else. Their courtship had been conducted at a rapid-fire pace, like they'd been too nervous to miss a second of forever, so all I knew was he wooed my mom quickly and she'd changed a lot. She spent all her time with his friends and spoke like him, emphasizing the same words, speaking with that sudden lilt in her voice. She had moved out of our quiet, cozy home in East Northport and into his raucous, dark house in Smithtown, where my new room had no windows and where people communicated through an intercom. She hadn't even told me she was moving. But one day I called her from school to tell her I'd just signed up for the GREs, and the machine picked up. It was his voice telling the caller to call over to the new number, his number, because that's where everyone would be living from then on.

In my room at the house were huge garbage bags stuffed to capacity with wool sweaters, jeans, satin formal dresses, cotton underwear, unmatched socks, flannels, fleeces, lacy bras, spandex workout clothes, heels, sneakers, and fluffy yellow slippers in the shape of elephants. I didn't pack "effectively" as my mom said, so each bag contained some of every item, which made packing a quick, messy activity and would make unpacking a dismal chore. We all carried the bags outside to the car and smooshed them into the trunk, which filled up quickly. My television and dresser went into Cathryn's truck with my CD player, my VCR, and boxes of odds and ends that included photo collages of my friends, mugs with the sorority letters emblazoned on the side, and stacks of the textbooks I'd chosen to keep instead of selling back for less than a third of what they had cost in the first place.

A scribbled list lay on my windowsill next to one last empty trash bag telling me to remember to pack the following:
—Sheets, pillow, blanket (still on the bed)
—Jean shorts (in closet)
—Dress and heels I was wearing for grad
—Sleep tee
—Bottle and Cork dress
—Makeup
—Hairdryer
—Mr. Gerber

***DON'T FORGET: Roll up & throw out carpet and refrigerator (check fridge for possibly still-there-from-April grilled chicken sandwich)

We went out to a lovely place for dinner that had been recommended to me by one of my sorority sisters who was from Delaware. The restaurant looked like the inside of an airplane; the food was amazing, and the service was horrendous, but we were all having fun anyway. My family was leaving and going back to Long Island that night, and they figured if they left right after dinner that they'd beat the traffic. It was kind of early, only five o'clock. Kim, Justine, and Rachel had come to dinner with all of us, and it was funny seeing Kim, usually such a potty mouth, speaking respectfully. But my parents loved her, especially my mom, and when she and I got up to go to the bathroom at the end of the meal, she held me close and told me that she adored my friends and she could tell how close we all were and she knew that these would be the ones, my friends for life.

I wish I could have said that I wanted my parents to stay and go out with us that night as Christina's parents were doing and Jessica's parents too, but I just wanted them to get going after dinner so I could get on with the night. I kissed them warmly outside of the restaurant and gave them directions back to I-95. I thanked them for the day and being there, and I gave my stepfather an extra squeeze. The warmth in his eyes touched me, and I knew that my dad would understand.

Back in Kim's car, sitting in the front seat, I wanted just one thing: a cigarette, and fast. As soon as my family caravan forked to the right and we veered to the left, I lit up the cigarette I had clenched in my damp palm, inhaling deeply and almost ferociously. The conversation in the car was getting kind of heated, because it turned out that some people were mad that I was leaving that night and going with Carley down to the Delaware Shore. I guess I didn't blame them for being hurt, because in a way I was deserting them on a pivotal, landmark evening, but it was what I wanted to do, and I knew if I didn't go, I would regret it for a long time while I played the I-Wonder-What-Would-Have-Happened game. I was done wondering, and I was done with games, and if it had taken me four years and a manila diploma to get to that realization, it had more than been worth it.

People were going out early that night to make the night last, and so the shower was already occupied. I figured that while I was waiting, I'd get my ensemble ready. I had only a few pieces of clothing left in my room. I laid out the short, frilly yellow cotton dress I had chosen, and I tried it on with my rope cork sandals, but when I looked around for my bra and underwear, I remembered I had packed them all and that all of my lucky undergarments were in the trunk of my mom's car.

I needed a thong! And quickly too, because Carley and I were leaving at seven thirty and it was already after five, so I asked Justine if she wanted to make a K-Mart run. We hustled out the door on a full-fledged lingerie quest.

I'd never bought K-Mart undergarments, but a trip to Victoria's Secret was unreasonable—too far away. I drove and Justine asked questions about Tim and what I hoped and what I expected and what he had said, and did he know that I'd be there that night, and was I nervous, and did I feel flutters, and what color undies did I want to get? By the time I got out of the car, I was so exhausted that I seriously thought about calling it a day, but I persevered and chose a pale cream satin set that was both classy and sexy. The whole thing cost only twelve dollars, and I realized that K-Mart might just be the best store in the whole wide world.

Everyone looked beautiful that last night at school. Cheeks were a butternut color from the sun and excitement, and I took pictures of the group before they left in a bunch. They were going to start at Kate's and end up at the Balloon, where a good band was playing, but I never found out what they all did that night. They said good-bye to me, and if I received any cold glances, I wasn't aware. I told them I'd be back by noon the next day, and they all said they'd try to still be there. After everyone left and the front door thudded closed, I went back up to my room and dried my hair, working gel through to keep it curly and tame. I got dressed and packed a sleep shirt and shorts and a toothbrush and makeup and the directions to the Bottle and Cork. I grabbed my wallet and my cigarettes and my composure and went to go get Carley.

Carley chattered away for the first twenty minutes of the trip about how she was going to have fun, but she didn't expect anything from Mike, so if he didn't shower her with love or affection or attention, she would be fine. And she meant it. Carley could remove herself from her emotions and go with it and not sulk. I thought that made her brave and strong, but I didn't know if it was honest. She insisted it was and since she was calm and collected and I was a basketcase, maybe she was better off. I was terribly nervous. I just envisioned a scenario where we got to the bar and Tim was all over some other girl. Or maybe I'd walk in and he'd be like, *what are you doing here?* Or maybe he'd be so psyched to see me and I'd feel nothing, which of course, out of the three, would be the best scenario, but certainly not worth a two-hour trip on graduation night. Carley told me I was nuts, perhaps even certifiable, but she wasn't going to let me get away with any woe-is-me shit and told me that Tim had begged both of us to come down, and he wouldn't have just said that, and get over myself, because tonight was going to be my night and I needed to get ready for it.

I'd heard about the Bottle and Cork for four years from older friends who had spent summers down the Delaware Shore, but I still wasn't ready for the sight that greeted me. The place was enormous, an outdoor Balloon that was *crushed* with people, and the line to get in stretched to eternity. It took fifteen minutes just to get a parking spot. Carley and I checked our makeup in the car, popped some gum, and got in line. As the line moved, I could hear the music coming from inside. I heard the band play "Freedom," which usually closed the first set. It was nine thirty. We got stamped for admission and paid our cover charge and walked in. Mobbed. I could sort of see the stage up ahead and to the left, but throngs of people blocked my view. I thought I could make out Jimmy since he was so tall, but I couldn't see Tim. Carley and I grabbed hands and tried to thread our way through the swarms. I was determined. I needed to get up to the front of that stage. A manic force took over, and I moved with a purpose. As the song ended, the band said they'd be back after a short break, but were still onstage talking to people. As I got closer, I saw Tim talking to some girl in the front row, and he didn't see me. I pulled Carley hard and we made it, we got to the front, and I yelled for Jimmy. He looked over at us and got this huge smile on his face and bent down and said, "Oh, my God. Tim is going to be so happy! He hasn't stopped talking about you all night. It's driving the rest of us crazy!" His comment squeezed my heart and it felt so good, and I asked Jimmy if he could go get Tim and bring him over, but not to tell him I was there.

I watched Jimmy go over a few feet to Tim, and the seconds moved like slow motion. I saw him lean down and heard him say that he had a surprise for him. He led Tim over and pointed at us. Tim just looked at me and crouched down and didn't say anything. I felt this weird vibe, like maybe he was disappointed I was there, since he wasn't saying anything; but all of a sudden, a second later, he grabbed my hand and pulled me onstage and hugged me so tightly that everyone in the place turned to see what was going on.

I was shaking when he let me go. Literal shakes and tremors were racking my body, and I almost couldn't talk. He kept touching me, my face, my hair, my hands, and he was so sweaty from the set. He went over to Carley, still on the floor in front of the stage, and helped her up. Mike came over to say hello to her, but the greeting was perfunctory, not warm. Tim just kept saying that he couldn't believe I was there, he'd been hoping but he didn't think I'd make it, and he just couldn't believe it. The second set was about to start, and he had to go change shirts because the one he was in was drenched, so he placed me delicately back in front of the stage. He said the crowd was rough, and if I started getting crushed to tell Billy, who would be in front of us playing guitar, to get us out of there, and he'd put us in the wings. Then he walked away toward Jimmy, who in full view of everyone, put an arm around Tim's shoulders and said something in his ear. Tim looked so happy and still amazed, and it was perhaps the most perfect moment of my entire life.

Before the set started, I needed a cigarette, so I got one from my pack, but I didn't have a light, and Carley didn't either. I walked around our vicinity and saw some guy smoking, so I asked him if I could borrow his cigarette for a second to light mine. As I did it, my hands were still shaking. When I gave his cigarette back to him, he said, "You seem to be very popular tonight." I just kind of looked at him and when he'd spoken, it hadn't sounded warm or complimentary. I wondered what he meant, if he thought I was some cover band groupie or something, and I squelched the faint desire to tell him I wasn't, I was much more, but I didn't. I just thanked him again for the light and walked back to Carley.

When the band started playing, Carley and I were way up in the front row, leaning against the stage, feeling important. The rest of the guys had stopped above us to say hello, and when the music began, Chris thanked us for coming down and then started singing some Dave Matthews and the place just exploded in a rush. The crowd was into The Assassins, and they all jumped and pushed and fell about with abandon. Tim had not been kidding, because we were two small girls quickly crushed against a wooden stage, and I thought that if I didn't get trampled, I'd surely come away with some splinters. We managed again and again to regain our footing, and we held tight to each other for support. Tim wound his way over several times to yell down if we were okay, and we nodded, good sports that we were. They sounded fantastic, and it was apparent that they loved how everyone was getting into them, but Chris did have to stop a song and tell the crowd to stop pushing because the people in front could get hurt. We spent that set holding tough and feeling protected by some supreme force that loomed above us.

And then it was time for Tim to sing a song, and he walked out to the center of the stage with his guitar and looked at me and Jimmy looked at me and everybody to my left looked at me and he smiled and said clearly into the microphone, "This song is dedicated to my good friend, Jaye." The girl next to me grabbed my arm to wave it high, and I grabbed it back because attention was great, but I was a little embarrassed. But then he began plucking out the first cords of "Black" by Pearl Jam, and I no longer cared about being embarrassed. I just wanted to take him off the stage and quickly into bed.

They finished playing at twelve thirty and went to change into new, nonsweaty clothing before coming out to get a beer and hang out. Tim and I stood close together. It still seemed unbelievable to him that I'd come down and equally unbelievable to me that he seemed so overwhelmed by my presence. He was making me feel so good about myself, like I was the most important person in the room, in the state, and my insides soared as my smile grew huge. We went back to their hotel with them, and the guys went to bed quickly and alone. Carley set herself up on the pullout couch, and Tim and I had a big futon in the living room to sleep on, but we never slept. It was another nonstop talkfest, revealing dreams and ideas and secrets and strange hopes and impossible expectations. We kissed and whispered, and touched each other beneath the blankets and tried to stay quiet and I felt even more drawn to him than before. We made bologna sandwiches at four o'clock, mine with mustard, his with mayo, and I liked that I felt comfortable enough to chow down with him. I hadn't always been that way. I used to be so self-conscious when I had to eat in front of a guy that I often didn't, feigning that I wasn't hungry when I sometimes wanted to rip the slice of pizza out of the guy's hand and gobble it down. I hated being that way, but it was hard not to feel it, and I don't know why and I don't know how, but those feelings never surfaced with Tim. Not once.

We heard Carley start to stir around six, and we wanted to talk more, so we went outside the door of the room and sat down on the cold cement. I was wearing my gym shorts and a T-shirt and Tim's sweatshirt, and we sat close together with my legs under the bridge of his. He wasn't speaking, just smoking his cigarette quickly, and I didn't know what was wrong. Then he looked at me for a long beat and said that he felt he'd found something so special in me, but it was just about impossible that it could work out. Relationships, he said, needed to form when people could be together constantly. He wanted to see me every day and go to the movies and run errands to the dry cleaners and make me soup when I was sick, but that could never be between us, because we lived a state away, and he played four times a week, and it couldn't work. I felt ice surround what I guess was my heart, but it felt cold in my stomach and my back too, and I did agree with him. I'd done long-distance relationships. I'd done one for four and a half years, and I wanted togetherness and convenience and immediate gratification and local phone charges, but I wanted Tim more. I was working up the nerve and muddling through positive wording when he looked at me deeply and stated simply, "But I don't think I can give you up." And outside on that chilly cement, we hugged tightly and vowed to make a go at it, no matter how painful it could be.

A few hours later everyone rushed around getting ready to go. Carley and I got dressed, and I wondered to myself about the intelligence of bouncing from one serious relationship right into another, especially one that was encased in logistical problems from the start. I knew part of it didn't feel right, but as I said good-bye to Tim, knowing I'd see him in a week after Christina's graduation party right near where he'd be playing that night, I willed us a chance because I felt that we deserved it.

We drove home without incident, stopping only once to get a bag of Baked Lays from 7-Eleven, and then we were back at school, and I was dropping Carley off at her house. I hugged her tightly, so grateful to her for being my friend and understanding me and my needs and my flaws. I told her I'd see her at Christina's party, but that I'd call her from Long Island during the week. Then I drove back to my house, expecting to see everyone there, but they were all gone. Everyone had left and the house was dark. There was a note on my bed from Jessica and Lee saying good-bye. I walked into all the bedrooms; the mattresses

190

were bare, and the carpets had been removed, and it was a weird feeling. I felt like I was the one living pore inside of a dying shell, and it took most of my strength not to sink down onto the wooden floors and cry. I couldn't believe how quickly the four years had passed by. I had sometimes longed for an end to them, for the never-ending parties to cease, for people to stop being superficial and silly. I wanted to get on with life, move forward, and here I was with no choice. My time was up. I was going back to a home I didn't much know and parents who often weren't around. Most of my friends lived in Jersey, and I had no plans until the Film Academy in July. I felt lost. I contemplated going back over to Carley's and asking her if she felt like staying at her house one more night to prolong my college experience, but I was just so tired. I knew I needed to be realistic, so I walked back into my room, and I tore the *Sesame Street* border I'd put up the previous autumn off the walls and checked the closet and did a quick sweep. Then I slung my knapsack over my shoulder and caught a glimpse of myself in the full-length mirror that still hung on the back of the door and contemplated myself and the moment, and then I left. I walked down the stairs, my footsteps echoing behind me. I pulled open the heavy front door and walked outside, and it closed behind me with a thud.

I never would have made it home without cigarettes. I smoked like a madwoman, not because I needed the nicotine, but simply to keep myself awake because I was so tired and my eyes felt heavy. The drive wasn't too bad, only three and a half hours, and the only traffic was on the Belt Parkway. The music was good, and I listened to a mix that Rachel had made me. I kept rewinding "Fast Car," listening to it over and over again, mouthing the words, wanting so badly to, like the lyrics said, *be someone.*

Part Three
June–August
Long Island and New York City

My parents weren't home when I got there, so it was my second dark house of the day. I pulled into the driveway, pulled up the emergency brake, and left all my stuff in the car. I just took my knapsack and my new house keys and went inside, turned off the alarm, and raided the fridge for a soda, since all those Baked Lays had made me thirsty. I went down the stairs to the room I wondered if I'd ever feel was mine, took off the clothes I'd been wearing since last night, pulled on a sleep shirt from my knapsack, got into bed, and slept for fourteen hours.

Without windows in my room, it was almost impossible to tell what time it was or what the weather might be, so when I woke from my extended slumber, I was in a state of confusion. I stumbled from my bed and went upstairs, experiencing some trepidation about what was going on upstairs, outside. I found my family lying in the sun, my stepbrother in the pool on a big float. I sat on a lounge chair next to my mother, who didn't really greet me warmly. She asked for a kiss and continued reading her book. I felt uncomfortable in the space we all shared, not certain how much of the space I was allotted. I sat with them for an hour or so, not saying much, answering only the questions posed directly to me. I felt the security and waves of contentment I'd so recently won begin to wane, and needing to compensate for the iciness I felt, I got way too sunburned.

Later that day I called my best friend from home, Gwen, and asked her if she felt like getting some dinner. I pulled on a sundress and my sandals and said good-bye to my parents, who were going out to dinner with some friends in the city. They said they'd be home pretty late and didn't ask when I'd be home. I wasn't sure if I was relieved by the non-question or hurt by it.

Gwen lived in East Northport, the same town I had lived in my whole life before my mom moved to Smithtown with Jeff. I had known Gwen since I was a fetus. Our moms were pregnant at the same time, and Gwen was exactly a month and a day older than I. We had been best friends our entire lives, even when I moved to the other side of town after my parents divorced to a smaller house with a tiny backyard. Gwen's family was a lifeline to me. Her mother, Rebecca, was someone I confided in and I listened to her and trusted her judgment. She was teeny skinny, weighing in at maybe a hundred pounds, with a personality that reverberated around any room she was in. She was easier on me than she was on Gwen or her sister. For them she had so many opinions that translated to edicts, but they never questioned and never crossed her. My mom was still friends with Rebecca, but I got the impression that Rebecca and Jeff didn't much care for each other, so the bond was unraveling. Gwen had just graduated from a school in Connecticut. She had been friends all four years with the same group of girls, and though the two of us were close, we'd never visited each other at school. We talked about it endlessly, but it never happened. In high school Gwen was considered to be moody and a little judgmental. People joked about how I was friendly to everyone and she was friendly to no one, but I just felt that people didn't get her. And she didn't care. I was anxious to see Gwen and tell her all that was new in my life and hear about developments in hers. I couldn't wait to leave my new house and return to her home that felt to me a secure, bustling haven.

Gwen looked fantastic. Her straight blonde hair hung thick and all shiny down her back, and she had lost the few pounds she needlessly agonized over. Her green eyes were bright, and she looked older. We hugged and then I moved into the kitchen to hug her mom and help myself to the Diet Coke that was always on the counter, adding ice from the freezer to make it cold. We went up to her room, where I walked around looking at the pictures in frames of the people I didn't know too well, their arms wrapped around my first friend, their smiles sharing secrets I'd never know, stories that wouldn't be funny when told later. It was odd that we shared separate lives and only connected periodically. I sat down cross-legged on her carpet, and she sat on her bed with a pillow tucked under her knees. I asked her about school and her boyfriend, Scott. She was sad to leave him in a week when she and a friend were going off to Europe, but she was excited for her trip and showed me the dresses her mom had bought that could be rolled up, folded, shoved into a backpack without becoming wrinkled. I wished a bit that I was going with her. My friend Mike was going to Europe with some cute AEPi boys, but I would be doing the Film Academy thing instead. I told Gwen about breaking up with Clay, about graduation, a little about Tim, but I was less talkative than I imagined I would be—not sure why, but wanting to just listen to others and not reveal of myself. We left soon after and went down to the town of Northport, smoked some cigarettes on the docks of the harbor, talked about hanging out there endlessly in high school. I thought of Luke while I was down there, standing in the exact same spot where I used to speak to him. I wondered where he was and if I'd see him and how I'd feel about it, because no matter how much time had passed, he still sent me fluttering. Gwen and I had dinner at Wok on the Dock, the Chinese place in town, lingering over hot tea and crispy noodles. As the time passed, I began to feel like the old me, the happy me, and I was grateful to her, to the meal, to the nighttime air.

The days of that week crawled by. I couldn't wait for Saturday. Christina's party would be during the day at her house, and that night Kim, Rachel, and I were going to drive a little south to the bar where The Assassins would be playing. I had spoken to Tim twice during the week. I still felt unsure of our whole relationship, and I was kind of scared it would just fade away as so much else just had, but on Tuesday while I was finally doing my laundry, the phone rang. I was expecting Rachel, telling me that she'd pick me up for the beach in an hour, but it was a male voice, a slightly timid male voice. Tim. I was so happy to hear from him; we spoke and laughed and counted hours until the weekend. He told me he'd been playing, and I told him I had been too, but my playing constituted different meanings, like trips to the mall and late-afternoon smoothies and casual bars with friends. He wanted to know how things were with my family. I felt it was a bit too early in the relationship to reveal all the conflicts and dysfunction, so I told him it was great to be home and I couldn't wait for him to meet everybody.

Thursday morning I walked down the long driveway to pick up the mail. Inside, buried between the Victoria's Secret catalogues and the water bill, was a letter for me that had a hard object inside. I opened it as I walked slowly back up the driveway. The letter was from Tim, telling me he'd been thinking of me and wanted to write about his feelings and he hoped I didn't mind. I took deep breaths as I read about my exact emotions from the perspective of another mind, another pen, and then I placed the large silver ring that he'd put inside the envelope on my thumb as I read the part about how he just wanted me to have a piece of him when we were apart.

Christina's party was amazing. We were all there. It was old times, like last weekend. Her dad barbequed, her mom sat around with us, and we dove and swam and gossiped and ate, and it was exciting and comfortable and like yesterday.

We left at eight to get to the bar. Most everyone else stayed at Christina's for some night swimming, but I was ready to go. I was decked out in black pants, a black strapless shirt, a silver belt, and my hair was straightened by a patient Rachel, who pulled and pulled on my head to get the glorious effect I could never achieve on my own. With Tim's directions we only got lost once. As Kim and Rachel navigated from the front seats, I sat in the back praying and chanting that this time would be as wonderful as the last two times. I didn't need to be pulled onstage, and I didn't need to have a song dedicated to me, but I needed to feel that I wasn't the only one diving in, heart first.

Popping gum on the way in, I first saw Jimmy. He told me I looked hot and pointed me toward Tim, who was bent over the bar, checking out the song list. He got a big smile on his face, kissed me hello, and hugged my friends. He got us drinks and told me he had to go play, but he was glad I was there, and did I need anything? I couldn't help but wonder who had trained him to be so accommodating, so attentive, and why hadn't Clay taken those lessons? My friends watched the exchange with rapt attention, impressed. We went to the bathroom and checked ourselves out and put on some lipstick; we looked good, all of us. And we got some attention back in the bar from people around us. I could see Tim watching from the stage as he tuned up, and I shot him a smile so he'd know nothing was up, but he didn't look pleased. He had told me when I first got there that he needed to tell me something that evening when we were alone, and when I told Kim and Rachel, we brainstormed what that something might be. Inside, deep down, in a place I wouldn't yet reveal, I thought that maybe he wanted to tell me that he loved me. Yes, perhaps too soon, but I felt the stirrings of an emotion too rushing to just be tenderness. Kim said maybe he wanted me to meet his family. Rachel thought he might need some space, which wasn't exactly what I wanted to hear, plus that was pathetic if true, because these days all we had between us was space, miles and toll booths of open, sterile space. They continued to shoot out ideas until they got bored as I just sat back and couldn't wait until the next day when I could relay to them how his eyes had looked when he told me that he loved me.

Watching the crowd grow and then seeing the throngs go wild for Jimmy, Chris, Tim, and the rest of the band got me excited. I loved knowing that the people that everyone clamored in front of for a look or a smile were my friends and my possible boyfriend, and the whole scene gave me a sense of importance. I would watch from a few feet back as Tim stepped offstage to dance with a screaming girl, and I felt no sense of jealousy, no pang of territory. I just had the feeling that what everyone longed for was mine, mine, *mine*.

At the end of the night, band members began to pair off with some of the girls there. It was a little weird for me to see that, since I knew most of them were in serious relationships with loyal girls, but since everybody pretended it was no big deal, I guess I had no need to be concerned. But I was. It wasn't possible to witness the cavalier hookups and not wonder what could possibly go on after shows that I didn't attend. Would Tim be the lone guy in the sea of couples? I wanted to believe that; his sweet looks that swept over me consistently should have helped me doubt that any indiscretions would take place, but I knew what the deal would be. I knew that I too could be free any night I wasn't "the girlfriend" to do as I pleased. I had wished for that freedom so often in college when my significant other resided several states away, but I had hardly ever indulged, and I had looked down upon those who had who weren't morally supposed to. I just didn't believe in cheating when your heart belonged to someone, and promises were made, and intentions were clear, and tomorrows were planned. It just didn't seem fair.

Kim and Rachel drove behind Tim's car, and I was with him. We drove behind Jimmy, and he followed Chris to the hotel we'd all be staying in. As he drove, Tim placed his hand on my leg, almost between my legs. It wasn't a fresh move, but a familiar one. I told him how excited I was for the Film Academy and how I would live in the city at my aunt's apartment while she was in Paris for the months of July and August and how I'd get to make four films, each one increasing in length and technique and how I couldn't wait to put all my theory into practice. He told me he had decided not to go to school in September and just play with the band and decide on his next step at a later date. Half-made plans hung in the smoky air of that car as my straightened hair started to curl in the crushing humidity of the night. I silently begged myself to hang in there and stay in the moment and not to withdraw, not to analyze. But I started to feel unsure, because we both had so many plans, immediate plans that really had no room for each other in them.

I got Kim and Rachel a room and paid for it myself, since I figured they were doing me a favor by being there. They didn't argue. Tim paid for our room. I offered to split it, but he waved my money away. We went up in the elevator, and it was going to be the first night we'd spent just us since that first Delaware night, and I couldn't wait. I wondered if we'd have sex and if he'd be any good and if I should have brought condoms with me. I also wondered what was on his mind and what he so badly needed to tell me when we were alone, and while much of me hoped it was declarations of love, I was a little afraid of that too. I tried not to acknowledge that I liked Tim more when he was stage-Tim, dancing, prancing, lit by a huge watted bulb. What did that mean? I wondered if he liked me more when I danced in front of him, adoring.

We didn't have sex, but once we got into hooking up, I wanted to. He said we should wait a little, and I told him I agreed, but inside I was like, now, please, let's go. I wondered if the difference in our ages was creeping up in the most annoying of times. But we kissed and cuddled, and I figured the time was right, so I lifted the covers from his body and smiled at him as I went below them, leaving the light on so that he could watch.

Later on we were watching some cheesy HBO movie, and I asked him what it was he needed to tell me. I braced myself and tried to figure out if I should say that I loved him back. He seemed reluctant to get into anything and tried to get me to back off, deflecting words, trying so hard, but that made me more curious and less tolerant. I just hedged a bet and came out and asked him if he was involved with anybody else, like his lovely ex-girlfriend. He swore it was all over between him and Jamie. He said when they were together (in a group of other friends, of course), all he did was think of me. He said he had been in love with her, but *had been* were the operative words, and I should know that and keep an open mind, because the thing he needed to tell me was that he had some upcoming parties to go to in the next few weeks, and he and Jamie had decided a long time ago that they would go together. And the plan was still on. Not as dates, he repeated. Nothing would happen, he knew that for a fact, and he wanted me to believe in him and trust in him. I was stuck in a hotel room with him, and it was only three o'clock in the morning; I still had at least five more hours to go, and I wanted to believe him, and I wanted him to believe himself, and mostly I just wanted not to know about the scenario that I now had to live with. I told him that I had no choice but to believe him, that if he said he's not interested anymore, fine. I told him I couldn't tell if he was lying and obviously I hoped he wasn't and that he'd better not be, because I didn't have the time or patience for that bullshit. I sounded more secure than I felt.

The next morning kind of sucked, because once we said our good-byes and it was just me and my friends, I had to tell them what the deal had been, and their sympathetic gazes almost killed me dead right there. Sympathy I didn't need. I wanted assurances that there was no way he'd look at anybody as he did me, that we were soulmates, joined by a spiritual force, joined for good—but none of us believed that and none of us said it.

The next few weeks, I waited anxiously for messages and phone calls from Tim, loving especially the ones that came late at night, which told me he was home and alone and Jamie-less. I tried not to completely panic when two days passed and he hadn't called. On those days I wanted so badly to call him, just to see if he was there, but he had caller ID, and I'd look more pathetic than I felt. I tried to keep busy. Lots of mall trips. Daily pilgrimages to the beach. Lunch with Gwen and Rachel, but separately because they'd known each other since they were little and at Hebrew school, and they'd never been fans of one other. Dinner a few times with my parents, trying, all of us trying, to get into a comfortable family groove, but more often than not, it just felt like hard work. I saw Mike before he left and drove Gwen to the airport when she left. I visited Brian at his new city apartment, going out to the neighborhood bar, doing shots that left me sick for thirty-six hours. I tried not to run to the answering machine when I was home, which was good, because the blinking lights were becoming more and more infrequent until the week before I left for the Film Academy, when they just finally stopped blinking all together.

I packed for the city with a breaking, bleeding heart, embarrassed from the inside out, blushing ferociously each time I thought of Tim's betrayal. I knew he must be back with Jamie on a permanent basis, and I knew they had a much better chance at a relationship. They had two years under their belts. They were the same age. They could go to the dry cleaners together! But I couldn't help thinking that while of course she had those pluses in her favor, what was wrong with me, and how come he'd forsaken me, and wouldn't I ever be happy? Would he ever acknowledge our time together with a phone call or a letter? Didn't I deserve that much? I wrote him many letters, barraging him with all of my unanswered questions and misery, but when I went back over them with a critical, puffy eye, I sounded like so much of a loser that I never sent them, burying them in the bottom desk drawer in my room.

I lost weight when I was depressed. Food made me nauseous when I was awake. Besides, I spent so much time asleep when I was sad, so I arrived at the beautiful apartment my aunt and uncle were letting me live in for the summer at the weight I was in high school. I may have felt lousy, but I looked fantastic.

The only person I knew living in the city that same summer was Brian, and he was always fun to be with. He was starting work on the same day that I was starting class, and we were both a little nervous. We went out for a nice dinner at the Blue Water Grille down in Union Square, literally a hop, skip, and three or four jumps from the Film Academy. Over Chilean sea bass, Brian obsessed over starting at William Morris, heading into the mailroom, and did I know that's where so many studio heads had begun their careers? Brian was the only friend I had who wanted to live the film world like I did, but he wanted to *live* in it and have brunch with the people, and I wanted to study them and teach what came out of those power meals. He said he'd be at Sundance in ten years or less, selling a property that people would line up for. I didn't doubt it and told him to bring me back a totebag. Brian had an intensity and a drive that I wished I could cultivate, and he thought it was crazy I was so down about Tim. He tried to get me to see he wasn't that great, reminding me of his age and that he earned a living playing *other people's music,* and that I could do so much better, and if I just let myself be open, I could have my pick of anyone in the city. He was being so patient with me, certainly more so than my friends, who told me they'd thought it was all a little strange from the start. Carley had been kind. She'd called every day for a week to make sure I was okay. I usually got messages, since I was sleeping so much of the time. But she still called. Carley had been there with me throughout the whole thing that I couldn't believe had lasted less than a month; it had seemed like forever. She'd watched it bloom, grow, and die, suffering with me during the wilting phase. But she also told me it was all for my best, no matter who had taken control of the end. I think she knew that's what hurt me the most—that I hadn't broken it off, but been the recipient of the pain.

My first day at the Academy began early, as the days would for the remainder of the summer. I needed to be there by eight, which meant leaving the apartment at seven to allow myself time to grab the One or the Nine from Columbus Circle to Times Square, where I could transfer to the N or the R. The "Never" and the "Rarely." By the time

I got there, I was sweating and felt grimy from being underground in ninety-degree heat. I promised myself that on days that I ate well, no fries or chocolate, and limited my thoughts of Tim to seven or under, that I could reward myself with a ride in a taxi, windows cranked open. But since I had woken up thinking of Tim's face and gotten dressed wondering what he'd think of my outfit, and in the ten minutes before class started, I had grabbed a chocolate chip muffin, I knew the subway would be how I'd be getting home.

The instructors introduced themselves to the group of incoming students in the screening room on the top floor. I guess there were about eighty of us. There were editing teachers and cinematography teachers and directing teachers, and it was hard to keep everyone straight. I sat in the second row, way on the side, and just knew I was the only Long Islander there. Everyone else looked like they were cosmopolitan New Yorkers or from some faraway land, and I found out I was right when we all had to stand up and introduce ourselves. The first girl was so tall and thin that she had to be a model. As she tossed her perfectly straight (and perfectly natural, I just knew it!) hair over her shoulder, I could see she was wearing amazing leather pants like they were jeans. And when she opened her mouth, it was obvious she was from London. Her name was Gillian, and she was so cool, I both fell in love with her and hated her immediately.

We were allowed a short break before we broke up into our seminar groups. There were four groups of twenty, and we'd be in them all summer long. I was in Group C. Taking advantage of the minutes to collect myself, I went down to the entranceway to have a cigarette; there I realized that film people are a nicotine-consuming bunch, because the space in front of the building was so clogged with inhalers that I needed to step a few feet down to light my cigarette without lighting anyone's hair on fire with it. I had just bent my head to the match when a voice asked me if I could light hers as well. It was Gillian. I gave her the match and watched her light her Marlboro, breathe in, and exhale through her nostrils. On her it looked good. She smiled and said thank you and asked me my name. I told her, and I asked what hers was, even though I already knew. She was truly breathtaking close up. She kind of looked feline, and she glided instead of walked; she seemed older than me, though she said she was only twenty-two. I was just about to tell her I liked her pants when another girl came over to us, a girl with wide hips and screaming red hair and a gaping, painted mouth. She said her name was Kate and what group were we in, and oh, good, she was also in Group C, and did we all want to get lunch later? Gillian and I nodded at Kate, and Gillian seemed genuinely sweet to her, though Kate's aggressive persona put me off from the start. Her voice was like a shriek, and her face was no better, and her personality, in five minutes, almost sent me over to the two guys from Kuwait for shelter. But I wanted to be near Gillian, so I put up with Kate for the time being.

Our instructor for directing was Alex: thirty-eight, baseball hat hiding thinning hair, gray T-shirt, huggable body. He was a filmmaker/teacher, an NYU graduate, a lifelong New Yorker. He seemed cynical and bright and witty, starting us off right away with explanations of camera techniques to invoke moods. I listened to him and felt transported back to a classroom in Delaware, and my heart started beating, because I finally felt free for the first time since had Tim hurt me. I realized that I was in just the place I needed to be, and if I had no other choices, Alex might be a fine person to have an innocent crush on during those hot summer months.

After the directing workshop, we were hustled down the stairs to the room where we'd have our first training in how to operate the Ariflex cameras we'd be using for our projects. We sat around a long table, one camera to be shared between two people, and since everyone was kind of in a circle, it was a good time to check out the rest of the people in Group C. There were many tall, bronzed men who spoke with accents I'd never heard. One guy was from Sweden. A brown-haired male with a sweet face and muscular arms was from Germany. Two were from Mexico. Two from Kuwait. But even more foreign to me was the perfectly groomed blonde girl across from me. She couldn't have been more than seventeen, but she was easily the most self-assured person I'd ever seen. She sat up straight and had a haughty look on her pretty face and tossed her hair back with aplomb. I overheard her say she lived on the East Side, on Park, had for her whole life, and was spending the weekends in the Hamptons. I wondered how someone that young owned such confidence, but when I bent over the camera next to her and saw her sunglasses were Armani and her purse was Prada and her jeans were Helmut Lang, I knew how she'd gotten that way.

Lunch came an hour later, and I was starving. Gillian, Kate, and I crossed the park and ended up at Coffee

Shop, a restaurant where models served grilled cheese and fries and charged fourteen dollars for it. Kate didn't blink when the bill came, but Gillian and I exchanged quick glances at the steep prices. All through the meal, I had been anxious to get to know Gillian and see if I liked her for who she was or just wanted to be around her because she was so stunning that being next to her almost got me tanned. I didn't figure it out at that lunch, because Kate wouldn't shut her mouth except to ingest some of my fries without asking for permission.

That night, after I got home and showered the city's filth from my body and ate a turkey sandwich from the deli on Sixty-Second Street, I turned on some music and opened the door to the terrace. The view was amazing. I could see Central Park on my left and Lincoln Center straight ahead and a white-haired woman walking a matching poodle below. It was kind of late, eleven thirty or so, and I just stared at what was around me, at the bustling, the incessant movement of the city. The floor beneath me was cold, and the lights from all of the surrounding buildings were bright, but I was in a trance. It seemed to me all of a sudden that the city was like the ocean, and you had to learn to be afraid of it and respect it for all of the uncertainty and pain it had the power to bring to you.

Our first filming exercise came later that week. We were separated into groups of three, and we were told to get the camera together, go across the street to Union Square, and shoot specified footage. I was in a group with two people I didn't know yet, Lance and Kelsey. We grabbed our stuff and quietly made our way down to the park, where we set up a few feet away from Gillian and the boys from

Mexico. I kept looking at Lance out of the corner of my eye. He was strange. He whistled continuously, off-key, and he looked unbelievably nervous. He was twirling his hands and making box steps with his feet, and I wondered if it was the camera that freaked him out or the fact that he was in close proximity to girls or if he was on something. I moved farther away from him and spoke to Kelsey about angles and distance and tried to figure out how she was reading the light meter. It was such a simple thing to do, but I could not figure out how to do it, probably because it involved numbers, and I'd been afraid of math since the day my high school teacher had written "x=" on the board. I'd gotten a tutor that day. I hung near Kelsey and looked at her too, and she was kind of soft spoken and funny in a reserved way. She was pretty masculine looking, with short hair and boyish clothes, and I figured she was probably a lesbian. I found out the next week that I was right, but by then we'd grown close, and she told me so, and I was pleased and honored she felt comfortable enough with me to want to share. That day, though, we shot the prescribed footage, and I got much more comfortable loading film and listening for the telltale click sound that indicated the film was done. The sun was out, but it wasn't too warm, and all around us merchants were setting up the Farmer's Market, and passersby stopped to check out what we were filming. Kelsey and I laughed a lot, and it was a close to perfect day.

We watched the footage we'd shot later that day in the air-conditioned screening room. Ours was okay, maybe a little static, but what surprised me was Tess, the Prada-Armani-Helmut Lang girl, because she was attractive in person, but my God, her group had got her on film, and on film the girl was luminous.

In less than a week, Gillian and I had grown close, which was odd; a week was a relatively short time to grow comfortable with a stranger, and we were different in every way from each other. I was dark, and she was light. I was short, and she was tall. I was American, and she was English. I was cute, and she was beyond gorgeous. I was silly, and she was reserved. And yet somehow, some summer day early in July, we just connected and spent the rest of the warm days and many of the warm nights speaking without breaks, rolling around in hysterics, shopping at weird stores, consuming fattening food, sharing our histories, and by being with our polar opposite, learning about ourselves.

When it came time to break into official filming groups we'd be tied to for the rest of the summer, it seemed natural that Gillian and I would get together, and we had a spot for one more. Kate approached us and asked to be in our group, but the very thought horrified me. As the days had passed, she had become even more annoying to be around, loud, opinionated, selfish. I spent some days more focused on getting out of having lunch with her than paying attention to the art of filmmaking. But I found I didn't have to worry, because Gillian was tougher and more assertive than I was, and she told Kate she was sorry, but Kelsey had already joined our group. Actually, Kelsey hadn't joined at that point, but as soon as I heard Gillian's clever excuse, I rushed up to Kelsey and begged her to please, please, please be our third member.

And from that day on, we were a threesome, going everywhere together, sitting in class together, a bona fide trio. If I thought that I couldn't have found anyone more different from me than Gillian, well, the three of us were the strangest group I'd ever seen. I sometimes thought about how it looked, all of us walking down the street together. People must have stopped and stared and not just at Gillian's beauty, but because we looked so incongruous together. I think it was part of our charm.

The days were long. Sometimes when I got home, it was late, especially if I was editing, and all I wanted to do was sleep. I didn't have much time to speak to college friends, but I wrote Rachel letters at the camp where she was a counselor, and I emailed friends at night. I was always tired, always hungry, and I started to put back on some of the weight I'd lost following the Tim debacle. I still thought about him constantly. The feelings just were not subsiding, and I felt worse a few weeks later. I missed him, the actual him, the idea of him. My busy days were not assuaging hurt, and making friends wasn't doing the trick either. I decided I would take another route toward self-medicating in a sense: find someone else to take his place.

The pickings were slim. On the one hand, I was in New York City, a place infested with beautiful men, dark and cool looking. On the other hand, I was stuck all day long, six days a week in the Film Academy, and not one boy in my class even made me blush pink when he looked at me, let alone a scarlet-maroon color. The guys in the other sections weren't much better, and I never saw them to begin with, because the sections were always separated. I could certainly have had some exciting random hookups when I was out at night. I could've kissed someone against a bar uptown or blown some nameless guy downtown, but that route would undermine the whole point of getting someone new, because what I yearned for was not physical contact, but constant awareness of someone else's presence.

I got nervous when I did something new. I wasn't paralyzed by fear or anything, but I would get uncomfortable and quiet if I did something or went someplace that was out of character for me. That summer in the city, I challenged my fears and myself. Every day presented something new: new people, new ideas, new subways. I dealt with my nerves by keeping up the mantra I'd adopted for myself at the end of college. I would chant it aloud when I was alone and silently when I was around others. That mantra: *it's all an adventure, it's all an adventure, it's* all *an adventure.* And it worked because my new life was so off-course and it was a true adventure, and somehow those words tended to get me through.

But before I could find the guy who I would invite along with me on my new adventure, Gillian got herself into an adventure all her own. She called one Sunday morning from the battered hotel she was staying in on Seventeenth Street, asking me if I felt like going to a movie with her. I told her all I wanted to do was spend the day sleeping and watching movies that none of my film classes had ruined for me yet, and I'd see her tomorrow. I thought she'd gone to the movies alone. It was her intention. But that didn't happen. According to her, she went up to the coffee shop a block up from her hotel, a block down from the Academy; and there, as she sipped dark coffee and smoked a Marlboro Light, who should walk in the place but Alex, our directing professor. How he wound up there, we never knew, because it was Sunday after all, and he lived a-l-l the way downtown in Battery Park. But there he was, in for coffee and a corn-raisin muffin. They ended up dining together and later went to the movie together. He told her that day, late at night down on the boardwalk of Battery Park, that she had blown him away when she'd walked into class, and he thought about her a lot. He tried to kiss her that night, late, when the sky was dark and her guard should have been down. But she didn't kiss him, wouldn't kiss him, and he acted okay with it, but she said she could see he looked rather destroyed. The next day was Monday, and I met her in our spot, the Korean deli next door to school, and there she was, looking quiet and nervous; she wasn't eating when she told me what had happened. I couldn't get over it. Alex was in his late thirties. He was a man! A damn cute man too, and I thought, once I got over being skeeved out that such a grown-up wanted me sexually, that I'd be flattered, and why wasn't Gillian? She lowered her eyes and didn't speak for a long beat and then lit a cigarette. She inhaled and blew smoke ferociously out of her nostrils and said, "You know what? I'm just sick and tired of men wanting to fuck me."

Questions rose that day for me about Gillian's life, the parts she hadn't shared with me. We were extremely close, but there were lots of times when she just wanted me to talk and she got to ask all the questions, never revealing of herself. I knew a little about her family. They lived in London. Her dad was a big businessman who would be in

New York for a weekend over the summer, and Gillian planned to see him then. Her mom was supposedly quite beautiful, and I got the feeling that she went out a lot and spent more time looking at clothing in couture houses than looking at her daughter's face. Gillian didn't live at home. She lived off King's Road, a place I'd read about in books about the Rolling Stones, and she worked as a chef, which I found weird, because she never talked about recipes once that summer. She said her specialty was sauces. She said she had come to New York after winning a free trip on a London radio station and had chosen the seedy hotel downtown, because she'd read about it in a magazine and thought it sounded interesting. When I went there to hang out for the day, my adventure mantra had flown out the window and died, just as I'm sure several former hotel guests had. The place was disgusting. The lobby was tiny and run-down, and strange-looking people of all ages lingered about in a haze. The elevator was thin and slow. Gillian's room had no bathroom and a small window; there wasn't much around but some clothes in the open space that doubled as a closet, the leather pants she'd been wearing when I first met her tossed over the one chair, some makeup on the rusty sink, and a half-smoked joint in the ashtray. She didn't have a toilet in her room—she used the community bathroom down the hall. I was sure the floor of that bathroom was also covered in pubic hair of various shades and various lengths, and the hotel to me seemed a sorority house on mescaline.

But what really got me curious was the comment Gillian made to me about men and them always wanting to fuck her. I knew she knew she was beautiful, but she was never conceited about it. She knew men wanted her. But it was the way she spoke of men, that time and others. She didn't speak like they wanted her or adored her; she spoke like they used her, like she had been used over and over and over again and she'd had enough.

I was strangely caught in the middle of the May-November wouldn't be/couldn't be romance of Gillian and Alex, because she went to me to tell about his pleas of devotion that she rebuffed, and he came to me to tell me of his unwavering devotion. I adored Alex, and it made me sad to see him looking forlorn. It also amazed me how close we'd all gotten so quickly, like we were young camp friends, not supposed-to-be adults. Alex told me he was drawn to me from the start too, but in a familial way; I reminded him of his younger sister. I died a slow death as I stroked his hair and told him that he needed to move on, that Gillian was a crush for him that wouldn't ever work, and that he had to get that through his thirty-seven-year-old head. Sometimes I would tell Gillian what he had said and sometimes I wouldn't, probably for a couple of reasons. First, if I let her in on his obsession, she'd just sigh and roll her eyes. She did like him, but for him to tell her that he knew at once she was perfect for him reeked of the fact that he'd been blown away by her already-adored-the-world-over physicality, and I think she wanted to be more than that. I also didn't always regal her with Alex info because I kind of felt jealous of the connection he wanted with her. I valued our connection, even if it was based mostly on her, and I wanted to keep a little of him for myself. I didn't feel romantic feelings toward him, but it was that whole Dr. Harris thing going on again, where I was so appreciative of the older man teaching me, educating me in the ways of Film and in the ways of my world. I guess my father had died too early, and I was trying to compensate. I was Freud's wet dream come true.

But before long I had an obsession of my own. It was a planned, calculated obsession that took fruition the day after I broke down one humid night and called Tim from the terrace. At first he had sounded so happy to hear my voice. He told me he missed me. He told me he saw someone the other day that looked like me and he'd felt sad. He told me that I sounded great, and I definitely played up my happiness to make myself sound strong. But after a few minutes, he just sounded bored. I was asking the questions, and he was answering in brief words. Then he said that he had to get going, that he was going out for the night, and he'd give me a call soon. But he wasn't specific about when "soon" would be; I had to ask him if he wanted my city number. I doubt he even wrote it down, and when I got off the phone, I felt so rejected and so hopeless that I cried for hours, tears puddling down my sleep shirt, and I felt like dying.

The next day I was exhausted from the tears and from questioning what it was about me that was so lacking. I got to class late because I'd spent extra minutes scrutinizing myself in the bathroom mirror. To get into the door to the classroom, you had to get buzzed in by someone who worked at the Academy, but usually everyone kind of showed up for class in a bunch, and we all held the doors open for each other. By the time I'd made it off the R train and rushed across Union Square to school, the bunch had already gone inside. I buzzed the intercom impatiently a few times, feeling haggard and out of sorts. Finally the door opened and Jake, the equipment guy, was looking down at me with amusement, letting me in and asking if I was okay, because I looked pretty damn shitty. I just stopped in my tracks, shifted my knapsack to the other shoulder, and took my first clear look at his blond ponytail and his slow smile. I wondered if he knew my name, and I smiled and said, "Thanks, I feel pretty damn shitty." And as he let me in and I ran up the stairs to class, he called after me, "Don't worry, Jaye. There's always a silver lining."

I walked into editing class, mumbled an apology to Liza, the teacher, for being late, and found a seat at the back of the room. Gillian tore off a sheet of paper from her notebook and passed it back to me through the rows. *Are you okay?* it asked in her flowing blue penmanship. *I am now*, I scrawled back.

And that day was the start of my Jake days, one of which I was always so sure would end with us having raunchy, very nasty, very sweaty, *re-e-a-lly* slow sex through the night and into my immediate future. The crush was made easy by the fact that I didn't really like him. I just wanted him to like me. I didn't often want to merely obsess over anyone. It made me feel kind of like a child. But it did take my mind off Tim. Jake and I saw each other every day, since I went to school at the Academy, and he worked there, and we started to speak frequently, flirting through our words. But I could never figure out what he was thinking. Some days I would be positive he wanted me. He'd give me that look. God, I loved that look. But then the next minute, he was aloof. I always tried to look pretty, because I knew I'd be running into him, and I made frequent walks past the equipment room, even when I didn't need equipment. And I longed for camera-checkout day, but I was kept wrapped in the pitch-black dusk about how my new intended prince thought about me. Or if he thought about me. I loved being preoccupied with thoughts of an unsure thing, especially because I didn't care nearly enough to get hurt—I thought. I liked having a boy to obsess about to my friends, and I lapped up the advice they shared. Gillian told me to invite him out for a drink, get both of us recklessly drunk, and the rest should come naturally. Kelsey told me to look deep into his eyes and speak slowly and seductively. She was the romantic one of the three of us. I didn't know whose advice to listen to, jaded Gillian or my girl-loving friend Kelsey, so I just bided my time and trimmed my pubic hair every two days.

Our favorite place to talk about relationships, burgeoning or doomed, was the coffee shop down the street from school. We went there almost every day for lunch, Kelsey, Gillian, and I, and we'd sit for the whole hour, eating and confiding. We all ate a lot that summer, and though the grilled cheese at the coffee shop was the best, on weekends we went to other places around the city. We had the Caesar salad at Pete's Tavern on Irving and amazing tapas at a great restaurant around the corner from Union Square, the place attached to ABC Furniture. I took them to my favorite pizza place, Mariella's, where we consumed many cheesy slices. We went up to Serendipity and had frozen hot chocolate and foot-long hot dogs one rainy Sunday, and we decked ourselves out one morning to have a fancy brunch at the Peninsula Hotel. We got ice cream cones down on Christopher Street, and while Gillian and I were enthusiastically consuming the delicious treat, Kelsey was looking amazed at the small community in the heart of the Village, where homosexuals walked honest and free.

Lots of times when we went out, we were joined by Beth, Kelsey's girlfriend, whom she'd met at college. They were loving with each other, holding hands and kissing, and both Gillian and I were envious that Kelsey was in such a solid relationship while we were both floundering in the romance department. But people on the city streets didn't always find Kelsey and Beth's relationship beautiful; many snickered as they walked by, seeing two girls' hands entwined, and some mumbled ugly words at them. Beth blew the comments off. She was older and had been proudly out for more years than Kelsey, so she could give two shits what random people said. But Kelsey would stare at the ground after one of the wordy assholes walked by, wishing she could be accepted by the world, and she was still young and optimistic enough to believe that she could be.

Though I was truly growing that summer, living entirely on my own in my (sort of) own apartment, going places on my own, finding out how to get to those places, making friends, embarking on urban adventures, I still found it impossible to leave my past behind me. Yes, I was in a place I'd never been, but that place brought me full circle to the most conflicted, horrific portion of my life. The Academy was literally two blocks from the apartment I had lived in during ninth grade, the one I lived in with my father and my stepmother. That year was so strange for me. I'd moved from suburbia, where all should have been well, to the city, trying to escape a bad relationship with my mother, bitter at me for enjoying my relationship with my father. Her fondness for him left when divorce paper had been signed when I was almost six. My sister complied with the road to an easy post-divorce life by hating my dad, as was expected. The two of them, my mom and sister, bonded over a mutually created hatred; and I was left out in the rainy, harsh cold. When I reached the age of thirteen, I'd had enough of defending my dad to unhearing family members, of being told to ask for the child support checks, of being shrieked at to clean my fucking room when her anger was certainly not about my fucking room. I started yelling back that year, standing up for myself to her face, hysterical alone when I was set to my room. I never wanted either of them to hear my sadness, so I'd hold Cookie Monster to my face, pressed really tight, and I'd sob and wail in stifled gulps. Hours later I would emerge, pretending nothing had occurred while the other two glared at me over dinner. I never said I was sorry; I couldn't because I hadn't done anything. The problem was that they never apologized either. Home became fake, a most uncomfortable venue. It felt like war. When I finally confided to my father that I felt dead inside because I was so caged in, he did something to help me. He had a court transfer custody of me over to him, and I moved into the city with him and his wife.

The year I moved was difficult. I transferred to a city school, complete with security guards and bars on all the windows. I rode the bus to school down Fourteenth Street, and I learned about the subway system—how to walk straight ahead, blank expression, to always hurry, hurry, hurry, because in the city, time moved quickly. I tried to keep a relationship going with my mom because she was my mother, but I was resented, and I knew it. We tried to make each other happy, but that took so much energy, and it was a year or so later when we stopped trying so much, and reconciliation just evolved naturally and quite honestly out of necessity. The reconciliation came about the day my father died out of nowhere from a heart attack in front of me on an East Hampton beach at the age of forty-six. My entire existence, my soul, my sanity, and my heart dropped on that beach and were washed away in minutes; a few hours later, custody of me was transferred back to my mother. The day of his death, I moved back to Long Island and began the confusing process of reentering suburbia just when I'd begun to view it with the learned cynicism that breeds in Manhattan. I went to Northport High School with the same people I'd grown up with and hung out in basements on weekends and drank wine coolers and learned to talk to my mother and learned to listen for the nuances of love that I know she wanted to offer me. I hadn't been back to East Fifteenth Street since. I'd learned to love the cocoon of the quiet Long Island town I lived in. But the summer of my college graduation, I walked down the same streets that I had called my own for too brief a time. Though my ninth-grade city days seemed dim and far away, they would rush back so quickly that when I would round the corner near the Academy or buy a pack of gum from the Korean deli I used to go to, I would be momentarily transported to another time, and those transports left me spent.

Alex had finally recognized the implausibility of becoming paramour to Gillian, and instead of desperate glances, he bestowed friendship upon her. It could have been a ploy, I suppose, to play the sensitive-friend-and-later-I'll-go-in-for-the-kill thing, but I chose to view his actions as genuine. The four of us, Gillian, Alex, Kelsey, and I, would get together outside of class often to go get drinks or run raucous around the hazy streets. We were careful not to tell the rest of the class about all of our extracurricular activities, worrying they'd resent us or get Alex in some kind of trouble, so we'd play it cool and professional during the day and go wild at night. Kelsey wasn't always around; she liked to spend most of her downtime with Beth alone, so often it would just be three of us. I could tell in his face that Alex loved being with us, his small but adoring harem. Little by little we were let into his life, starting with the day Gillian and I decided to surprise him at his Battery Park apartment. Wearing sweats and T-shirts on a rainy Sunday, we knocked on his door and proceeded to spend the day lolling on his plush couch, drinking fruity white wine, smoking cigarettes until you couldn't breathe, and watching *2001: A Space Odyssey* from his extensive movie collection. We learned that day over pizza that he'd never been married, but had been engaged. He was working avidly on a new screenplay. He wanted children. His mother had been an actress. He was a neat freak. His toilet paper was blue. I would avert my eyes from the film and from the pizza to him when he wasn't looking and wonder why women his age failed to see the beauty of this man. I wished I were older, and I was so happy that I chose to do the film thing. I wanted to be friends with both Alex and Gillian forever, because they were so different from me, but I found them fascinating, and they found me wonderful, and we just brought out beautiful things in one another.

Including perversions. One balmy night we were back again in the Battery Park apartment and somehow we got on the topic of blowjobs. Gillian and I compared our techniques. She told me she was heavy on the teasing and the stroking, and I told her I was all about just going for it and fuck the teasing and I could deep throat with the best of them, and only if the guy was really huge would I gag. I loved when the guy would start caressing my hair and would be all into it, but I couldn't stand when my head would be pushed forward. I liked being the one in control. I knew Gillian had much more experience in all sexual matters than I did. I was proud of my few partners, and I knew I wasn't a prude and sex talk never grossed me out. But when Alex joined the conversation and the subject turned to foot jobs, I was physically taken aback. I mean, sure, I could stick somebody's dick in my mouth after a sweaty night in a bar, but stick that same person's foot in my mouth so I could snake my tongue between his toes? Thanks, but no. Gillian and Alex laughed at me, simple, naïve, toe-jobless me, and I figured, fuck it, I'll give it a go, and out of nowhere I instructed Alex to take his socks off, and I'd do my first one on him, my good platonic buddy. I've never seen socks come off so fast. I felt brave, but then I remembered that we'd all walked a lot that day, and it was the middle of summer, and his feet would probably be dirty and smelly; I politely requested that he please go scrub his feet and *then* I'd go down on them. I could see him step into the tub and rinse his feet from my place on the couch. My heart was pounding like I was doing something pretty dangerous, and Gillian was staring at me with her mouth open a little, and the air seemed weighty. But when Alex came back and sat on the couch and propped his foot up on my lap, I told him to look away. I closed my eyes and opened my mouth and just started sucking away, pulling at his toes with my mouth, wrapping my tongue around each toe, making sure he felt both the front and the back of my tongue, getting all into it. Gillian said she'd do it to him also, and he should judge who was better. And the next thing I knew, I was all over one foot, and Gillian was all over another, and it was getting dizzy and intense. I felt myself and my inhibitions sliding away, and I felt a weird stirring inside of me. But then I looked up. I looked up and I saw a pillow over Alex's lap and his head back with his eyes closed, and it no longer seemed exciting; it just seemed dirty, like it could all lead to something dangerous, so I moved his foot away, brushed the hair out of my eyes, and stood up, disorienting both him and Gillian. I told them I was tired of the whole foot thing, so let's all put our shoes back on and go out and get a beer.

I'd like to say after the toe night that it was the same between the three of us, but I can't. Though we hadn't kissed or held hands or fondled intimate body parts, a line had been crossed; when Gillian and I shared a cab home that night, we sort of kept our eyes averted from each other, because we just knew Alex was hoping that the foot job would have led into a threesome of the typical variety, and we both knew we'd come awfully close to engaging in one.

I stayed in the next few nights, hibernating and confused. I fell back on some old behaviors: eating an entire package of Oreos—all three sleeves—in one sitting, smoking too many cigarettes, and writing a letter to Tim that I thought I wouldn't send, except I did. Not one of those vices brought me even a moment of solace.

Dear Tim,
Hey! Long time no speak, see, or think, huh? Actually, it hasn't been all that long, but it feels like a lifetime. How's your summer going? Playing a lot, I'm sure. Long, sweaty nights with the band, giving your very

genuine-looking fake smile to tons of girls and your amazing real smile to a few special ones. Some days I wish I could see it. Some days I don't even remember it.

What I do remember is how you told me once that you were nervous for me to live in the city—and how right and wrong you were. Wrong, because I've never been so happy as I have been this summer. I'm challenged by my school, my new friends, and my surroundings. I've found a confidence inside myself that I'd forgotten was there. I've met some amazing people, made some decent movies, and I haven't slept nearly enough. Those are the good things. The bad? I'm moving so fast, falling out of synch, really learning who I am, but that's just creating more questions and very few answers. Enlightening, yes, absolutely—also very fucking scary. This city really rips you up, unapologetically, and you have to stitch yourself back together before anything valuable falls out. I thought I knew myself so well. I thought I was so stable, and I guess I am in a way. But while I've gone deep to really figure out who I am, I haven't yet reached that bottom layer where all the truth is and now it's covered in dust, begging for some Windex to clean it off, and doing so can be painful.

So Sunday was my professor's birthday. His name's Alex, and he turned thirty-eight. My two friends and I took him out for dinner at this great seafood place in SoHo. We drank way too much wine, talked a little bit too much about sex, and left the restaurant around midnight. Alex and I put my friends Gillian and Kelsey in a cab—they live close to one another on the East side—and then he and I walked a bit to flag down a cab for me. Somewhere between walking to get one the plan changed, and I found myself back at his apartment, listening to a Springsteen bootleg from the year I was born, and getting a little too high. Alex and I have a very cool relationship. There's a familiarity there, like we've known each other for a long time instead of only a few weeks. He told me once I reminded him of his younger sister. And yet...it got a wee bit weird that night, but maybe only in my paranoid mind. Bruce started singing "Candy's Room" a little too slowly, time began to move in baby steps, and Alex started telling me that he thought that I was gorgeous. That's when I decided it was time to leave. He hailed me a cab and I tried to act natural. Then I told the driver where I lived and sped off into the night, away from something that felt too odd and too exciting.

As for the work I'm doing, I love learning how to edit, but I think I'm much more intrigued by studying Film rather than making films. I'm not surprised. I belong in a classroom. I think I always knew that.

And as for you, Tim, you broke my heart in three, but I've recovered and I'm over it. I do miss you though as a friend, so stop being an asshole and call me some time. Hope you're doing well, that you're happy, and that everything is working out with you and Jamie. Tell the guys I said hello, especially Jimmy and Mike.

Talk to you soon?

Love, Jaye

Maybe I was trying to make him jealous. Maybe I wanted him think that I was living a life so exciting that he would want to be part of it again. Maybe I just hoped that seeing a letter from me would bring me back into his daily thoughts, even just for a second. Maybe it was just me being pathetic and masochistic. All I knew for sure was that everything in that scrawled letter was true—except my being over him. He never wrote back.

I hadn't told Gillian or Kelsey about the second part of the night of Alex's birthday, and he never brought it up. But the two fucked up nights with Alex and the lack of a response from Tim made me move ahead in my Jake plans because I craved the normalcy of wanting someone my own age and of the opposite sex so I figured it was time to get busy. I dressed really carefully one morning in a lightweight sundress in pale green and straw sandals and I made my way past the equipment room and asked him sweetly if he could help me figure out some of the technical parts of shooting, that I couldn't figure out the light meter, didn't remember which was a key light, and I really made myself sound kind of stupid but he agreed that he'd meet me after class the next day and we'd work on what was confusing me.

I went home that night and tried on different outfits for over two hours. I was looking for something slimming; something sexy but not too blatant; something sophisticated. My entire closet was literally strewn across my bed, and I was growing frustrated, because I was not nearly as thin as I had been when I had gotten to the city. And even though I knew I'd been so skinny because I had been heartsick over Tim, I still admonished myself for putting on some pounds. I finally pulled together an outfit that would work for a full day of class at the Academy and for my seduction later. I would wear a low-rise Citizens denim skirt and a tight black tank that had a sexy neckline. The important decision of wardrobe made, I went out and took a cab across the park to Brian's apartment. The two of us went to Dorrian's down the street from his place and ordered wine and sat in one of the tables on the porch. I confided to him that I was interested in somebody and he was cute and seemed funny and he had a ponytail and he was a mysterious city kind of guy. I said we'd be meeting tomorrow to talk about equipment, but I planned to lure him away on a real date. Brian said I seemed excited and giddy and more like myself than he'd seen in a while, but he also told me in no uncertain terms that I should learn to be happy for just who I was, and that I should remember why I had broken up with Clay. It hadn't been only because the sex was lousy, but because I had realized that my life depended upon what I could do for *myself*, not on what some guy could do for me.

The next day class dragged. We were supposed to be working independently on ideas and storyboards for our final film that could be up to fifteen minutes long, but I couldn't get any ideas. I had toyed with the idea of making my movie about the end of my senior year of college and how much I'd grown up, but when I looked at my present life, I couldn't find much evidence that I was now a grown-up. It was kind of scary to think about. I mean, I'd reached the age in life where society tells you that you should be a mature, responsible person, an adult, but at the stage in my life where I was, all I knew for sure was that I had a lot more growing to do.

As the long August day at the Academy wound down, I cornered Gillian in the cavernous hallway outside of the projection room and asked her how I should approach the whole Jake thing. We were meeting under the pretense that I needed help figuring out how to operate the light meter, perhaps the simplest piece of film equipment ever invented, but it had numbers on it and required basic math skills, and I actually had no idea how to use it. But should I act all interested in the light meter? Should I flirt? My read on him told me that coy glances wouldn't work with Jake. I didn't know a whole lot about him, but I'd compiled my own little dossier on him in the last few weeks using the investigative prowess I'd learned from watching *Charlie's Angels* avidly when I was seven. The information I'd acquired:

1. I found out from Alex that he was originally from Pennsylvania but had lived on his own, legally emancipated, since he was seventeen.

2. He'd traveled and settled for a time in Seattle.

3. He'd headed to Manhattan on a whim and had taken the film course and then had gotten a job at the Academy, and that's where I came into his life.

He seemed to strike me as someone who'd lived, someone brave, and I hoped that some of that courage would literally rub off on me, perhaps later that evening. Gillian told me I should play it calm and cool and tell him we should go get a drink at Heartland across the park and just hang out there and get comfortable and wait to see what would happen. She reminded me that my new Jake-obsession had nothing to do with Jake. It was about me trying to move beyond my Tim-obsession, whether I wanted to admit to it or not. She was so smart sometimes. That amazing ease of hers probably came as a package deal with her gorgeous face, but I couldn't deny she'd given me sound advice. I checked my makeup again and fluffed my hair up. Gillian fixed my bra to make better cleavage, and I went to the equipment room and rubbed my damp palms on my little denim skirt, leaving marks that only I could see. Jake was just putting the last camera away and smiled when he saw me. I opened my mouth, practiced-bravery abounding, and said, "Why don't we go get a drink at the place across the park? We can talk about all of the technical stuff there." And those two sentences had taken so much energy out of me that I almost had to sit down for a second, but he just shrugged and said, "Why not?"

Heartland was a long, narrow bar with a large red sign outside. Inside it was nothing special, but its location facing Union Square made it worthwhile. Jake and I got a small table and sat facing each other on high bar stools. When the waitress came over, he ordered a beer. I got a glass of wine, and I'm pretty sure I saw him smirk. The moment hung; it actually felt heavy. I kind of drifted beyond myself and looked down at this strange scene and just knew he was looking at me and seeing a long-haired, wine-drinking, dimpled-faced suburban girl. I didn't know how to show him I was more, and I didn't know if I found it necessary to have to show him anything. I couldn't figure out if I liked him as a person. We seemed to have nothing in common. And he made me nervous. He had the ability to look at me and not feel the urge to look away, while my eyes were flitting wildly around the bar if they settled on his face too long. Every time I stared directly at him, he seemed to develop a new physical feature. Were his eyes this green all summer? Had his stubble grown since my last sip of wine? The moment felt so existential and unreal that all I wanted was to make it through a half hour or so, thank him for his equipment help, and book across the park and up to the editing suite in the Academy, where I could put my third film together with Gillian by my side and decompress in the comforting darkness of the editing room. I had told Gillian I'd probably see her there later, so convinced I'd been that this non-date would just feel unrelentingly awkward. I was thinking of how to word my exit, of how to get away before he tried to get away, when Jake touched my fingers lightly and asked what I thought of the program that summer and why I'd taken it in the first place. That led into a natural discussion of college and my classes and graduation and my uncertain future, and he told me of his strange past, of his beyond-liberal upbringing, of his desire to make documentaries. I told him that I loved *Trainspotting*, which he had recommended I see the week before. He told me he had thought I was cute all summer, that he'd noticed me immediately. I asked him what his favorite books were and somehow in his answer about literature, I found out he was a vegetarian. He asked if I had really been president of a sorority because the thought terrified him. And four glasses of Pinot later, when he got up to go to the bathroom for the fifth time, I looked at my watch and realized through my buzz that I was not going to be meeting Gillian anytime that evening.

One of the hundreds of things we'd spoken about over what felt like hundreds of drinks was his final film. As we left the bar and I was thinking, okay, what now, Jake asked if I felt like coming back to his place. He said we could just hang and watch his film. And whatever.

In the cab on our way farther downtown than I'd ever been, we were quiet and sitting close together on the large backseat. It wasn't a crushing silence like it had been earlier, just quiet. I took the time to caution myself against feeling too much. I repeated my "it's all about adventure" mantra to myself, psyching myself for the rest of the night and whatever would happen. I told myself that yes, we'd had compulsive, deep conversations all night, and no, I hadn't felt that open with anyone since that first mystical night with Tim, but this was a totally different situation, and I should remember that the reason I even got myself into this in the first place was to get over one relationship, not completely wrap myself in another.

Third Street and Avenue A. We got out on the corner and walked a few feet to Jake's place. He unlocked the three locks, and when we walked in the door, I began to feel really uncentered. The front door opened into a bedroom, and from the pictures taped up, I saw it was Jake's bedroom, and I was scared because who was he? Where was I? What was I doing? Was experimentation like this what it meant to be a grown-up? Or did my experimenting just further prove I was a stupid child? Shake, shake, and put the thoughts out. I'd gotten good at that; I was like an Etch a Sketch. I walked around his room, checking stuff out, working on looking nonchalant, trying to stand up straight through the alcohol haze that was so strong, I felt I could actually see it surrounding me. It's a weird thing to walk around someone else's most personal space, especially when you really haven't earned the right to be there and own his secrets. But I found out a few things by his room. He didn't make his bed, but the rest of the room was clean—no dirty dishes or ashtrays or cobwebs around. He was obviously fond of music clubs like the Bitter End because he had promo postcards on the dresser. I'd never been there. He had a small sticker of Ernie from *Sesame Street* on his mirror—I liked that. And there were lots of pictures of this grungy brown-haired girl who looked young. She was always in the pictures alone, just a shadow of whomever took the photo across the ground, and I wondered who she was and what she'd meant to Jake, but I didn't ask him, just paused in front of them for a while and then moved on. I did realize by looking at her that if that girl was his type, he must have been feeling as experimental by being with me as I was by being with him.

We watched his movie. A sexy girl and a thin guy moved around to P.J. Harvey, and it looked cool, really shadowy and dangerous. Then we went into the tiny kitchen, where he had some Fruity Pebbles and I had some water. Then we went back into his room, and I was nervous because I could tell he couldn't completely figure me out, and he didn't really know what to do with me—kiss me, send me home, throw me on the bed, talk more. He was stuck, and I felt stuck too, but the videotape of Ben Harper appealed to him, and we lay down and watched the guy sing and perform. As we watched, my eyes started to close, and he started stroking my hair, doing it off and on in a kind of strange rhythm that I couldn't quite predict. I whispered that I was exhausted and I should probably get going, but he told me I should crash there. And the tape was still playing and both of us started to sleep and we were turning toward each other, but I couldn't get comfortable, and I kept fidgeting, and I moved the pillow again, and that's when he grabbed me. He just rolled on top of me and held my hair all tight in his hands and pulled me close and kissed me so hard that I felt momentarily suffocated. Then he untied my tank and unzipped my skirt and took off my underpants and pushed up my bra and did all of this so quickly, I couldn't even pull the blankets around me for cover. And he was kissing me everywhere and flipping me over and back again, and I felt grip marks being formed on my wrists and thighs, and he was still completely dressed, and I wasn't wearing so much as an earring, and I started to freak out because this no longer felt fun, it just felt aggressive, and it surprised me because he had seemed so gentle, but then I guess I really didn't know him well enough to know what he was.

I finally gained control of Jake when I rolled on top of him, locked his hands to his sides with my knees, and leisurely took his clothing off. He was skinny, hairless, and his skin was so smooth, almost like flattened velvet, and he was *so* into hooking up. His primal instincts took over, and he lost all inhibitions. Sometimes it got a little rough and lots of times he got a little loud, but I kind of liked it, and I figured out that holding him tightly for a few seconds, like hugging him, calmed him down so his aggression stayed in check. He was completely present in what was happening, and I was not. I was sort of watching it as it happened. I was recording in my head the sequence of events: how frequent his moans were, what my hips were doing, how the balls of my feet dug into his mattress, where on the bed we were at any given moment. After an hour or so of being on the bed, against the bed, of throwing each other all over the bed, facing the opposite direction we had started in, he got back on top of me and started to push himself in. And I wanted him to. I felt it would complete something, but then something changed, and I just didn't want to anymore. The desire literally passed in a flash. I felt kind of over it for some reason, and over him too, and for the life of me, I couldn't explain why my emotions changed so suddenly. I just know that I came to my scattered senses and shook my head faintly. He slowly stopped pushing against me and kissed me on my forehead and breathed the word, "okay," and his breath blew across my cheeks.

We slept with our arms around each other and my thigh was stuck to his, and I kept waking up, looking at his mouth, his nose, and my skirt and bra in a crumpled pile on the floor. It had been an interesting night. I'd wanted and gotten this guy—and it had been beyond simple. I grew more mature and confident as I lay beside a stranger and the sun broke through the city sky.

But when I said good-bye just past dawn, pulling last night's clothing back onto my naked body, I lost a bit of the pride I'd felt a few short hours before. Something about the early-morning light bouncing off the concrete made me see things, see myself, admit how childish my motives for last night had been. As the cab shuttled me up to Sixty-First Street, I stared straight out the window at the city rolling by, focusing on everything and anything but myself.

I showered at my apartment uptown, changed clothing for the first time in twenty-four hours, and left immediately to go back downtown to school, my heart thundering in my chest the entire time. I kept thinking back on the night, remembering every word and glance, trying to remember it all accurately. But the many drinks I'd consumed blurred some details, and my fierce embarrassment over what I did remember worked to blur the others. I had been open with my thoughts and philosophies with a stranger. I had murmured filthy sexual things in his ear just a few hours after our not-really-even-a-date had begun. I was sure he thought I was a bit slutty, and maybe all of a sudden I was, but wasn't he kind of a whore too? In the sweaty subway, I pondered why men never had to face these soul-searching repercussions. Or did they, but women never got to see it happen? I damned the movies and books that had served as the bulk of my worldly social education; they only portrayed females as anguished and ravaged. I was scarred from all I did and didn't know.

While I'd been on my adventure, the rest of the class had been editing their music videos, and now I didn't have a finished one to screen. When Alex asked why, I mumbled that my extra help tutoring session with Jake had run late, and he raised his arched brows and excused me.

Gillian had set her film to the song "Perfect Day." We had shot earlier that week in the crazy hotel she was residing in. It was pouring out as Gillian donned a black sheath dress and lots of dark and sloppy eyeliner to play the star of her short film, a young girl who looked glamorous but was falling apart emotionally to a sweet song. Kelsey aimed a harsh key light at her while I climbed atop the cupboard-like closet to point and shoot the camera as Gillian flailed and twisted about, throwing books, makeup, ravaging the hotel room she was paying for with the money she'd supposedly earned as a chef. Kelsey worked hard not to flinch as Gillian roared from-the-belly screams and threw her possessions about, almost cracking the light bulb. As the room became unrecognizable from before, Gillian sank to the floor in a heap, and I kept filming because I wasn't sure if she was still in character or not.

When Gillian's strange and disturbing film was shown to the class, nobody said much, but I felt the stares that must have burned through her thin shirt. All of these unanswered questions presented themselves. What was this breakdown inspired by? What rage lived inside such a beautiful creature? Would she break down for real? But nobody asked her anything, and she offered no explanations, no invitation to understand, and no eye contact with anyone for the rest of the afternoon.

And that whole day, every time I turned a corner, every time someone knocked on the classroom door, I was convinced it would be Jake, and I was both disappointed and relieved that it was never him. I'd told Alex, Kelsey, and Gillian all about the evening, even letting them in on his highly aggressive nature, and now we were all anxious to see how he would interact with me the illustrious day after. But midway through the afternoon lighting class, Alex came in to whisper to me that Jake wasn't at work that day. He'd gotten a last-minute callback for an independent film and was somewhere in Midtown trying to woo two directors not even out of their twenties, when I'd looked forward all day to him coming down the hall to woo me.

I finally saw him the next day quite by accident. The whole morning felt dramatic, and it just got more so as the minutes raged on. We were in class discussing high and low points of our third film efforts, the music video. I wasn't saying much because I hadn't even turned one in, and I felt guilty for that. I had paid all this money for a class, turned my back on backpacking through Europe so I could take this class, and here I had chosen to hook up in a dark apartment rather than "hone my craft," as the brochure for the Academy had promised. As everyone offered critiques of the work, I came to the understanding that I was much more a regular girl than an artist. I had always expected that I was both, and maybe I was, but I had no proof, because I had no film and I had no guy, and I was starting to pout when Tess turned her tragically hip attention on Gillian's film. Tess said she love-love-loved Gillian's choice of song, she'd even loved it in *Trainspotting*, which by the way she'd gone to the premiere party in Tribeca for, but what was Gillian's film really about? What was she trying to communicate to her audience? Why all those sharp tilts? When she took a breath and her lips painted with brick Mac lipstick closed, my cool and collected friend Gillian got up and literally ran out of the room.

We all just sat there for a second as Tess turned purple with embarrassment or regret or both. I left the room in a hurry after Gillian, having no more idea than anyone else about the cause of her outburst. It was so unlike her to behave anything but composed and stylish, and her behavior in that screening room was the exact opposite. I booked out the classroom door and down the main stairs…and right into Jake, who was carrying new editing lamps through the front door. I stopped breathlessly and said hello. He asked me what was going on, and I told him I didn't really know, but asked him if he knew where Gillian had gone, had he seen her, was she crying. He pointed out toward the park, and I said that I had to find her, she was sad, really sad, and I'd talk to him later.

I saw Gillian hunched over in the park on a bench. I sat down next to her, and she looked at me through her hair and mumbled a request for a cigarette. I had run out of class so quickly that I didn't have one, so I told her to hang in there and bummed one from the guys on the bench next to us. Then I sat with her on the bench in the hot August sun, and neither of us said anything.

When she finished the first cigarette, she bummed another, this time from a different guy, who ended up giving her two. She handed one to me, already lit from the guy's lighter, and apologized. She didn't know what was going on inside of her, but she'd felt all screwed up all summer long. I told her that I wanted to help her, but I didn't know what I could do. I revealed that I always felt she was keeping so much in and that, close as we were, I hadn't even scratched the surface of who she was and why she had so many secrets that haunted her. I wanted to tell her that I'd love her, no matter what the secrets were. I felt like I already knew anyway, but she just said it was better for her to hold things in, at least better for those who wouldn't have to hear it and pretend to be okay with it but judge her anyway. She said she was okay now, and I pretended to believe her, even though her breathing hadn't yet returned to normal and she still looked puffy, weak. Whatever haunted her would continue to stay in, and my only course of action would be to be there if she ever decided to exorcise herself and, until then, bathe her in my secrets to take her mind off of hers.

Jake called me that evening to ask if Gillian was okay. I was shocked to hear his voice; he'd never called before. Then quickly he told me that what we had shared that night was cool and that he'd had a good time. He said I was different from how he'd expected me to be, but he couldn't get into anything serious because he had just gotten out of a relationship with the girl I'd seen in all those pictures in his room, and he wasn't emotionally ready. I was all prepared to snipe back that if he wasn't ready for anything, then why did he have his face down my pants the other night, but I realized something. It was actually okay with me that he wasn't ready and didn't want me, because I wasn't ready either. And besides, sure, we'd had a good evening together, it had been exciting, but we weren't right for each other, we weren't soulmates, for God's sake. He had been a distraction, an experience. He was a story to tell in retrospect.

The other thing I found out from Jake was that he'd gotten the role he'd auditioned for the other day and he had secured three weeks vacation from his boss at the Academy. He was leaving the next afternoon to go down south to film this movie that had no set script and where he would be paid close to nothing. But he said he was going anyway, because it would be good for his resume and kind of an adventure, and that I understood.

And that was the last I ever spoke to Jake. Until a year later when his supposed-to-be small film premiered big in New York. I was there with Brian, a beleaguered assistant agent at William Morris by then. We greeted each other pleasantly as he made his rounds, a publicity guy leading him through the throng, and he looked better than I ever could have imagined he would. He'd moved to LA by then, and he was wearing a tailored suit that I knew he hadn't picked out. We spoke for about three minutes about life and people we knew in common and then kissed each other on the cheek and went our separate ways.

But back to that summer. My mother kept calling the apartment and asking what I was going to do after the course was over. Was I looking for a job? Did I have any leads? I wanted to tell her I'd given no thought to after-Academy life because I felt shards of fear attack me when I did and I was vehemently holding onto my last few weeks of allowed escape. But that wouldn't make her happy, so I told her that I was going to come home that coming weekend, go to the library, research all the film companies, and send my resume to every single one of them.

It felt good to get out of the city. It was nice to sit in a big house and go in the pool at night and go to sleep with nothing but the sound of crickets chirping. My mom and I went shopping for a business suit for me at the mall for my hopefully soon-to-come interviews. She kept putting me in skirts that felt too long and colors like navy and gray, and I felt so constricted with those shoulder pads, and I sincerely regretted taking time off before graduate school.

Then I got a strange phone call. My sister called me up late one night when I was still at my mom's house and told me she'd just found out that our old sleepaway camp, the one we'd gone to for six years when we were younger, had not been torn down and made into luxury condos as had been the talk those years ago, but was still there, barren but standing. It wasn't a camp anymore, and some company had bought the land, but it was untouched. The cabins were still there, the buildings were there where we'd last seen them. Camp had always been my favorite place in the world, replaced recently by my sorority house as the place I felt most safe and warm, but camp had held that designated place inside of me for over twelve years. And

244

the thought that my beloved childhood summer home hadn't been torn down but was still there made me feel this amazing surge of hope. I begged my sister to take a drive up there with me so we could walk around the land and search for relics that would tell the story of who we had been.

With no shooting going down, just preproduction for our final films, Kelsey and Gillian gladly told me to take the weekend off. My sister and I piled into her squishy Saturn and made the pilgrimage back to camp. We'd gone online and gotten directions from this map site, so we knew how to get there. We'd asked my mom, who had come up to camp for visiting day every year, always being the first mom there because she'd left New York at two in the morning, but she couldn't remember the way. It had been a long time, but we were now armed with directions, making the trip for the first time by car and not bus. On the way up to Massachusetts, we sang the camp songs we remembered, told the camp ghost stories that always involved the haunted Girl Scout's camp across the lake and wondered aloud what had happened to those people who were summer staples of our childhood. We had been driving for about four hours when things started to look familiar. The roads went from smoothly paved to potholed to gravel to just dirt, spinning behind the Saturn in soft waves. And then there we were. There was a gate up at the end of a dirt road; we got out of the car and locked the doors and stared. Beyond the gate, which we promptly climbed over, was the dining hall. Straight ahead was the huge rock where I had once auditioned for *Plaza Suite*. Down the road was the flagpole where we'd all gathered for announcements each morning. The pole was still standing, only now hundreds of sleepy kids weren't gathered around it; severely overgrown grass was. The bunks surrounding the pole had once housed the youngest boys, and the bunks, wooden and sturdy, still stood. Instead of trying the door latch and going inside, my sister and I decided to check out the girl's side and look for our old bunks. Our pace was brisk as we walked up the hills, but inside I felt like time had stopped. I kept seeing myself as a young girl everywhere I looked. I saw my close-knit group of camp friends standing outside the dining hall on the day of the marathon, me holding a *Sweet Valley High* book. I saw myself perched on the fence that seemed to have rotted away over the years, watching the counselors run in a panic down to the waterfront when the announcement, *all staff report to the waterfront immediately*, had thundered over the loudspeaker. There had been a fear that a girl had drowned in the lake. She hadn't, just forgotten to remove her swim tag from the board, and was thus presumed missing. But I remembered those counselors, who years later I realized were only about seventeen years old, running scared toward a responsibility they weren't close to equipped to handle. And I saw what was the camp store to my left, where my sister had bought me candy when my tooth had fallen out, because she knew if the tooth fairy didn't come, I would grow suspicious. The bathroom buildings were there, and the same trees stood, and the grounds were a mess, but it was the most beautiful thing I'd ever seen. When we finally reached the girl's bunks, Cathryn ran off to find the one she'd first been in, and I went to one I'd been in. The door creaked open. It was dark inside, with bugs everywhere as I stood still on that threshold, tears streaming down my dirt-smudged face. I just felt this overwhelming emotion, and the tears spilled. I leaned against the wooden bed built into the wall that had been mine and thought about the picture of my family I'd tacked up there, the letters from my father, and I just wept.

I met Cathryn at her cabin, and she showed me the spot on the wall where her name was, still there all these years later, written in indelible silver paint pen. She just kept shaking her head, disbelieving. Then she rummaged through her backpack, located a pen, and the two of us wrote our names together on the wall and put the date commemorating our visit below.

We walked the overgrown hills. We went to the waterfront. We saw several buildings that we recognized, like the arts and crafts building, that just looked too spooky and abandoned to enter. We traded stories about our camp experiences, things we'd never thought to share before, and laughed through our tears. Cathryn took three rolls of film, and I used my video camera to literally capture the past. A timeless amount of time later, we climbed back over the gate, unlocked the Saturn, and pulled away, leaving a trail of dust behind.

Something changed in me that day. I had seen myself as a child all around that camp where I wandered as an adult, and I felt this new sense of inner peace and strength. I was proud of who I was and the roads that I'd taken, for making the smart choices and for living with the ones that hadn't been so smart. I'd come full circle, and I was ready for what was next, whatever that would be.

In the next two weeks, the last we'd be together before the course ended, we worked at a killer schedule to collectively shoot all three final films and then individually edit our own. We shot Kelsey's in one dawn-till-dark day, running all over the city for interiors and exteriors. We used my uncle, just back from Paris, to portray the father in her piece. He was quite good. The movie starred Kelsey and dealt with her big life issue: coming out of the closet. Most of her films were about that. I privately thought that she was a talented filmmaker, but was maybe pigeonholing herself by only playing the lesbian artist; but I also knew she was using her filmmaking to explore the moments of her life she was seeking to understand. We all did that. Our films became our therapy.

Gillian's film took longer to shoot than Kelsey's. She was using a child actress someone had recommended for part of the movie. The mother was there as we filmed, and we treaded softly, because none of us had ever worked with a child before. She was quiet and beautiful and looked like a young Gillian, which I suppose was the point, since Gillian played the grown girl in the film. The little child listened intently to Gillian's directions and would nod solemnly as Gillian spoke to her. She was darling and got her scenes done in very few takes. We used her for only one day, but that day of being on our best professional behavior was exhausting, so we all agreed to call it an early night and meet to complete the film the next day. The next day's final scene called for Gillian's character to be fucking some guy, some nameless, faceless guy. The shot was to be just her, square in the frame in a medium shot, where you would see her face and her hair and her bare breasts, and she would look haughty and bored and blank and a little bit broken while she fucked away. We'd discussed the disturbingly harsh scene before, but Kelsey and I had left out two crucial questions. The first was whether this was an autobiographical sketch of her life, a recreation of an actual devastating moment; but we were kind of scared of the answer, so we went ahead with the second question: how were we going to shoot this?

I lay flat on my back, four flimsy pillows supporting my head, the camera tilted upward. I knew Kelsey was near the door adjusting the lights, but I couldn't see her from my position. I was focusing the lens when Gillian appeared in my sightline. She took a drag off the joint on her dresser and pulled her tank top off to reveal her breasts. She asked me once again if I was okay with this, and I tried to nod under the weight of the camera and the moment. She climbed on top of me, and we both giggled a little. Then she started moving, and I set the thing to record. I tried to just concentrate on her face and the tightness of her mouth, and ignore her body and how close we were and what she was recreating and how strangely sad and unreal this whole experience was; but pretending this was all a movie didn't cool the sweat on my back and my legs.

My movie was filmed last. I had racked my brain to figure out what I wanted my final piece to be about and how I wanted to express my issues. I came to the conclusion that losing my father and constantly looking and appraising myself to gain clarity were things that had defined me for an awfully long time. I finally felt ready do battle with them. When my dad was alive, I had sought reassurance from him about everything. I wanted him to reaffirm that I was intelligent and pretty and worthy. He was the smartest, most hilarious person I had ever known, and I knew a lot of little girls felt that way about their fathers, but I felt I had proof that I was right in my assumptions about him. At least once a year, he would take me to work with him, because I liked to be on campus and watch him teach. I never slept well the night before—I was too excited. I loved every nanosecond of those excursions. We would wake up early and drive to his campus. We'd stop by the dining hall and get a bagel and some orange juice, and he paid for it with a card that had his picture on it. Then we'd go up to his office. I loved how the hallway would be kind of dirty, and he would bring me down to the department office and show me off to the secretaries. They all seemed to be in awe of him, but maybe that was just me. Then we would trek across campus, and he would sit me in the back of a classroom. Often he would introduce me to some of his female students and ask them to keep an eye on me, and they had always seemed so glamorous to me, what with being twenty years old and having car keys resting on top of their spiral notebooks. Sometimes the class I saw was an English course, sometimes it was his Comedy class, and my father was simply riveting as he taught. It was confidence and wit personified, and I knew even then that not every ten-year-old was lucky enough to know about Joseph Heller or John Updike or to have such a brilliant and engaging father. Besides going to work with him, I also loved seeing movies with him next to me. I would feel a sense of gratitude when he laughed and I laughed at the same time. I'd feel satisfied that I got it. Whatever *it* was. When he died, it had been tragic, yes, of course it had been, and being a witness to his actual death had never fully ceased being haunting. But I was also quite aware that he knew exactly how much I loved him. There was nothing unrequited between us; I was grateful for that immediately, and I tried to move on by reminding myself that I had fourteen years of life with a great father. What I maybe didn't consider and couldn't understand then was that there would be residual consequences for me due to my loss. When he died, the yardstick of approval for me had also ceased to exist, and I felt I didn't know how to measure myself anymore. Whose standards should I use? In the following years, I searched for it endlessly and thought I'd found it in the men I passed through. I went through boyfriends, professors, band members, stepparents, just looking hard to these men to give me inspiration to improve and grow into what, by their estimations, would be positive. These men, without their consent or awareness sometimes, served as muses for me, and their judgments pushed me along while I continued to engage in near-constant self-appraisal. I looked into mirrors and into storefronts and back through past journal entries at my reflections, but I had a hard time trusting myself to choose my own path. It became hard to ignore that what I needed to do in this next stage of my life was to take all my past muses, blend them up into a nice, frothy concoction, and for the first time pour myself into the mix and learn to measure success on *my* terms. It would be like breaking a habit, but it was time, and I decided to make my film a trial run.

We shot at my parents' house over two long days. The young character lost a parent and searched through people until she found herself. Instead of music, I used a voiceover narration of the old high school poetry that I had been so proud of. I believed it helped show the evolution of a girl learning to accept loss and pain and figuring out how to let fear inspire her to grow. *A Blended Muse* lasted just over ten minutes when it was screened for students and family of the New York Film Academy on August 30. And even though the film received applause and I received compliments, it didn't resonate nearly as much as my pride in myself finally did.

Part Four
September
Long Island
and
The University of Delaware

September came, and with it the end of summer. Not much to say about September, except it sucked. I bid my newest safe place, the Academy, good-bye and came back to Long Island. Before I left, I drove Gillian to Kennedy Airport for her flight back to London and hugged her hard at the gate, waving to someone I knew I'd never see again. We'd crossed paths for a fated and lovely moment in time, but I truly believed that our moment was over. Neither of us had any idea just what was in store for our futures, so we were both kind of quiet, but I hoped my hug said what I felt for her. I felt her gratitude and love for me in her embrace. Alex and I stayed in touch on the phone for a while until the conversations got shorter and shorter and then just faded away. I kept good thoughts of him and his feet and moved on. I spent lots of nights on the phone and lots of days on the computer e-mailing my friends and found that Jessica and Christina had both gotten entry-level buyer jobs in the fashion industry; Callie got a middle school teaching job; Erica was still in interview hell seeking a job as a nutritional counselor; Kathleen had left for graduate school in Atlanta; and Rachel, Carley, Allison, and Kim were headed back to Delaware. I had sent out all my resumes to stop my mom from screaming, and I got a second interview with a company that produced health-care commercials. I put on my navy blue suit that I'd had slightly shortened and got on the Long Island Rail Road to head into the city, site of my could-be job, and practiced phrasing until I was dizzy all the reasons they should hire me as a production assistant, knowing if I got hired that I'd be waking up five days a week before dawn to ride the train, and my mom would have to teach me to make coffee so my bosses would find me worthy.

Three days later I received a call from the vice president of the company asking me to come in two weeks from that day for a final interview with all of the producers. My first thought when we hung up was that I needed another ugly interview suit. My second thought was that I was scared I wouldn't get this job, because no other prospects loomed in front of me. All those resumes, all that postage, and no other prospects. I woke up morose and increasingly penniless every day. But I was also scared, because I didn't feel excited by the job. I didn't belong in a company environment, everyone peeking around their cubicles, not even if it involved filmmaking of some kind. I wanted something different. I just didn't know what it was. All I knew was that in September I felt displaced, like I should be back at college, I should be seeing my friends, I should be feeling happy, and I absolutely wasn't. I wanted to feel like a part of something again. But all I'd felt since the end of summer was alone, tired, and afraid.

And then, a week before my final interview, the day came for me to go back to school for a visit. I knew that it was time, not because the day was circled three times in flaming red on my calendar, and not because I had to pack up my prettiest and most flattering outfits, but because I felt trembles through my entire being. Some of my graduated friends would be meeting that weekend for a catch-up session of condensed friendship, and as a bonus and for us, Rachel called the week before to announce that The Assassins just happened to be playing the Balloon that weekend. So nerves, anxiety, preparation for high drama, excitement for muted hysteria abounding, I boarded the train bound for Newark and prayed with all my might that I would feel happy again, if only for a lovely lapse in time.

The trees and fields that had yet to be built upon looked far greener than I remembered them ever looking, even through the dirty, murky windows of the Amtrak cruiser. My knees buckling under me, I hoisted my huge bag from beneath my seat as I felt the train begin to slow, and made my way through the narrow aisle, my nerves brushing each of the passengers on my way. And I knew when I jumped down those steep train steps and was engulfed in the warmest of hugs that I had received in far too long, that my hysteria didn't show in my painstakingly painted face, and that my friends thought I was the same person as I was when I had seen them last.

Kim, Justine, and I went straight from the station to Salad Works for dinner. As we drove down Main Street in Kim's shiny little Jetta, it absolutely floored me to look out of the window and see so many people my age in one place at one time. Their faces screamed a peace that I wanted to grab from them and run away with, far away with; and when I finally would stop running and sit to catch my breath, I would bandage myself carefully with adhesive tranquility and lift my smiling face to the sun, which would ease the shivers that had become constant and were scaring the living shit out of me.

At Salad Works I ordered my favorite salad with my favorite fat-free sun-dried tomato dressing and sat with my sweet friends like it was last year, talking about the same people, laughing over the same jokes, bubbling over with the same enthusiasm. I told them about my possible job, and also what it was like being home, and that I was starting to feel more comfortable with my mother. We were figuring out how to live together again, and it seemed that my stepfather was turning out to be a very kind man. And I looked again out the window, this time not in astonishment, but in search of all of the cute boys I wanted to see and hug and say, "I'm good! How are *you* doing?" and play the game all over again. Reset.

We pulled into the still-unpaved driveway of my old house, the house that I had lived in longer than my house in Smithtown, and Amy and Alicia jumped off the porch swing and sang out "Welcome home!" It made me feel so good and so wanted, and I hugged these girls that I was never really close to, and I wanted to hold them to my burning heart for longer than I did. I walked in the front door and saw that the new composite had arrived. My face was at the upper right-hand corner of it, which made me smile because the top row is where all of the big people went—the old people—and I saw that in sorority terms at least, I had come of age. I dropped my bags in Kim's room, which I had lived in junior year, and went to Rachel's room, which I had lived in last year. Or did I, for here was a frilly, completely carpeted, very clean room, drowning in plants with nary an Elmo in sight. I looked at her bed and at her window and at her radio, and with a real sharp and jarring twist, I remembered Tim smiling up at me, right before I leaned over to kiss him for the first time. Suddenly I just wanted to be alone; my newly hard-won strength began to fade, and I wasn't so sure I would be able to handle this weekend.

My precious Carley, my Assassins partner in crime, wrapped her arms around me. She was the first to see through my façade, and she squeezed me extra hard and gave me that wide smile of hers. I threw back my long hair and closed my eyes with a sigh of submission. I was here, I wanted to be here, and it was time to just deal. We sat on Kim's floor, the door to the fire escape pushed open, and we smoked too many cigarettes in a row while I became reacquainted with my friends on a minute-to-minute level. I looked in their familiar faces and saw the unmasked love in their eyes, through their lashes, on their chins; and despite my heaving heartache, I did feel welcome at home.

At about seven we all began getting dressed for the night. I realized I would be way too sweaty in my jeans and my long-sleeved tee, so I started going shopping in other people's closets. I loved that a sisterhood could share love, loyalty, and shoes, pants, shirts, and bras. Off came my shirt and on went Justine's pretty strapless bra and Carley's halter top. I stepped back from the mirror in my oldest of my rooms and was alternatively repulsed and pleased with my reflection. My hair looked okay and my makeup was fine, but putting that mascara on with my shaking hands was no easy task, so I spent more time fixing the smudges with a Q-tip than I did putting on the rest of my makeup. I smoked many cigarettes and took many deep breaths. I talked to all the girls from the house, and they all asked me if I was excited to go to the Balloon that night, and if I was excited to see The Assassins. They all knew about Tim, because he had said something to them when he had come by after they had played last time. I acknowledged my nervousness with an openness that I loved having again, and I felt supported by these girls, my sisters. A piece of me had always mocked the whole sorority thing. I had spent the entire summer in the city downplaying the importance of it all, but now I realized that being in a sorority wasn't about leasing your friends for four years, and it wasn't in any way contrived or fake; instead, I was the one who had been fake for discounting the comfort that sisterhood had afforded me.

Carley kept smiling at me, and at one point when we were alone in the kitchen, I whispered that I felt off. It was weird being at school, and that was an awful way to feel because I had so desperately wanted to be back there, but now I didn't know where I should be. As for Tim, even if he asked me to get back together with him, I wouldn't because we never would get to see each other, and I didn't trust him anymore, and he had disappointed me so much, and he was too young, and blah blah blah, but I still wanted him, and *why?* Rachel's friend, Derrick, who had also graduated last year, was visiting this weekend with his friend, Pete. They were staying in the sorority house also, and they had brought with them cases of horrendously hard alcohol as a housewarming present, and just looking at the alcohol out of the corner of my twitching eyes made me nauseous. But they had brought a bottle of Pinot, which seemed to be the only thing that I could drink without getting horrendously sick or a bloated belly, so as I felt my insides jumble and jitter, I forced myself to down a few Styrofoam cups of fruity ego endurance.

I couldn't stop looking in the mirror, remembering what I looked like in those brief breezy days when Tim had seemed to be on the verge of almost loving me, when I had felt so present and so free, and I wondered if I looked the same and how he'd react when he saw me. Kisses and hugs? A sharp slap on the clammy palm? A furtive glance in my direction? And would I be smart and cool, or would my longing for him seep through my pores and hit him hard enough to hurt? Maybe I wouldn't want him when I saw him. *Oh, God, please don't let me want him when I see him!* As my friends kept wrapping me in warmth, I felt the sliver of frosty rejection puncture my almost-healed heart, and I knew all of a shocking sudden that I shouldn't be here, I shouldn't see him, I couldn't pretend, I might actually be in love with the kid. I couldn't even comfort myself with the fact that, okay, I was still in love and I just hadn't gotten over it yet, because I had never admitted to myself that I was in love with him in the first place, and—fuck—now I had to deal with that too.

About nine o'clock I ushered everyone out of Kim's room, urging them to put down the shot glasses and the cans of beer in favor of a mug of Bud Lite served over the wooden Balloon bar. I just couldn't handle it anymore; I had to go. Enough already. I was in town, he was in town—*help!* Everyone laughed at my eagerness, remembering that I had never the one to rush, rush, rush to the bars, and I laughed also at the ridiculous situation I was about to place myself in. I suddenly remembered how stable I used to be and how boring I had thought that was—and how I should never have let it all go, that adventure might be overrated, and my lungs already hurt from all the smoking that I had done that day.

Kim needed to hit an ATM machine before she went to the Balloon, so I offered to go with her, delaying the confining moment of confrontation. I couldn't stop shaking. Every inch of me was trembling. My hands, my voice, even my hair, and beneath it all, I could feel the grip take hold of my heart and start to pull with a vengeance that frightened me. I asked Kim if she thought anyone would be able to tell that I was shaking, and she said probably only Rachel would notice. She touched me lightly on my shoulder, and that small touch meant so much. We walked the remaining feet to the Balloon, and right before we got to the stairs of the bar, she suddenly stopped and asked me again if I was ready. I nodded slowly, trying to convince myself more than her, and she softly leaned in and said to me, "You know, I'm not sure, but I think how you're feeling might be about more than Tim. I think being here is kind of hard for you. I'm sure I'll feel it when I come visit next year. Just try to have fun tonight." I wondered if Carley had spoken to her about what I'd confided in the kitchen, or if she'd just figured me out on her own. The noise from the bar hit me then. I was ready, almost; because just for a second, I had this urge to sit by myself and take ten deep breaths, *in through my nose, out through my mouth, pretend I'm in Lamaze class.* I wanted to rest my head against something cool, close my eyes, and flash back to a time that was not so long ago, when this was my life— when it had felt right being here, when I knew what tomorrow would hold, when I was adored beyond recognition or reason by the boy who was inside, tuning his guitar, who had probably forgotten my name.

The curtain that separated the stage area of the bar from the rest of the dingy, dirty mess was still up, and though the curtain was flimsy and see-through, it made me feel as unwelcome as if it were constructed from rusty steel. I walked in, grabbed a cup of beer that someone thrust into my flittery, fluttery hands, and went straight to the bathroom, where I couldn't pee, even though I felt like I had to. I thought, great, I'll probably get another urinary tract infection from this. I knew that when I finally saw Tim, he would give me a hug and tell me that he missed me, but then he'd probably spend the rest of the night being distant toward me, and I would have to drown my disappointment in toothy smiles and fake enthusiasm and energetic dimple flashing. The pain that swept through me as I stood up straight in front of the Balloon mirror, twisting my hair away from my face, was undeniable and crushing. I felt hollow and I felt heavy, and surrounded by everyone that I had missed so very much, I felt alone.

But then I put my glass of beer down on the vanity and steadied myself. I managed for a minute to hurdle myself over the bullshit I had fenced myself in with. And I remembered that the psychic Carley and I had gone to had made sure to tell me that my father needed me to remember the nickname he'd given me. It had been "Tuffy"—and he was right. I *was* tough, and I was smart, and I would be just fine. And even though I was starring in my own depressing drama, deep down I knew it was just an act to ease the boredom and the uncertainty of this newest stage of my life. I was obsessing about my past because I didn't yet want to participate in my future. I gave myself a break for a second and realized that Kim was right; being here momentarily felt weird, and not a good weird, but I would be okay. I took one last look at myself in the mirror, saw my eyes and my lips and the created insanity of this night, and I actually laughed out loud and realized I didn't have to care so much.

I left the bathroom and looked around the Balloon for my friends, and I saw that the curtain had been taken down and the stage area was open. All of them had gone into that area and were sitting on bar stools near the railing that separated the stage from the rest of the bar. They were lighting cigarettes and sucking down horrible beer. The band wasn't on, and I just didn't feel like going in there yet. I went over to the bar and hung around with Derrick and Pete, refusing shots from them and talking about how much it sucked that we had graduated. I was so relieved to hear that being back felt weird for them too. Derrick was such a sweetheart, the cutest guy. He used to go out with Justine way back when, and then he and Rachel had this whole hush-hush flirtation thing going on, so he was definitely off-limits for me. We both knew that, but I hung out with him for a while at the bar, letting him hug me a lot, letting him make me laugh a lot.

Then Carley saw me and walked her little self over to me, grabbed my hand, and pulled me over toward everyone else. At that moment the side door leading to the upstairs whooshed open, and Jimmy and Tim came sauntering out and onto the stage. My stomach dropped for a fraction of a second and I stared at him for what felt like more than a fraction of a second, and then walked right over to the stage. His back was to me, but Jimmy turned around and gave me this huge smile, and I yelled, "Tim!" He turned around and walked to the edge of the stage, crouched down, and without saying a word, he just wrapped his arms around me and hugged me for a long time. I tried to pull away, but he just kept on hugging me, and I touched his hair and it felt the same. We let go of each other then and smiled. I told him it was good to see him again, and he said he had hoped I would be there that night. The trembles that had left a while back resumed, and when I lit my cigarette from his burning one, my trembling was obvious.

All of my friends had watched our greeting like an avid audience, a burning collection of held breath, and when they saw that it went well, they came over to say hello. I left Tim for a minute and walked over to Jimmy, who gave me a big kiss hello, and it was so great to see him again. Then I walked back over to Tim and asked him how things in his life were going. He said everything was going well and was pretty much the same, and then it just seemed like we had nothing left to say to each other. And it wasn't sad, but strange, because I couldn't stop thinking about the nights we had spent together and how we didn't even want to go to sleep because we wanted to spend every second awake and talking and snuggling, and that crazy, immediate connection that we had seemed to be gone. So I left him and walked back over to my friends. They smiled wide at me, willing me lots of luck and tons of love, and I just smiled back and started dancing to the music that the band started playing.

The set list had changed a lot since I had seen them play last. The music seemed harder, less poppy, but they still sounded great. All of the guys in the band saw me and said hello or waved from the stage. I remembered it had been really fun to hang out with them, but it had been so much nicer to just have Tim hold my hand. I watched him play, and it all came flooding back in a cathartic burst that I let myself sail away with. The pangs I felt were the loss of those lazy, crazy days gone by; I was definitely still attracted to him, but the pangs were not of love. I knew that what I had felt in the bathroom earlier that night as I stared at myself was true: I wasn't in love with him. I had never been in love with him, and he had never been in love with me, but had we been, it might have been really beautiful and special. And it might not have worked out at all. I realized then that uncertainty didn't have to be a bad thing, and looking up at him as he swayed and played, I was happy that I'd gotten to experience him for a short while.

Rachel and Kim and Carley kept asking me if I was alright, and I assured them that I was fine, thrilled to be genuinely sparkling from my company and from my finally collected conscious. We let ourselves go and neatly pressed our inhibitions down while we rediscovered the comfort and the hysteria that we brought to each other and that this band brought to us. Those moments, dancing and singing on that dirty, sticky bar floor, brought me way, way, way back and gave me the courage to push myself way, way, way forward.

When the band took a break, Jimmy came over to speak to me. He told me he'd been back to the sorority house the last time they had played, and he had seen my composite picture, and I had looked good. He was so cute, and he said he was single again; I wondered why none of my friends had sunk their hooks into him and carted him off to their frilly boudoirs, whether by force or by consent.

Then someone touched me lightly on my shoulder, and it was Tim. He sat down with us, and Jimmy left. I think he thought I wanted to be alone with Tim, but although the two of us may have been sitting alone, cross-

legged on the stage like we were in a privately dim corner
banquette, there were still 807 other people in the bar, so it
wasn't any sort of intimate environment to begin with. Tim
leaned over to me; I thought he was going to whisper
something, but he just smelled my head and pulled back,
looked down, and said, "It's still the same." I don't know
what fixation or fetish he always seemed to have about my
shampoo or my conditioner or whatever, but the fact that he
remembered made me think that maybe he had cared, if
only for a little while. We were quiet for a moment, and I
could tell how uncomfortable he felt. I told him I hoped he
didn't feel too awkward with me being there, and he said he
didn't, but I could see a tightness in his mouth, and I could
hear it in my voice. And then he said, "I'm not saying this
seductively, but I do think about you a lot and I do want to
call you, and then all of these other things come up, and I
always think, 'Shit, I didn't call,' and I'm sorry. I got back
together for good with Jamie. She specifically requested
that I not speak to you. She said it would make her
uncomfortable. She knew that I had begun to genuinely
care for you." The truth was that I didn't really blame
Jamie for feeling the way that she did. And it was nice
hearing that my face did still swim momentarily across his
crowded little head, and I couldn't help but wonder how I
looked when he thought of me. How did he remember me?
When I thought of him, I always thought of his look of
astonishment that night I surprised him at the Bottle and
Cork, right before he pulled me onstage to hug me, and of
how he looked later on that night as the two of us sat
outside the motel room at six thirty in the morning on that
cold concrete ground, my shorts-clad legs under the bridge
of his, wearing his sweatshirt that smelled like him, while
the two of us discussed how impossible this situation would

be and how it couldn't be and how badly we wanted to make it work. Or I would remember lying on top of him, kissing him, staring down at his face, his eyes closed, wondering what he was thinking, and knowing for sure that I knew.

The break ended, the music resumed. The Balloon had gotten so crowded. It just floored me to look around and see all of those younger girls I used to see on campus or at Rush, but who I never ever had to see out. But now they were twenty-one, and they were all gaping up at the band. Tim was playing to all of them. I had always thought of myself as being a pretty jealous person, but for some reason, I found it funny watching him sing to other girls. Sometimes when he was singing, he would come over to where Rachel and I were standing; he would look down at me and try to act natural or maybe flirtatious, but it felt like an act, and I didn't quite see the point.

Then the music ended and the band said good night. All I wanted was to get out of that crushing, sweltering bar, so I walked to the outside deck with some of my friends, and when I had finally pushed the throngs of people aside to gratefully gasp some cool September air, I realized Tim was still inside, and there was a chance one of us would leave without saying good-bye.

But then Tim came walking up to me, and asked me to come inside for a while. We sat down on the cement steps, and I told him a little about my summer and about my movie and about my professor and about my friends. I sat there with him on those brittle steps, and he leaned over and pushed my hair off my face. I got self-conscious and turned away from him. Then I crumbled for a second, because it all of a sudden felt right, felt so achingly familiar, and I looked into his sweet face and said, "I'm not saying this seductively…but do you want to come over and hang out for a while?" He looked down and told me he had errands to run in the morning and Jimmy had to go home and they had driven together. I shrugged and said, "It's cool. You don't have to make excuses to me." I went to get up, and I shook my hair back into a ponytail. He gazed up at me and asked when he'd see me again. I told him that he wouldn't, that I wasn't going to be around—I'd graduated, and my days of touring with them were over. I leaned down to where he was still sitting and gave him a one-armed hug. I didn't say anything as I waved good-bye and walked down the steps and tried to silently come to terms with the fact that I'd probably never see him again.

I went back outside, where I found Justine. I asked her if she felt like going home, and she didn't, but I managed to steer her out of the bar anyway. She was so drunk and so annoying, and she was telling me some long, intricate, boring story about her ex-boyfriend. I pretended to be interested in her plodding anecdote, offering the expected, "No way!" and the "He said that?" while leading her home at about ninety miles per hour. And when I saw my sorority house looming in front of me, lit from within, I was so relieved to be there and so relieved that I had survived this night that I just wanted to sit down and close my eyes. I went inside and pulled on sweatpants and a T-shirt. I looked around at the mess I had already made of Kim's room, and then I heard someone knock on the door.

I ran downstairs and stopped short on the bottom step when I saw Jimmy and Tim at the door, but I recovered and let them in. Tim kissed me hello. Derrick and Pete came in right after them, Derrick shaking his head at me, announcing he was off to prepare macaroni and cheese in the kitchen. Jimmy, Tim, and I climbed the stairs and went into Kim's room, since I didn't officially have a room anymore. Jimmy lay down on the carpet, Tim sat on the bed, and I sat on the fire escape, lighting Tim's last cigarette. I was surprised the pack was just about empty, since I had seen him unwrap it earlier in the evening. He was smoking a lot more than I remembered him smoking in the past. I wondered what else about him had changed. I looked at him sitting on Kim's bed, packing a bowl, and he looked so cute. It all felt so familiar, and I felt comforted, but something about him and the moment itself seemed surreal. I couldn't explain it, and I didn't want to. He started smoking and asked me if I would still write to him once in a while—he liked the fact that I still sent actual letters—but I answered him honestly that I wasn't sure. I finished the cigarette, and he finished smoking and offered me the last hit, but I didn't feel like it. I sat back on the bed and grabbed a pillow and put it on his legs and lay down on him, my head nestled in his lap. Jimmy started asking me how it had been living in the city and about places I had filmed and what my movies had been about, while Tim played with my hair and rubbed my back. There was something happening, but I didn't know what it was. Jimmy said they had to go soon and excused himself to go see who else was around. When we were alone, we stayed lying like that for a few minutes more. And then he pushed me off of him, a weird look that I couldn't read on his face, and he picked up my hand and held it. He was looking

271

down at my ringless hand. Quietly I told him that I still had the ring he had given me, but I didn't wear it anymore. I saw he was still wearing the necklace I had sent him. I squeezed his hand. I knew that part of him wanted to kiss me, but I also somehow knew that he wouldn't make the move. I knew that I could lean in and do it, that he'd kiss me back, but I knew it would just make everything more difficult, so I held myself back.

Jimmy came back into the room and said they had to go, and I walked them downstairs. Tim and I went outside. He pulled me close, and we just hugged tightly for a while. We stood there on that back porch, in almost the same exact spot where we had said good-bye on that fateful first morning, hugging each other in the same clenching way. I knew that tonight was over, and so were we. I walked them to their car and waved to them as the headlights bathed both me and the back porch in light. I made myself go back inside and close the door before they pulled away.

Over the next twenty minutes or so, everybody else came through the door in groups of three or four. I was sitting in the kitchen, perched on top of the counters like I used to. Kim made me a cup of cocoa with marshmallows while Rachel and Carley heated up food. While it was cooking, they asked me what had happened with Tim. I recounted the events honestly, feeling both embarrassed, like I'd been visibly rejected, but I also felt this unexpected sense of calm for the first time during my visit. Later, sitting in Kim's room, we continued resurrecting the evening, and I remembered, oh yeah, this is how it was: we always ended up hyping the night into more than it had been. Everyone finally wound down and Kim helped me set up the futon on her floor with blankets and pillows and then she got into her bed. As she settled in, I told her I was going to sit outside for a while; she should go to sleep. I desperately needed some hard-earned, by-myself time, and I hoped she didn't take it personally. She just laughed, pulled her hair into a bun, and drew the comforter around her body. It was nice to be understood.

The air outside was silent and still as I walked over to the wooden swing and sat down. In all the fantasizing I had done over the last few months about being back at school, I had never created this moment in my head—me on that porch, alone at dawn—but it was exactly what I needed. I remembered sitting on the ground in front of that swing for the graduate school prayer session, and I knew it had been fear of moving forward that had kept me from going to Miami, but I didn't feel afraid anymore. My acceptance was valid until January. I would hold out on Long Island until then, and then go and do what I'd originally planned. The thought alone, that I was going to venture forth and do what had so recently paralyzed me with utter trepidation, fulfilled me; it made me feel strong, like I'd learned something, learned a lot. And sitting there on that swing where I'd once made so many decisions, big and small, I could feel that everything was starting to fall into place for me—my thoughts, my feelings, my past. I thought about Tim and seeing him again. It had been what I wanted it to be, in that it was dramatic and exciting, but it wasn't Tim that I missed. It was the illusion I hadn't wanted to move beyond. The swing I was sitting on creaked, disturbing the perfect quiet, and I thought then about the summer noise of New York City. I had been brave there. I had befriended strangers and explored the person I might turn out to be. There had been days it had felt frightening, and moments that were exhilarating, and times I had never felt more tired, and evenings I had never felt more alive. That's what was waiting out there for me: confusion—beautiful, scary, mind-altering, potentially-reckless, smile-inducing uncertainty—and my heart began to beat faster as I got up and went inside to climb the winding stairs. I crawled into my makeshift bed on Kim's floor, and, as she snored quietly, I looked up at her ceiling fan that spun around and around, and, there in the darkness, I smiled.

Hugs, Kisses, and Gratitude:

Writing this acknowledgement page is even more fulfilling
than the acceptance speeches I sometimes give while
standing in the shower, holding aloft the Pantene bottle that
I pretend is my Best Original Screenplay Oscar. This time
it's real -- but I still plan to snag that Oscar one day too.

My radiant mother, Harriet Kulka, is one of the finest
people on the planet, and everyone who meets her, even
briefly, knows that's true. Geetle, your enthusiasm,
wisdom, support, and selflessness shine from your beautiful
face, and I am so blessed to be your daughter. You tell me
often that you are proud of me; that sentiment is more than
mutual.

My stepfather, Jack Kulka, came into my life many years
ago now, and he has bestowed upon me new perspectives,
amazing political debates, Yankee playoff games in
unbelievable seats, trips to Sundance, and the rare second
chance to have a father. I appreciate it all wildly.

Leigh Becker is a wonderful big sister and friend. I am
grateful for the closeness we've cultivated on our own
terms. I thank you for your humor and your honesty -- and
for creating the game "Leigh and Nell" that we used to play
on Saturday mornings when we were little as we built forts
in the den. I think it's so funny that all it involved was you
pretending you were me and me pretending I was you.
Crazy that such a simple concept kept me occupied on
Saturday mornings and allowed our parents to sleep in. I
love you for your very presence and for bringing Rich,
Michael and Jadyn into my world.

I would have not published this book without my best friend. Becky Mendel Bradley, everyone should be blessed with the kind of friend you are to me, inspirational and beyond hilarious. Seeing the person you have become makes me so proud, and I admire you as a wife, mother, and writer. Thank you for the college years, for allowing me to be a non-rent paying roommate all the years you lived on 22nd Street, and for being the best friend I have ever had.

My former Chairperson at Bay Shore High School, Nina Wolff, is the epitome of what a boss and mentor should be. Nina, you instilled the confidence in me to become a brave, innovative teacher by allowing me the freedom to grow and to sometimes fail, and I always knew that you believed in me and supported me unequivocally. You have more energy in your tiny body than anyone I have ever known, and education as a whole would benefit significantly if you ran the show.

All of my teachers have left a mark, but Dr. Harris Ross and Dr. Thomas Leitch inspired me for all four years of college and beyond. Your collective brilliance kept me riveted, and you both challenged me intellectually in ways I hope I have emulated in my own classroom. Your lessons have never left me, and I have unabashedly stolen from all of those syllabi and I have passed your combined genius off as my own. You brought me Hitchcock, B movies, an understanding of bloody Italian horror, and an evening with John Waters. It doesn't get any better.

Going to work is a true joy, and I know it's because I work at Bay Shore High School, a place that values educational freedom and creativity. I am so fortunate to work on the same hallway as some of my favorite people in the universe, and I learn from all of you and laugh with all of you on a daily basis. I want to especially send thanks to Michael Hochman, Shannon Handley, Walt Fishon, Joanne Dineen, Dave Mayo, Jose Rodriguez, Kate Hughes, and Pauline Smith for your support and friendship. I also want to say thank you to Matt Pasca. Your publishing of "A Thousand Doors" inspired me to open one of mine.

I want to give a massive thank you to some people who read early drafts of Student and offered me helpful feedback: Pete Palumbo, Katie Mosier Carlson, Nicole Sysler Ryback, and Beth Thomas. Suzanne Litrel always inquired about my book's progress as she was powering ahead to publish her own manuscript, and I appreciate her words of encouragement. Nicole Galante read an early edit as well, and she was key in reminding me to get off my ass and revisit what I had started. She also took my author photograph during a recent afternoon, and I had so much fun with her as she shot pictures of me climbing trees at the arboretum. Her loyalty and humor are appreciated every day.

My students, both current and former, embody intelligence, compassion, talent, and ambition, and I am lucky to be able to spend my days with them, even though those days begin at the ungodly hour of 7:20 AM. When years go by and I get an email from one letting me know that the newest slasher on the market *totally* follows the theories laid out in Men, Women, and Chainsaws, down to the phallic weapons used, well, there's no cooler email to receive. And if you'd all stop that incessant texting while in class, I'd love you even more.

I appreciate the unwavering support of my aunt, Marjorie
Kalter, my uncle, Robbie Wasserman, and my brilliant
cousin, Sasha Kalter Wasserman. I know my father would
be thrilled that you remain a constant presence in my life. I
also want to send love to Paula, Amy, their husbands, and
their adorable children who have allowed me to be an aunt
several times over. I want to let Devin know that I miss
him. And though he is not immediate family, I want to
send love, thanks, and appreciation to Henry Davidson,
who is always there when I need him.

I have never met him, but I would like to thank Bruce
Springsteen. Your lyrics have informed every stage of my
life and they have changed in meaning as I have grown.
You are a true poet and every time I'm at one of your
concerts, I am stunned silent for more than a millisecond
that I get to be in the same physical space as you, breathing
the same air. Your music has soothed me, inspired me, and
has defined significant moments of my life, and I am
grateful that I get to share this planet with you.

I appreciate all of the boys and men who have taught me
about what it means to grow and grieve from love,
especially Craig Schissler, who I will always consider my
first real boyfriend -- the best first real boyfriend a girl
could ever have. Chris Messina inspired me way back when
to embrace my creativity through writing and to share my
early journal scrawlings with him over the phone for hours
on those long ago nights. I am so proud of all you have
accomplished. And Jim Damon...I'm not yet certain of the
role that you were meant to play in my life. I'm still

figuring that out. Maybe it was to teach me about lake-effect snow and the modern need for windmills. Possibly it was to introduce me to a vodka-based drink that I could finally enjoy. Or perhaps you came into my life to remind me of how madly and completely I can love someone—and how much strength I have inside. All of them: lessons learned.

Made in the USA
Lexington, KY
08 January 2012